Pavement

By Rafael John Ayala

Chapter 1: The Boardwalk

Bale slept past his alarm that morning. He couldn't have been tired though, he laid down in his motel bedroom around seven and slipped into sleep before eight. Bale knew his flight didn't leave until seven thirty the next day, and his motel was right by the airport. So why rush? He stood at the counter, bagel in his hand, suitcase in the other. His hair was greasy and unkept. His suit was still too baggy for him, but he would look ungrateful buying a different suit. His mother saved a lot of money for this one. Sweat stuck to his forehead and clung his cowlick between his eyebrows. His teeth felt foreign, with a film of filth permeating his mouth. Maybe he shouldn't have mixed toothpaste with Jack Danials.
Slouching, he asked when the next available flight would be. He had half the day, so on the bus ride into town he knocked around a few ideas. He could stare out into the ocean and watch the beautiful people be beautiful. He could buy some fried dough. The boardwalk had games and caricature artists and men on stilts. Bale had a day to do whatever he wanted. Bale hadn't thought about that in a long time. What he wanted. Somewhere down the line, it just stopped being about that.

Bale was sipping some fruity drink near a tiki bar when his phone went off. Maybe it was his mother. Maybe it was his girl. Maybe it was someone who cared about him. He answered the phone assumedly and was greeted by a voice he had never heard before, but somehow had heard a million times. It was the soft voice of a woman, probably an older woman, who wanted to ask him about his car insurance. Bale told her he had insurance. He told her he didn't need any new insurance. He told her he would hang up. But she kept talking. Maybe it was an automated call, Bale thought. He hung up when the woman asked for his card information. Three fruity drinks later and Bale felt brave. He danced with total strangers until a strong-looking man pushed him off of some girl who grabbed his tie. Probably a good thing, Bale decided. His mother bought him the tie too. Before the strong man could hurt Bale, a mass of thirsty party-goers flushed in and sent Bale spiraling out of the bar. He fell onto the boardwalk and was trampled by the people running in and out. Someone helped him up. Someone asked him if he wanted another drink. And another. And another.

When he woke up, Bale was laying in the back of a bus. He was woken by the sound of people rushing out of the bus and towards their next adventure. His suit was covered in bad smelling liquid, his tie had been cut in half, and his suitcase was gone. There was a sharp, stinging sensation on the side of his stomach. He assumed the worst and lifted his shirt. No scar or string, just a tattoo of a name: Vana. Bale didn't know anyone named Vana.
He shot up from the moist seat and glared out the window. The sun was red and low. And time was running out. The bus ride back to the airport was longer than Bale would prefer. He ran into the terminal and approached the counter. He was asked for his ticket. "Of course, of course," Bale said as he began patting his pockets. He was worried he lost the tickets along with his suitcase. He still had his phone, though it was full of missed calls. He continued to search himself and stumbled upon a small, black, plastic toy. It was a kaleidoscope. As he briefly looked down into its prismatic glass, parts of Bale's memories came back to him.

"I won it at a ring toss game," Bale told the tattoo artist.
"That's all you won?" she asked.
"Yeah," he chuckled, "it's got pretty colors" he offered it to her.
She pushed it back to him. "I'm not supposed to tat you up if you're drunk".
"Tat me up" Bale laughed harder, "Do you hear yourself?"
"Do you hear yourself? You're slurring and talking about colors".
"I'm having a good day".
She watched him for a moment. This loser. Drunk, lost, playing with a toy in a tattoo parlor. He looked beyond the toy and at this woman. This force. Free, fearless, talking to him like what he said mattered even a little bit. He put the toy down and looked at her straight on.
"What are you doing here?" he asked.
She scrunched her face briefly and sat beside him. "Giving you a tattoo? Where do you want it, by the way?"
"I dunno. Here," Bale lifted his shirt and pointed to a spot on the side of his stomach. "What are you doing here though? Like, do you like being here?"
The woman padded against the spot of skin and answered, "I like it here, sure. Why do you ask?"
Bale leaned back. "I used to feel that way too". Bale studied the ceiling, the bright static lights. "I don't feel that way anymore. I don't feel anything".
"Well, you're about to feel something" the woman readied her equipment and asked, "What do you want?"
"I don't know. I know what I have. Maybe that's not enough. Maybe I want to not know what I want".
"Dude. What do you want tattooed?" she snickered.
"Oh, uh" Bale looked at her nametag quickly. "Vana".
"Yes?" she replied.
"I want your name. On me".
"No" she laughed, "Come on, what do you want".
"I want you. I want your name on me".
"Are you married, Bale?"
"Are you asking, Vana?"
She snickered again. Maybe he was charming. Maybe he was so drunk he could make a nun bust a gut. But she wasn't unimpressed. She had been listening. And she wasn't alone. Hesitant as she was to share her life story with every drunk slob to stumble in there day-to-day, Bale said a lot of things she had thought about. Was she here because she liked it here? Or because all she knew was here?
"Okay," she finally said, "I'll give you my name. Just make me a promise".
"I'll promise anything" the words slipped and fell out his mouth as darkness approached the corners of his eyes again.
"Wherever you take me, don't leave my name behind".

"Sir" the airport attendant called. Bale stood still for a few minutes. "The plane is about to leave and your ticket is in your hand. You can get on" she waved her hand towards the shuttle door. Bale looked at the ticket. He looked at the toy. He felt his skin burn. He felt his phone vibrate. He felt everything. Bale looked outside the window to his left and saw the city in a way he never did before. The colors were so bright. Lights blasted out of buildings like ribbons of heaven. The red celestial mist hanging over the ocean kissed the dark sea. There was something hypnotic about that world. Something full and real. Bale had to know what he saw. What he felt. "Sir," she repeated, "the plane is about to leave. Will you be boarding?"

The ocean didn't look as dark from the pier. But the heat from the falling sun caressed Bale's cheek as he leaned against the wooden railing and listened to the flight back home scrape across the sky. His ticket was in a trash bin somewhere. His home was where that flight was going. And his worries were nowhere to be seen. Eyes closed, Bale listened to the seagulls and the waves. He smelled the salt of the Earth. What was he doing and why didn't he care that he was doing it?
The serenity of the ocean was split by the ringing of his cell phone. Work again. It went to voicemail. Shaking as he opened his phone, Bale listened.
"Bale. We need you to come in tomorrow…"
"Honey, where are you? Your father and I…"
"We're calling to inform you about your car's extended warranty…"
"Give me a call back…."
"Smith called out and we need you to…"
"If this is what I have to look forward to, I don't think I can…."
"You were supposed to be…"
"Last chance. You need to come in…"
"New medical opportunities…"
"I didn't even want to get back together…"
"Your father can't get his medication by himself…"
"Pick up or you're on suspension…."

Bale screamed loud enough for the dead to rise and squeezed his phone. He was angry enough to crush it, but not strong enough. A flurry of voices that echoed in his soul screamed out for him and in his rage Bale threw his phone into the ocean. His consistent screams turned into bouts of laughter. He reveled in the weight that was off his shoulders. He cried at the reawakening of his spirit. The chains fell from his wrists. His world was gone, swallowed by the ocean.
As he cleared his tears, Bale looked into the endless sea and thought about his new world and how big it was. How much of it he had to see. How much of it he couldn't see alone. He sprinted across the boardwalk, eagerly laughing and greeting people who walked by. The drunks and the easy, the thin and the burnt, they all smiled back at him. He turned a corner and found the tattoo parlor from hours ago. He grabbed the front door and pulled. He pulled and pulled, but it stayed locked and closed. He peered in and saw only darkness. No lights or sounds. Facing nothingness, Bale began to fear his decisions. Remembering the pit he crawled up from.
"Did you forget something," Vana asked a few feet from the parlor.

"You're here" Bale looked stunned.
"Yeah, I left my keys inside. What did you forget?"
"Vana. I figured it out. I know what I want".
"Okay," she crossed her arms.
"I want to eat fried dough".
Her eyebrows lifted, "That's it? You know you can just make that shit at home".
"No. No, I want to buy it and eat it. Here".
"Here?"
"Here. There! Anywhere!" Bale shouted and lifted his arms. "And I wanna play games on the boardwalk. And look at clowns and stilt-men walking around. I want to watch beautiful people be beautiful. And I want people to draw me with a big nose and a weird snaggletooth and I want to laugh and drink and walk. I want to throw my phone in the ocean a hundred more times!"
Bale stumbled closer. Vana kept her arms locked and watched skeptically, "You didn't look in the kaleidoscope, Vana," Bale said to her, "But I did. Do you know what I saw?"
"Pretty colors?" she replied.
"I know what I want now" Bale looked deep into Vana's eyes.

Vana laughed. It started with a small chuckle and then a sharp, piercing giggle. Bale's face sank. The darkness taunted him again. But to his surprise, Vana reached out and took his hands. Before he could say anything stupid, she got close and whispered, "You're so stupid". Vana kissed Bale like the sun kissed the ocean. There was distance, but the swelling of passion wrote songs on gondola rides. The most beautiful sounds, the flapping of an angel's wings, the hum of a newborn Goddess. Nothing could compare to the quick "flip sound" of Bale's bottom lip snapping back into place after Vana pulled it with her teeth.
She kept her arms around his shoulders and whispered, "You know all that stuff you said you wanted to do?"
"Yeah?"
"Can we do all that tomorrow?"
"Okay".
She let him go, but grabbed his hand. "Let's get my keys".
"And then?"
"And then I'm going to take you back to my apartment," she turned to open the door, "and I'm going to show you my world".
"Vana. After tomorrow…"
"What, Bale?" she glanced over to him, "What do you want to do?"
"I want to go everywhere. With you".
She smiled as they walked into the darkness of the parlor together. Bale didn't think about the lack of light or color. There was nothing scary about the dark.

Static noises whispered from the surface of the ocean. As night rolled in and the stars scattered the sky above, not even the loneliest of debaucherous men, women, or children walked the cold, coarse beach. With a steady pace, it walked up from the ocean and stepped through the waves and the sand. It fell to its hands and knees as the water left it on land. It looked up to the stars and made eyes out of their glow. Its skin reflected the flat, black surface above. Its hair was wet and raggedy, its suit drenched but fitted, and while its right hand was larger, square, and heavy, its left hand glowed. A small, white screen appeared on the palm of its left hand. The screen displayed several missed calls.

Chapter 2: Tapetown

"This place is boring," Vana remarked.
"We just parked," Bale replied.
"Yeah, well, I've been staring out the window and I am not impressed. This town looks like it was put together with tape".
Tapetown prided itself on being the largest tape manufacturer in the country. Everyone who worked there made tape, sold tape, and built with tape. As Bale and Vana left their rental car they were greeted with a banner above city hall. It read, "Tapetown. Don't cut your finger". The shops of the town sold roses made from tape, phone covers and license plate frames also made of tape. Snow Globes full of white, chopped up pieces of tape.
Bale purchased a novelty cowboy hat made from green tape and wore it proudly. "You look stupid" Vana laughed. Bale took it on the chin.
"Well, I think it looks mighty fine" a voice shouted. The two were greeted by a tall woman in a long, blue dress made from tape.
When she saw her, Vana asked, "Doesn't that hurt to take off?"
"Ask my husband," the blue woman quickly answered. "My name is Patty, I'm the mayor of Tapetown. What do you think?"
"I think it's boring," Vana replied.
"I think it's neat," Bale replied.
"Well, I bet you'd love to know how this little town got started".
"No, not really," the two of them answered.
Patty seemed thrown off, she sighed, "Yeah, nobody seems to care how we got here. Just that we're here".
"Amen to that, sister," Vana replied, "You guys got a bar here?"
"Well, yes ma'am we do! Right between the tape museum and the tape drug store and across the street from DD's".
"What's DD"s? A tape music shop?" Bale asked.
"It's a coffee place. You know the one where America runs on it? That one".

After a few embarrassingly named drinks at the "Tipsy Tape Roll", including the "Stinky & Pink" and the "Adhesive Cleaner", Bale and Vana checked out the Museum of Tape next door. Animatronics made from tape represented Doctor Horace Day, a German surgeon who created pressure-sensitive adhesive in 1845.
"Wow, imagine being the surgeon who watched a different surgeon invent tape," Bale stated, "I bet that guy was pissed".
"Miranda Bailey invented a machine that looked inside your butt," Vana replied, not really concentrating on the conversation.
"Oh, he didn't even make tape. He just made the sticky stuff that goes on tape," Bale continued, "Why even include this guy?"
"It was so dumb when they put Ben in that firefighter show," Vana murmured, "Like, I'm already watching this show, why make me watch another".

In the next room was a tape sculpture nearly 30 feet tall, its head pointed towards the second floor of the museum which surrounded it. Little strands of tape wisped off its body and stuck to the carpet. More and more tape came off the giant as Bale and Vana simply marveled at its size.
"You know who he looks like?" Bale said quietly.
"Who?" Vana asked.
"Bob Barker".
Vana was quiet for a moment. "I don't see it".
"Help me," the giant requested.
Bale and Vana's eyes widened.
"You two. Help me. Please".
"It's talking," Bale said quickly, "Bob Barker is talking".
"No. It's probably a trick" Vana reasoned.
"Please," it begged, "Help me".
"There was an episode of South Park like this" Vana trailed off, "but it was a whale in that one".
"I'm losing tape. Help me".
The two of them looked at the floor. There was so much tape.

"Did you know your tape giant is alive?" Vana asked. She and Bale were at The Tipsy Tape Roll with Mayor Patty. She kept looking around trying to find her husband. "Patty," Vana called her.
"Oh, yes, the giant," Vana continued searching from the table as she spoke, "Found em' in '02. Started stripping him of his tape. Now here we are".
"That's how Tapetown started? In 2002?" Bale asked.
"Oh, now you care what our town's history is," Patty gave Bale a spiteful eye, "Besides, I didn't say which '02 we found it in".
"Can you stop looking around," Vana asked, "You're making me anxious. I can't eat when I'm anxious. I can only drink".
"My husband said he'd be here and he ain't. So, I'm anxious. And unlike you, little lady," Patty took her fork-which was made out of tape-and picked up a piece of popcorn chicken and popped it into her mouth, "I can eat".
"Yeah, you can eat," Vana replied.
"What's that supposed to mean?" Patty asked with full cheeks.
"Uh, Patty," Bale said, "We all ordered the popcorn chicken".
Patty looked at the table. There were two and half empty plates of popcorn chicken and neither Bale or Vana had eaten.
"Oh. Oh my," Patty blushed.
"Patty, isn't taking tape from a living creature like that, ya know, bad?" Bale asked.
"Aw hell, he don't mind at all. Grows the stuff like leg hair".
"Yeah, I'm pretty sure people don't go around begging for help when they shave their legs" Vana commented.
Patty settled in her seat to look at Vana. "I don't think I like your attitude, missy".
Vana sat up suddenly and shouted, "You're stripping a tape giant of its body parts".

Patty's husband never showed up to the restaurant. Or, at least if he did, Vana and Bale didn't stay long enough to meet him. Patty told Vana she wasn't welcome in Tapetown. She said a few rude things, among them a creative local insult "you're a pair of scissors in a tape shop". Bale laughed to himself whenever he thought about that. He and Vana decided they'd leave in the morning.

The two of them had a motel room as "The Peel". They laid on the carpeted floor and stared at the ceiling fan. Bale didn't want to use the bed because the sheets, the blanket, and the pillow sheets were made out of tape. He daren't not look upon the mattress. He considered it a miracle the coffee wasn't sticky and flat.

The ceiling fan was covered in various stickers, fruity cousins of conventional tape. What the fan lacked in speed, steadiness, or effectiveness, it made up with aesthetic value. The room was mostly silent, save for the jittering of the ceiling fan.

"How messed up would it be if this fan fell on us?" Vana blankly asked.

"That would be pretty messed up," Bale answered.

There was really nothing to do. No TV channels. No TV at all. Bale found a bible covered in tape in the nightstand under a loaded pistol. Vana spent a few minutes peeling tape off of a lamp and sticking it to the wall.

"Do you wanna have se-" Bale asked.

Vana cut him off, "Should we save the tape giant".

Bale nodded and gathered his thoughts. "Yeah, okay".

"Can I snip these ones?" Vana asked as she held a pair of scissors to braided bands of tape that held the giant up. She was standing atop a very high ladder while Bale undid leg braces that latched onto the giant's legs. Bale shrugged. He looked up at the giant, "Hey, tape giant," Bale shouted, "Answer her, please". The giant allowed Vana to cut the cords. He seemed to wince with every cut of the cords, but didn't complain regardless.

The giant could not leave the museum, he was too big to fit through the front door. Vana tried to get him to squeeze. The duo couldn't think of a solution fast enough and were frightened when they heard a shotgun blast behind them. Patty stood with a shotgun in her arms. "Get back in the museum, tape bastard.".

"What are you? Crazy?" Vana shouted.

"I am the mayor of this town," Patty yelled back, "And its future is my responsibility". She cocked the firearm. "Now, get. Back. Inside".

"Patrice," the giant moaned with his head outside the door, "Why are you doing this, my love?"

"H-Howard?" Patty tearfully whispered.

Bale grabbed Vana and the two ran off towards the motel. Patty desperately shot at them, but she missed and caught the giant in the face. She screamed in terror as Bale and Vana made a B-Line to their car.

Patty could hear the engine start up, but her focus was on the tape giant who blew strands of torn, red tape from its face. It groaned and cried at Patty as she shook with fear. Her shotgun fell out of her arms. From around her, the awoken townsfolk watched from their windows and front doors and breathlessly marveled at the town's beloved art piece as it shed from its innards the wounds of a man.

As Bale and Vana drove out of Tapetown, the tape giant fell to pieces and lost the shape of a human. Stripped from its body was enough tape to last Tapetown another fifty years of glorious memorabilia. Patty fell to her knees in the washes of tape and tried desperately to put Howard back together. But the tape would no longer stick.

I saw it," Vana said in the darkness of the passenger seat, breaking silence with her revelation. "You saw what?" Bale replied.

Vana turned as half of her face was lit by the dim blue light of the car radio. "The giant," she said, "he looked just like Bob Barker".

Chapter 3: Sendoffs

Vana had seen towns like this before. She actually grew up in one like this. The city seemed gray from far away, but the deeper you got into it, the longer you walked the seedy streets, the more shades of brown, green, and piss yellow you could find. There was little diversity as Bale and Vana trekked the city. Some people wore suits and carried briefcases and talked on cell phones. Some people wore rags and shook cups and held signs claiming "they tried". There was nothing in the middle. The busy and miserable. The poor and miserable. Same as they were, they would rather be a million miles away from each other.

Tucked away in this concrete jungle was a nightclub called "Sendoffs". Neon lights strung around the two-floor building like a tornado of luminescence. Long, velvet ropes cast a maze keeping the undesirables out. And posted in front of the entrance, a tall, wide-built man with sunglasses. It was 6:04 and the sun had set. There was no sun for Sunglasses.

"You can't come in," Sunglasses said.

"Why not? We're young and hip," Vana said. Then she looked at Bale and told him to floss.

"Are you with him?" Sunglasses asked her.

"Very much, yes," Vana said proudly.

"Then you can't come in".

"Well, how do we get in?" Bale asked, standing behind his lady friend.

Sunglasses shrugged and said, "Do something crazy".

Bale and Vana sat at a coffee shop for about half an hour trying to think of crazy things to do. Immediately, Vana considered streaking, but Bale knew that wouldn't be enough. He had spent his whole life playing it safe. Even when he went crazy in college, it was a safe type of crazy. No, what Sunglasses wanted wasn't to be impressed, it was to be disgusted. Vana's next suggestion was stealing a garbage truck and dumping it's collection of trash on an old person. Bale liked that idea. But it still wasn't enough.

Bale glanced out the window and saw a bank. But not just any bank. A twenty-four hour bank. Full of people either taking cash or leaving cash. This city was dim for a reason. All its life, all its energy, all its dirty, sweaty, light-shining, ass-grabbing, high volume tenacity sat in Sendoffs. It was a beacon of joy in an empty cardboard city. To get in there, you couldn't be a square. You needed to stand out.

"Well, what do you think we should do?" Vana asked.

"Let's rob a bank".

Bale had never shot a gun. He never held one either. So while Vana held the pistol at the teller, Bale tried to remember every bank robbery he had ever seen in movies and TV. Vana had to help him out. She whispered "Tommy Boy" to him and he told everyone to get on the ground. They did as they were told. The teller did not cry or flinch or move. She simply stood there bored. She even yawned as Bale assured nobody needed to get hurt. Bale walked to the counter and politely asked for a large amount of money. He threw a sack to the teller and went back to watching the room.

"This is going really well," he whispered to Vana.

"Yeah, I'm kind of surprised. Usually there would be-".
The bank door was kicked down by a foursome of police officers. Each of whom had progressively more prominent mustaches. The bushiest of lips ordered, "Stand down. Put your hands in the air and freeze".
Vana and Bale stood completely still, save for a glance back and forth.
"I mean it," the mustache shouted, "Drop the gun. Hit the floor. And stay still".

Bale half turned to Vale and somberly nodded. The realization that their journey was coming to an end had hit him. This charade, this pathetic attempt to escape reality was doomed from the start. He walked towards the cops and got on his knees. One of the hairy officers walked over to cuff him.
Vale did as she was told. She dropped the gun from her hands and as it sharply hit the floor, it bounced and went off. The stray bullet ricocheted off the walls and hit the sprinkler system above Bale and the cops. As tanks of water spilled out onto them, Bale grabbed the officer's taser and threw himself backwards. As Bale slid back across the tiled floor, he shot the taser at the officer who tried to cuff him. The electrical current traveled through each of the soaked officers, knocking them all to the floor.

The bank was silent. Bale stood up and looked over his work. For a second, it felt like he had nothing to live for. But right now, in this moment, he had never felt more alive. Vana walked over to him, gun in one hand, and bag of money in the other. She seemed frightened, but as her breath touched his neck, Bale knew there was something else in her. An electricity. And not the "knock out a bunch of wet cops" kind.

Bale slid across the front of the car, but came to an embarrassingly squeaky stop halfway across the hood of the car. Vana shouted at him to stop showing off. She then threw the bag of cash in the car and then swung herself into the car via the open car window. Bale drove like a madman across the city as police cruisers seemingly spawned out of nowhere. They drove over sidewalks and through trash cans, as did the police who blasted their horns and fired their pistols.
"Bale, this is like a "Fast & Furious" movie," Vana shouted, "But, like, one of the earlier ones with crime bosses and street gangs".
"Are we the crime bosses or are we the street gang?" Bale spoke quickly.
"We're Roman, dude. We're Roman all over".

Sunglasses did not move from his post. He stood with the stillness of an obsidian tower. The wind ceased to exist when it brushed against him. Sweat evaporated into vapor the second it appeared on his head. He had Flo-Rida's "Whistle" stuck in his head and pondered to himself what kind of sexual encounter could Flo have had to make him think "this is like blowing a whistle".
Bale and Vana came screeching down the avenue and unevenly parked in a parking spot. Vana grabbed the money bag and the two ran from the car, they ducked under and jumped over the

velvet labyrinth. Vana waved her pistol around and the gray businessmen standing in line parted like the Red Sea. She shoved the money bag into the arms of Sunglasses. The bouncer glared at the two exhausted bank robbers, then looked behind them as an army of police swarmed the parking lot.
"Well?" Bale asked, "Can we go in now?"
Sunglasses put the bag into Bale's arms. Stiff, he instructed, "Give me the gun".
"What?" Vana murmured.
"Give me the gun," he boldly commanded. He reached out and Vana quickly gave her the gun.
"I'll hold them off," he swore to them. Sunglasses stepped past Bale and Vana. "You two go inside".
Vana shrugged and walked inside the club. Bale went to follow her, but Sunglasses turned and added, "Do me a favor, kid".
Bale looked back at Sunglasses.
"Have the best night of your life".

Bale had heard some stuff about Sendoffs. He read a poster advertising it as "An everyman's heaven for every man". A man outside the bank was begging for spare change, hoping to bribe his way into the club. Even Sunglasses, who gave little expression, had glimpses behind himself, beyond the golden door, and into the oblivion of nirvana that was Sendoffs. Bale tried to picture the interior of the club all day. He imagined jet-black walls, blinding white tables and bright neon lights that wrapped around the rooms like dancing auroras. Waitresses who stepped out of Maxim magazines. A bartender so handsome he could peel the skin off a banana, who's encyclopedic knowledge of obscure and exquisite spirits rivaled only the professional courtesy and therapeutic social skills of God himself. Or herself. Or itself. He expected music that pulled bodies like puppets on strings, music that reverberated rhythmic ecstasy and would tattoo its dope ass beats inside his skull.
Vana was really hoping it was a bar that served good food. Good bar food was hard for her to find. Her favorite bar to eat at was Buffalo Wild Wings, but she never enjoyed going there. Somehow there was always a championship game on the televisions and the patrons were so damn loud. All she wanted was a Coors Lights, some barbeque wings, and stories chronicling idiots of Buffalo Wild Wings' past.

Their expectations were shattered and their senses overwhelmed. Waves of light traveled across their bodies, sounds of chimes and harps and pianos blasts out from inside their hearts. Bale felt the sensation of near sleep, the feeling you get as everything around you comes to a drowning slowness and you can feel the bliss of slumber just moments away. Vana nearly pissed herself.
Before the two of them laid an endless desert of sand. Grains of ruby, sapphire, jade, amethyst, and topaz intermingled into this beach of geodes and gemstones. Standing here was like standing on glass, but the sensation was separated from the pain. Pushing forward and back over the sand was an ocean, an ocean with water of a light, teal shade. It was bubbly and as clear as glass. If not for the bubbling waves and the smell of white wine, you wouldn't even notice it.

Bale and Vana held hands and walked slowly across the beach. They felt the gentle breeze of honey and apple brush across their skin. The red sun, larger than life, lounged at the end of the white wine ocean. Looking at it wouldn't cause blindness, simply the feeling of a sweater wrapping around your soul. The sky was orange and pink and purple and baby blue and yellow and through the darkest splotches of beyond you could spot stars brighter and sharper than any star before them.

Vana could see other planets as she gazed further into the nothingness. Red planets, ringed planets, planets made of cookies and planets consisting of ribbons of water overlapping one another. She could see spaceships out of the 1960's race side-by-side with handsome angels. Their wings of flower petals glowed from the graceful sunbeams of a golden nova beyond a warm Milky Way galaxy. This was beyond. This was heaven, as Vana imagined it.

"Can you see it," she asked, "can you see the angels?"

Bale wasn't listening. He kept looking at the sun. He was looking at something he couldn't understand.

"Bale," Vana called to him, their arms joined, but their minds further apart than they had ever been.

He looked at her in disbelievement. Could she not see the man against the sun?

"This is my heaven, Bale. I always imagined this".

"All of this? Or only the good parts?"

"Bale, there are only good parts".

"Are you sure?" Bale looked back at the sun at the man drenched in black.

Vana gripped his hand harder. He looked back at her. Her skin was vibrant and smooth, her eyes glistened like morning dew over an untouched lake. Vana was beautiful. She was his everything.

"Let me show you this world," she said to him, "Before we go back".

Bale nodded. Words escaped him. They went back to walking and watching the sky. They observed cosmic deities of fire and water as they danced and battled and made love, ending in a cascade of shooting stars painting multicolored spectrums of passion and carelessness across babylon. They were beyond. And the man, drenched in black against the black sun and standing knee high in white wine, was ignored. But he did not stop walking through the sea. Because his hand would not stop ringing.

Chapter 4: Hogan's Hotel

Vana fell asleep around two in the morning to the candid tones of MeTV's black-and-white war serials. Bale stayed awake, as he often did before this period of his life. He stood by the window and watched the neon lights of a casino sign flash and change. In college he would stay up all night like this. He would tell people it was because he needed to cram for a test, but the truth always was that he hated sleeping. Those nights he'd just listen to music and watch the campus from his window, like this. Although there he was living on the third floor and here he had to be at least three stories high.
The campus was never as exciting as he had hoped, or as crime shows made public places look at night. Nobody was ever kidnapped or murdered. Sometimes he would see some drunk students messing around, pissing in bushes. Once or twice he'd see people hooking up. Bale never considered himself a voyeur, but in his heart he knew everyone had better things going on than he did. Even when his friends would stay up late and party, he never expected anyone to invite him. He was too much of a bummer.
"You gotta lighten up, man," his friend Dole told him once over a drink. "When all this is over you're gonna find a good job and nice lady and you'll be all set".
Bale remembers he was six beers deep then, "And then what? Kids? A house? Retirement?"
"That's the dream right," Dole asked.
"Maybe, yeah. But maybe that's all it is. It's a dream".
"Maybe we should stop drinking," Dole laughed, "Before one of us does something stupid".

Bale hadn't talked to Dole in a long time. Last he checked he was doing pretty well. He married his high school sweetheart and bought a car shop from his father. Bale sipped his fancy drink and peeked over at Vana. Her arm was slung over the front of the bed and her drooling face sat comfortably on a pillow, as the rest of her body was haphazardly wrapped in a blanket. The empty plates from room service piled on a table in the corner, next to the mini bar Bale had treated himself to. He didn't consider himself much of a drinker, but alcohol helped him calm down. Before meeting Vana it was the only thing that calmed him down.

"Bale, honey, it's been a year already," his mother reminded him, "When are you going to propose to this woman?"
"I don't know, Mom. I just don't think I'm ready" Bale told her over the phone. It was a while back and he was juggling his phone, his breakfast sandwich, and his steering wheel.
"Well, you need to get ready. All the girls at the salon are saying she's gonna walk out if you don't show her you're serious".
"Mom, I don't really care what-".
"What the girls at the salon think. I know. You've had the same haircut for three months, I get it. But you should care what I think".
"I know".
"And I think this woman can make you happy".
"I know".
"And we both know you've never been good at being happy".

"I know," suddenly his sandwich wasn't tasting as good.
"Maybe marrying this woman will finally get you out of this funk of yours".
"I know," how long had he been parked at work? It felt like he was just driving a second ago.
"I mean if college didn't do it-".
"Mom. I'm at work".
"Oh! Well, what're you talkin' to me for? Get to it, honey".
"Okay, Mom. I love you".
"Love you too. Buy that woman a ring".

A few days after that conversation Bale got on a flight he'd never come back from. He was sure wherever his phone ended up it was probably full of messages from his mom. And from his girlfriend. And from his boss. The room got a little darker. Bale walked over to the only lit lamp and tapped the bulb. The light was restored and the room wasn't as dark, but the feeling stayed. Maybe this was a mistake.
Bale looked at the nightstand. Alongside empty wine coolers was his wallet, Vana's wallet, her camera, and all sorts of souvenirs. The nicknacks splayed onto the corner of the bed too. Among them was the kaleidoscope. Bale picked it up and rolled it around in his hand. He kept doing this as he walked back over to the window. On the small table next to the window Vana left her lipstick and some pocket change. Bale put the kaleidoscope into his shirt pocket.
Bale took a quarter and lined the edges with some lipstick, caking it into the divots of the coin. As he did this, he hummed along with the generic military music from the television as some actor nobody remembers went on and on about heroes and their sacrifices. As the trumpets blared from the program, Bale sat the coin on its side and flicked it across the ivory table. As it rolled across the table it left a red line along the path it traveled. The TV man began coughing throughout his speech. The coin rolled across the whole table and slowed down when it reached the end. It sat for a moment. Bale knelt down to look at it from the other end of the table.

The red line was straight with nary a deviation. The man on the TV couldn't talk anymore. He just kept coughing and wheezing. The music wasn't playing anymore. The coin moved again, now turning and leaning as it fell off the table and ripped through the floor like an ox through tissue paper. Bale stood up slowly and walked carefully towards the hole in the floor. It fluttered like paper in the breeze and beneath him was utter blackness. Bale heard a noise and looked at the ivory table as it slowly came apart. Both ends fell as if they were split down the middle. As both ends plummeted through the floor, more darkness creeped in. The floor began to give out. Bale looked at Vana. She was still asleep, but the light by bed went out and obscured her from Bale's sight. Outside the window, the whole city went dark. Nobody was awake anymore. And the casino was gone. Now, the only light in the room came from the television. Watching every footstep, Bale walked towards the back of the TV. He reached out and grabbed its sides. The light coming from the TV remained white, but had no dimension all of the sudden. As if the light wasn't coming from the front and was nearly a border, like a solar eclipse.

Bale looked into the square of darkness surrounded by white light. There were faint sounds. A whisper. Was it the actor nobody remembered? No, it wasn't masculine enough. There was a

softness to the voice, something comforting. Bale leaned forward to try and hear it more clearly. He was inches from the blackness when two orbs of light appeared in the center. The blinding white lights looked him in the eye and he felt hands gripping his shoulders.
"Call," the soft voice spoke.
Bale was speechless. He looked to his side to see long arms coming from the TV.
"Call me," the peaceful voice continued.
Bale felt himself being lifted from the floor. He hung in darkness as more long arms clung to him. His breathing began to strain and the screen wouldn't back away from his face.
"Call. Me. Back," the gentle voice commanded him.
Bale tried to answer, but he could draw no breath. The TV was higher than him now. It looked down on him. Its numerous arms wrapped around him and it repeated itself over and over. As "Call. Me. Back" went on and on, so did the sound of ringing, which grew louder. Bale found enough breath to scream. He screamed louder than he ever had before.

The ringing went on, but the voice stopped as Bale screamed out. The arms began to let go and Bale felt a warmness in his chest. He could see the darkness fade as a spectrum of light cut through it. The TV recoiled and its border of light vanished. The spectrum came from Bale's chest, but not his heart. From his pocket he took out the kaleidoscope, which glowed like a sun. Bale's breath returned to normal and the darkness seemed thin.
Bale held the kaleidoscope up to his eye. The shifting of colors and bending of light eased him. It reminded him of happiness. As the colors danced, he could hear the war music. He could feel the light of the neon signs hit his peripheral vision. He could smell the liquor on the carpet floor. Bale removed the kaleidoscope from his face and gripped it in his palm. He was on the floor and his drink had spilled into the carpet. But the carpet was still in one piece. The corner light was still on. The man on the TV was still talking about war and heroes and sacrifice. Vana was still asleep.

Bale got up and steadied himself on the ivory table. The red line remained, but the coin laid flat on the end of the table. Bale's vision shot to the lamp as it flickered and dimmed again. With a big breath, he walked over and shut the lamp off. Bale then sat on the floor in front of the bed, he looked over his shoulder at Vana. She slept like an angel. A drunk, drooling angel.

Bale rested his head against the bed and closed his eyes. He welcomed sleep. He hated it, but there were things he hated more. As he drifted off to another world, Bale thought of his mother. He wondered if she would ever live her own life again. Or if living through other people gave her what she needed. Perhaps that was her kaleidoscope. Bale became dead to the waking world. He didn't hear the TV man's speech. He didn't hear the TV man cry. The TV man screamed and begged to be saved. But nobody heard him.

Chapter 5: Longhill

With gas prices rising like they always did, Bale considered switching to electric someday. When he told Vana this, she laughed. "Electric cars," she told him, "they always remind me of those toy cars you set on a race track and drive with a remote". The two of them were stopped at a gas station. Bale had given Vana a handful of cash while he stood outside and pumped. When she returned with drinks and snacks, she had a disgusted look on her face.
"What?" Bale asked her.
"The clerk inside. He smelled like beer".
"You like beer".
"Yeah, but I hate the smell of it".
Bale made a thoughtful noise.
Vana tossed her supply in the car and went on, "My Dad smelled like beer all the time".
"Vana, what did I smell like when we met?"
Vana looked back at Bale. She made a thoughtful noise and got into the car.

Longhill looked like an eventful town on all the roadmaps Bale and Vana had found. But as they arrived in the sleepy town there were no fares or storefronts, simply boarded up buildings and stacks of dirt spread throughout. Bale drove slowly and parked in front of a diner. The two got out and looked in the window. However, the morning light made it hard to see. Bale cupped his hands to see into the diner. At first there was nothing, and then suddenly something. The face of an old woman popped up and startled Bale. He fell backwards into a small puddle on the street. Vana laughed and pointed and held nothing back. Bale tried to tell her about the old woman, but Vana begged him through laughter "just let me have this". The diner door swung open and the old woman peeked out. She held a wooden baseball bat in her hands and told the two to get inside. Vana helped the rump-soaked Bale up and they followed without question.
The diner was not lit, but full of townsfolk who all hid under their tables. While they seemed fearful each of them had a plate of food. The food smelled good too. The old
woman-Tula-reapplied some wood boards to the door and locked it shut. She waved her hand and instructed the two to pick a table to hide under.

Bale and Vana crawled across the diner and hid under an empty table. Tula crawled over and took out a pen and paper.
She whispered, "What can I start y'all on?"
"How fresh is the coffee?" Vana boldly asked. As she did, all the patrons shushed her at the same time. "Don't shush me," she beckoned. They all shushed her again. "Knock it off".
"Sweetie, you're gonna have ta' quiet down. On account of the monster," Tula told her.
Bale spoke softly, "What monster?"
"You wanna know more, I'll tell ya what I tell all the tourists," Tula explained, "order some lunch and save room for pie".
"What kind of pie we talking, lady?" Vana asked.

After a club sandwich and half of a pumpkin pie, Tula was ready to talk. Well, whisper. She told Bale and Vana about a monster that came to town quite a while ago. Nobody knew where it came from, and nobody had seen it hurt anyone, but it's terrifying aura was enough to force the whole town into hiding. Sheriff West has been trying to put a posse together to find and kill the monster, but everyone has been too scared.
"Tula, could I get the rest of this to go?" Vana asked, pointing at the pie.
"Sure thing, sugar" Tula crawled away.
"This is weird," Bale said while they were alone under the table.
"You're weird," Vana quickly remarked.
He gave her a skeptical look.
"Dude, you don't like pumpkin pie?" Vana asked.
"So?"
"So, that's un-American or something".
"I don't see what this has to do with anything".
"You're dodging the question because you can't defend yourself".
"Look, I just don't like pumpkin, okay?"
"Did you even try it?"
"What?" Bale snickered.
"The pie. Did you even try it?"
"No".
"Okay, so try it".
"No".
"Why not?"
"Because I don't like pumpkin?"
"But how do you know you don't like it if you-" Vana was cut off by some people shushing her.

There was a banging on the door. Everyone remained still and quiet. Vana slowly slid the pumpkin pie over to Bale. She mouthed "try it" and Bale shook his head and pointed at the door. Another bang. Tula stood up from behind the counter and opened it. Some of the customers were about to run for it, but several men marched into the diner.
"Tula, I have successfully procured a gaggle of men to assist me in the hunt of the monster which had done invaded our small town".
Tula smiled widely, "Good job, Sheriff. Are you on your way to kill the beast?"
"Correct. Prior to our extinguishing of the irreparable behemoth, myself and my cohorts would be mighty appreciative if'n we could procure some of your lovely caffeinated beverages. To keep us on our toes and such".
Tula nodded and began pouring coffee into to-go cups. Vana walked out from under the table and into a sort of crouch walk. She crouch-walked over to the counter with her pie.
"Hey, I still need a to-go box," she whispered.
"Ma'am, for what reason do you find it necessary to stalk over to this here counter like a ghoul?" Sheriff asked.
"Actually, I was going for a ninja movie kind of thing," Vana corrected him. "I thought we had to be quiet and careful to avoid the monster?"

"Shee-oot! Little lady that monster don't come near me no-how," Sheriff stated, "On account of my sheer muscular magnitude".
Vana stood up straight, "Are you sure it's not because you're carrying a gun?"
"I haven't the slightest clue what-" the Sheriff stopped talking and glanced at his hands. He was polishing his pistol without realizing it. "Oh, how did that get there?"

"Here ya go," Tula placed a few cups of coffee on the table and the boxed remains of the pumpkin pie into Vana's hands. "Sorry for the wait. Most of our staff fled town".
"Because of the monster?" Vana asked.
"Yep. Well, some sought better work opportunities, but mostly the monster".
"Babe, let's go," Vana called to Bale.
Bale shot up and bumped his head, "Sorry. I was counting the gum under the table."
"You're so gross" Vana smiled and shoved the pie into Bale's hands. She then looped her arm through his and they walked out the door.
They walked towards the parked car and discussed where to go next. But they were called out by the Sheriff. "Now wait just one God-lovin'-Satan-fearin'-beer-drinkin'-summer-lickin' second, you two".
"What does summer licking mean?" Bale asked.
"Seeing as you two were so eager to leave Longhill, why dontcha' join my posse here?" Sheriff waved his hand at his gang.
"Dude, no. We're leaving" Vana stated.
"Dontcha think others have tried, little lady?"
"I'm the same height as you".
"The reason passerbys like them customers in the diner stay here for such a varied extend of time is on account of the monster's precarious interest in travelers whom exit the town".
"Are you saying if we leave the monster will target us?" Bale asked.
"I think I'm trying to say that, yes".
Bale looked at Vana. Vana was not convinced.
"Lemme ask you this, Park Ranger Smith," Vana marched up, "Let's say we take your advice and stay here at the diner and we don't help your posse. Are we going to be treated differently for not helping".
"Well, I'd probably be upset".
"Upset enough to do anything to us?"
"Probably not. I'd still be upset".
"So if we don't help you it's okay, but you'll be privately upset".
"Yeah. I would not ever tell you I was mad at you, but you could tell by my general energy".
Bale stood next to Vana, "Vana, if we don't help him it's gonna be awkward".
"Good point".

Twenty minutes later Bale was in the back of a pickup truck which was following another pickup truck. He, along with four other guys from the diner, had been recruited into a war he had no right to fight in. For the soul of Longhill. At Sheriff West's behest Vana and all the women stayed back in town. Vana wanted to fight this, but according to Tula it was far more likely that Sheriff

and the men would retreat back with their tails between their legs than actually die. Vana gave Bale a passionate kiss before sending him off.
"If I die, what would you do?" he asked her.
"I dunno. Never thought about it," she replied.
Bale looked somberly at her, then down at the pistol in his hands.
Vana lifted his head by his chin, "Hey, I never imagined what I would do with you either".

The image of her smile lingered in Bale's mind as he traded stories with some of the guys in the truck bed. Some of them were on their way to bigger towns. Some of them were visiting family. One guy said he had been kidnapped and dumped in Longhill by some guys in tracksuits. Nothing was funny, but that got a laugh out of everyone.
The trucks pulled up to a cave on the outskirts of the town. Sheriff got out and shouted at the cave like he had done it a hundred times before. He claimed the beast's days were numbered and that today would be the day that it would die. As he spoke, his voice cracked and his body shook. At first it looked as if he would stumble, but his loud voice turned into a laugh. The townsfolk he wrangled up started laughing too.
"What say you, behemoth?" Sheriff giggled.
A loud roar came from the cave, followed by a deep voice booming out, "What say I, human?" Covered in black fur and the body of a bear, with a head resembling a goat, the monster walked out and asked, "Did you guys bring the beer?"
The men laughed and hoo-ha'd and grabbed cases of beer from their ammo bags. As Sheriff West walked up and high-fived the monster, the rest of the men followed. One guy even chest bumped the monster.
"Aye, aye, aye, you got some more friends" the monster proclaimed. The townsfolk hooted some more.
Bale walked in front of the diner boys, "Hey, uh, what the hell is going on?"
"How ya doin', man?" the monster stuck out a paw. "My name is Supay".
Bale was hesitant, but reached out to shake his paw. As his hand got close, Supay reeled the paw back and brushed back the hair on the top of his head. The townsfolk laughed.
Supay patted Bale on the shoulder, "Aw, just messin' with you, man. Please come in! All of you!"

Supay's cave was a wonderland of nostalgic euphoria. Against the back wall was a half pipe and a tall wall of skateboards which hung from it. This same wall extended away from the half pipe and further up the underground cavern and formed a rock climbing attraction, complete with a pool of foam cubes at the bottom. Spread throughout were piles of candy stacked next to old arcade machines. Behind three "Street Fighter" machines was a series of refrigerators all connected to a generation the size of a Sedan.
As townsfolk loaded the fridges with beer, Bale could see dozens of frozen pizzas inside. Against another wall was a huge TV, and across it multiple bean bag chairs, a recliner, and a segmented sofa. A pile of VHS tapes laid under the VCR which was connected to the TV. Bale could hear the townsfolk argue over watching "Jackass" or "Shark Week". Bale looked around and noticed how all the diner boys had joined the Sheriff and the townsfolk in reveling in entertainment. He stood there with Supay.

"Pretty cool, huh?" Supay asked, "Drinks, food, TV, video games, I got it all, man".
"Yeah. How did you get it all?"
"Aw, you know. Asking around and stuff".
"Yeah, but, how did you physically get it all down here".
Supay flexed his bear-like arms, "I'm wicked strong, man!"
Bale nodded.
"That's not all. Check this out," Supay lifted Bale up and held him under his arm like you'd carry a rolled up towel to a pool. They moved over to the fridges and Supay told Bale to put a pizza out on a flat stone pillar. Bale did as he was asked and Supay breathed fire onto the pizza, perfectly cooking it. Bale took a slice and had a bite. It was damn good.
"You spend enough time doing that you start to get pretty good at it, you know," Supay seemed pleased with himself.
"So, what is all this?" Bale asked between bites.
"This is my place, man! Sheriff and the boys come up here, like, every weekend to hang out".
"He told us you terrorized people in town".
"I mean, yeah, at first. But the first time the Sheriff came up here and threatened to kill me, I showed him my place and we've been kicking it like this ever since".
"Do you know what the townsfolk think? They think you want to kill and eat them or something. They say you hunt people who leave".
"Psh, that's just what the Sheriff says to people. You know why people really leave and don't come back? Because Longhill is boring as hell, man".
"So you don't eat people?"
"Oh, no dude, I eat people all the time. But nobody from Longhill".
Someone called for Supay to come play Dance, Dance, Revolution. "Sorry, man. Good talk, but I've been challenged," he handed Bale another slice, "Enjoy yourself".

Against all odds, Bale did enjoy himself. He played some arcade games, he raced Supay up the rock wall and fell into the foam pit. He spat beer out of his nose when Steve-O got hit by a bull. He ate pizza, laughed with the boys, and shared his story with Supay and the Sheriff. Sheriff West had been married for twenty years and nearly lost himself to his work. After he met Supay though, he realized that life was bigger than your career. He became closer with the townsfolk and spent more time with his friends and family, and eventually he felt like a more complete person.
Supay left the underworld when he was a teenager because his father didn't believe in his dreams. "I said to him, I said Dad, I don't wanna be the Prince of Darkness, I want to do something good for humanity". In about a month he'll have his online degree in massage therapy. You'd think the bear claws would hinder that, but apparently he's had a lot of practice on the townsfolk. Randy had a couple of scars on his back, admittedly.
Upon hearing his story, Supay told Bale that freedom is something everyone wants. Freedom from duty, freedom from age, everybody just wants to feel like they control something. But as soon as you take control of one part of your life, you eventually realize the foundation of that control is in the hands of people you'll never meet. True freedom is realizing you can't control anything. Anything at all. Life is just random. Bale really liked Sheriff West and Supay. And if he

didn't eat people, Bale might have considered Supay the nicest person he had ever met. But, hey, nobody is perfect.

Chapter 6: Route 404

Traffic backed up pretty hard West of Longhill. Bale and Vana had been sitting in the same spot for nearly ten minutes. The wait was annoying, but the heat was excruciating. Bale had one elbow on the windowsill to hold up his head, and his other hand was on the steering wheel tapping the top of the wheel. There were hardly any good radio stations, so it was obscure 70's rock music all the way down. Vana sat back in her seat, crossed her arms, and spied on people in other cars. She was squinting past Bale and into the car on their left.
"That guy looks like somebody," Vana said, keeping her eyes on the driver.
"Everybody looks like somebody, Vana".
"No, no, no. Look at him".
Bale turned to look at the driver. He was an average looking white guy. He had big ears and slightly graying black hair. He looked back at Bale and shook his head tiredly, likely feeling the traffic depressing too. He had his windows up and Bale could only imagine the powerful air conditioner his newly produced car probably had.
"He looks like the guy from those museum movies," Bale turned and said to Vana.
"See, I thought so too. But when I think of that guy's name I keep thinking of the guy from the office show".
"You're thinking of Steve Carell".
"Is he the museum guy or the office guy? I get them mixed up".
"Steve is the office guy. How do you get him and the museum guy mixed up?"
"I dunno. They both just have, like, the same energy or something".

Traffic started to move and the couple were ecstatic. Cars began moving. The heat was broken by strong breezes. The jaded old radio host was replaced by two sassy young DJ's who played some early 2000's hip-hop. All was right with the world. But, like all beautiful things, this tumultuous time came to an abrupt end. Cars began slowing down. The wind died. The radio began fuzzing and buzzing and the sultry beats of 50 Cent faded into the aether. Everyone came to a stop and as Bale looked to the left he could see Museum Guy cursing in his car. Museum Guy looked back at Bale and mouthed "what the Hell?" and shook his head again. Truly, they were in this together.

Ten more minutes had passed. The heat was getting worse and the AC in the rental car was half-assing its job. Bale unbuttoned his dress shirt another button down, nearly halfway open. The sweat from his forehead crawled into his eyes and salted his vision. Apparently his eyebrows were half-assing their job too.
He looked over at Vana and she looked like she had it worse. She had removed her band T-shirt and wrapped it around her chest to form a make-shift half shirt. Her hair was tied up into a messy bun, it lacked any formality and looked like a tornado of hair. Despite her sweat soaked skin, Vana continued to lazily lean back and watch other cars. She was annoyed obviously, but somehow kept her composer despite the heat.

Meanwhile, Bale felt like he was going to explode any minute. He swung his head back onto the headrest and asked how she was keeping so cool in this heat. Vana lowered her sunglasses like a cop in a 90's action flick and claimed "I'm always this cool". After a chuckle, she told Bale that she spent most of her adult life living in a hot city. Beaches, sunrises and sunsets, warm sand, the heat was nothing new to her. Bale revealed the opposite, having grown up in the North-Eastern part of the country he experienced long winters. Bale was one of those people who would throw on a pair of basketball shorts in the middle of December, step over snow piles just to cross the street and grab an ice coffee.
"Why would you drink iced coffee in the winter?" she asked.
"Why do people eat pizza in the summer?" he replied.
"That's not the same".
"I don't know," Bale glanced at the ceiling of the car, "My Dad drank a lot of coffee when I was growing up. He worked a lot, you know".
Vana nodded, her attention fully on Bale.
"I used to think drinking a lot of coffee meant he was a hard worker, and if I wanted to be like him I had to drink a lot of coffee too".
"I can see why you'd think that".
"Yeah, the thing is, one day my Mom told me why he really drank that much coffee. He had a problem with alcohol and the coffee was just to fix his head after a long night".
"That's terrible. How old were you when she told you that?"
"Let's see. Maybe fifteen? By then I had already gotten used to the taste".
"The taste of coffee, you mean?"
Bale didn't reply. Even here, trapped in a metal death trap an eternity away from forward progression it didn't seem like the best place to get further into this conversation.

Traffic moved once again. Yet another brief fling with open road freedom, Bale saw nothing on the road to justify this traffic storm. No trees fell onto the road, no car accidents, nary a police cruiser. But like clockwork, the cars came to a stop and the waiting began again. The Museum Guy was on the phone now. Poor bastard didn't know he could throw those away.
Bale kept glancing over at Museum Guy. Something was eerily average to him. Like he could be anyone he'd ever met. No, more like he was someone he had met. Museum Guy kept talking on the phone, but glanced over too. He smiled at Bale and looked at the road. But that's when it hit Bale. He knew this guy. All by the smile.
"Shit," Bale said as he looked back at the road.
"Yeah, it's pretty bad," Vana replied.
"That's not what I was talking about".
"Oh, do you have to poop?"
"No, I don't have to poop".
"Okay, good. Because we're in a moving car. Well, it's moving sometimes".
"I know who that guy is".
"Who? Museum Guy?"
"Yeah, I figured it out".
"Is he Ben Stiller?"

"What? No, I know who he actually is".
"But Ben Stiller is the guy in the museum movies, though. Right?"
"Yes, Vana. For God's sake. Ben Stiller is the guy in the museum movies".
"Okay, good. So who is that guy".
"That's Hank".

When he was a young man, Bale worked in a warehouse and spent every soulless hour of his life typing orders on a computer. Sometimes he got to scan barcodes and print stickers, but those were the highlights of his work experience. The suffering wasn't unique to him, though. Many of his coworkers understood the same mediocrity. There was a sort of unspoken sympathy between Bale and his coworkers. Except for one employee. He was not silent. His name was Hank. To himself, Bale referred to Hank as "The Human Sponge". The man just absorbed attention. But like a fat, swollen leech incapable of knowing how much blood isn't enough, Hank didn't know when to stop. Maybe he should have called him "The Human Leech", come to think of it.

Whether it was outside the building, or on the staircase, or in the hallway, or anywhere in the warehouse at any time, if Hank was there, everyone did their best to avoid a conversation with him. Bale even knew of this one woman who learned how to make herself vomit on command just so she could claim to be "very ill, but too stubborn to quit working" and escape conversations with Hank. It's not that he was a dick, quite the opposite actually. Hank was happily married for thirty years, he had three kids and a dog and he loved going on fishing trips. He had grandkids and served in Iran and vacationed in Cabo. He didn't even need to work. Every Christmas he'd donate thousands of dollars to orphanages. One time he asked Bale if he wanted to attend his wife's retirement party.

Hank was a nice guy. But that's all some people wanted him to be. Bale could recall multiple times he'd be walking down the hallway weary of where Hank was. If Hank was walking behind Bale, Bale would speed walk and get to the door long before Hank could. Bale could then go through the door without feeling obligated to hold the door open for Hank. Any closer to Hank and Bale would look like an asshole for not opening the door and waiting for Hank. However, if Hank was in front of Bale, Bale would walk slower and pretend to check his phone. Sometimes he would bend down to untie and retie his shoe, just to stall. Just to desperately hope Hank would lose interest and use the door without holding it open for him. But Hank was patient. No matter how far behind Bale was from Hank and the door, Hank would always hold the door open and look down the hall at Bale.
"Hey, no rush", Hank would tell him. "You don't have to run," he would assure him. But Bale needed no assurance. He never doubted Hank would leave him behind. And when Bale walked through the door, there was no escape. "Yeah, me and my oldest went down to the lake this weekend...I was telling Donna from upstairs they should put another cooler in...so my doctor said I need more fiber in my diet....it was the best steak roast my wife has ever made...the defense from Brady was wild...saw this deer in my backyard...damn phone won't make a sound when it rings...I love you and I'll never let you go...did ya see the crows out in the lot this morning...you'll never escape....that Katy Perry is a little firecracker, huh?"

Bale remembers hiding in the bathroom every morning after walking with Hank. Hank sometimes went in too to wash his hands and finish a story for the fourth time, adding inconsequential details that neither elevated or diminished the story. Bale would sit in a stall, put his hands over his mouth and scream. He would scream until he turned red and ran out of breath. Then he would get up, walk up to the sink, wash his hands, hate himself in the mirror, and walk out of the bathroom.

This happened for several years until Bale left that job. Occasionally he'd get Friend Requests from Hank and see the same profile picture of Hank on a boat with a fishing hat on. He would see Hank peek around on other people's pages too, often offering his guidance to people seeking sympathy and his judgment to people trying to live happy and free. Bale never thought he'd escape the distant memory of Hank. And now here he was.

Vana heard Bale's story and told him now could be the last time, truly, he'd ever see Hank. She told him that he should tell him how he felt and try to start over. Clearly if Hank was a nice guy, maybe they could be friends free from the shackles of corporate America. So, Bale took a deep breath and waved his hand. Hank looked over at him and said something into his phone. Hank put the phone away and rolled down his window, the brush of arctic wind pelting Bale like a New England winter.

"What's up?" Hank asked.

"I know you," Bale began.

"Okay" Hank furrowed his brow and kept looking between the road and Bale.

"I gotta get something off my chest, okay? I don't hate you. I never hated you, I just couldn't take too much of you. I know you're a good guy. Everyone keeps telling me that, but back then it felt like you were everywhere and everything involved you and you just couldn't take a hint and shut up".

Hank opened his mouth, but Bale kept talking.

"It's cool what you have and what you do and how happy you are, but for crying out loud I've heard it all before. I don't care about it. Any of it. I don't care about your wife or your kids or their kids or your hobbies or your home or anything you've ever done. You are irrelevant to me. I don't care about you. If I never met you I'd be happier, if I never saw you again I'd feel better, and if you were dead I'd feel safer knowing I'd never have to see you or hear you again".

"Look, man. I'm gonna have to call-" Hank was cut off.

"No, shut up! I'm not done," Bale yelled, "Knowing you has made me hate myself. Because I know if you and I were friends, you'd never let me down and I hate that too. You'd be the perfect friend and I'd feel like crap compared to you. That's why I spent every single day trying to avoid you, because you had to be so goddamn friendly, and so goddamn good, that nobody could stand next to you. We were all looking up to you and I know you enjoyed that".

"Buddy," Hank replied abruptly, "I don't know you".

Bale fell silent. He couldn't see Vana, but he could hear her swallow.

"Wait. What's your name?" Bale asked.

"I'm Ben Stiller".

Bale gasped quietly. He could hear Vana softly whisper, "I knew it was him".

"Yeah, I'm in movies and stuff and I thought maybe you recognized me".

"Oh. No. I'm sorry. Listen, I didn't mean-" Bale was interrupted by the sound of a car horn. He looked back at the car honking at him, then looked forward and saw the traffic was completely gone. He and Ben Stiller were just sitting in the two lanes. Piles and piles of cars behind them continued to honk, and before Bale could say anything else Stiller was gone, rolling down the 404 like an escapee from a mental institution.
"You better drive," Vana suggested.
"Yeah", Bale shifted into drive and sped up ahead of the mass of drivers.
"Do you think Steve Carell would have driven off like that?"

Chapter 7: Engine City

The heat from the Sun Sliver was hotter than it had ever been. Since the Cold Times, the Engies of Engine City knew little of the outside world beyond it being dark and cold. But now the light from the Sun Sliver sitting beyond the city allowed the Engies to see each other for the first time. To them there was little to discuss as they all looked the same. Metal heads in odd shapes, torsos made from wrapped twine, limbs made from clumped lead fibers. One of the Engies, known as Ore, could not settle with the sample of light. "I want to see more," he told his companions, "Don't you want to see more?"
The hundreds of Engies did not agree with him. They were happy with darkness and now they were contempt with light. Vision did not matter to them, as their duty carried on. Every day the Engies collected natural waste from beyond Engine City. Leaves and bugs. The Engie named Nale once pulled an entire centipede from a metal tube. When they did not work they rested and built energy for the next day of work.
The Sun Sliver did not slow this way of life down, but instead made it easier. Now the Engies could tell when it was day or night by the amount of light coming through the Sun Sliver. Before, they could only denote time by sounds in the sky. Their existence was not chronicled, but memories meant little to them.

Days had passed and Ore's passion became anger. He begged Elder Skarue for answers. "We could use the leaves as parachutes to fly towards the Sliver".
Skarue continued to pick up discarded seeds, "The leaves could break".
"Perhaps. What if we created a bridge from sticks?"
"The sticks could break," Skarue tossed the seed in a pile.
Ore huffed and puffed. Breathing hot air his species didn't need, "What if we used the sticks like a tree? We could put them all together and push the sky over".
"And risk letting more of the light in?"
"What is wrong with the light? The light helped us see".
"Seeing is a distraction, Ore. Seeing makes us slow. It makes us uncomplacent".
"And why is it bad to be uncomplacent, Elder?"
Skarue dumped the pile into a hole in the floor. Dooming them to incineration. "My child," he said slowly, "We are born from the Engine. We serve the Engine. That? Out there?" He pointed to the Sun Sliver, "That is not born from the Engine. That does not serve the Engine".
Ore looked at the Sun Sliver. A blue glow shone through. Ore felt no touch, nor did he taste or smell. This Sun Sliver blessed him with sight. Before now he knew only his work. And he heard only his work.
"Please, Elder," Ore looked back at Skarue, "I want more".
"Child. You were not born for more".

While the Elder did not agree with Ore, in time he found others who would. His fellow Engies formed into a Rebellion who seeked answers to their existence beyond serving the Engine. In mass numbers, The Rebellion marched through Engine City. They pushed over piles of seeds and dead bugs, they broke twigs into pieces, they wrestled with other Engies until their opponents stopped moving. They sieged the Red Funnel, the source of all heat. Without it, Engine City would drown in waste.

Ore led his followers into the Red Funnel with a clipping of red flannel cloth around his body and a silver washer over his head. He proclaimed himself The Leader, The Destined, and most of all, The Free. Skarue rallied the strongest Engies and ordered them to keep Ore away from the bottom of the Red Funnel. One side had numbers, the other had power, neither would bend, push, or fall. Ore stepped over his loyal followers and squeezed between larger Engies. Finally, he reached the rim of the fire pit. Beneath the fire was the core of the world.

"Not a step further, my child" Skarue appeared from above and landed on the rim next to Ore.
"Step aside, old man," Ore shouted.
"If you destroy the core, you destroy us all".
"Do not undermine me, Skarue! We were never alive to begin with".

Skarue drew his sewing needle. Ore drew his twig. Skarue made a sound similar to a laugh, but he never knew humor. To think, Ore went through all this trouble to get here with his army and all he could think to wield is a piece of trash. The two Engies ran into each other. Skarue lunged his needle into the body of Ore. Every piercing blow ripped twine from Ore's chest. Beneath the twine, red flakes of metal shot out followed by the occasional spark of metal grinding metal. Ore swung wildly with his twig. Unsuccessful, Ore fell to the ground looking over the pit of fire.
Skarue aimed his needle down at Ore, "What will you do now, Ore?"
"I could throw myself into the pit. Complete my mission".
"You will not do that, Ore. If you do, and you succeed, you will not be here to see the results of your actions".
"Yes. I could throw you in there. End both the Engine and its zealot".
"You could. But you would need to defeat me to do so. And, in your foolishness, you brought a twig to a needle fight".
Ore snickered. He knew humor. "You are mistaken, Elder. I have not brought a twig".
In quick motion, Ore lunged his needle into Skarue's chest. Through the twine, through the red flakes, through the Elder. As the Elder stood motionless, Ore rose slowly and twisted the needle deeper.
The Elder stuttered, "H-How? What magic is this? Your twig became a needle".
"This is no magic, Elder. It is the gift of sight," Ore began walking to Skarue's side, switching their placements.
"You see, you have lived in darkness for too long," Ore boasted, "And what you conceived as a sharp twig, was simply a needle, like yours. But the light from the fire pit changed the needle's color, and the shadows created hid the surface of the needle".
"C-color? Shadows….surfaces? Light has made you a foreign, my child".
"Old fool," Ore put his foot over Skarue's chest, "Light has given me more".

Pushed from the needle and sent into the fire pit, Skarue's body superheated and inflated. Pieces flung from his body as the bubbling flames devoured the Elder. Ore looked down into the inferno and took in his actions. No shame. Only progress. From here a new beginning could be forged. As Ore turned to leave and confront his people, a tower of flame blasted out of the pit.

The flames grew and enveloped the room. And before any admission of regret could come from Ore's nonexistent lips, he was devoured by red and orange light. In the end, light gave him more than he could handle.

"Yeah, the engine just blew up," Bale told the rental car agent. He and Vana were standing outside the car, whose hood erupted in smoke and flames. Vana was nonchalantly packing stuff from the car into their backpacks. From out of one bag fell a pack of hotdogs.
"Hey, do you wanna eat these with me?" she shouted to Bale.
"One sec," he told the agent, he looked at Vana. Then he looked at the hotdogs. Then he looked at Vana again. Bale held up two fingers to Vana. He went back on the phone, "Yeah, so if you could just wire me my money back...what? Well, no. I said no. I had no intention of driving the rental car back to you, that's right. Mhm. Oh! Well, okay. Goodbye".

Bale hung up and walked up to Vana who had four hotdogs over the flaming car. Two for her on one stick. Two for Bale on another stick. They stood there for a while watching their food darken. Bale informed Vana that the car rental place would not refund them and, frankly, said some pretty rude things about him. Vana recounted how some of the kids back home would call hotdogs "glizzies".
"That's the stupidest thing I've ever heard," Bale replied.
"Yeah," Vana said, "Sometimes I wish I knew less".

Chapter 8: Lillipatton

Lillipatton border patrol was pretty thorough. They asked the basic questions like date of birth and place of birth, as well as questions like "how much did you weigh when you were born" and "when you were born what was the last James Bond movie". The red flags continued when the border patrol separated Bale and Vana and asked more personal questions.

Bale was inside a room with a patrolman in a bright red baseball cap. Bale was exhausted from the walk to the town and already irritable. "How many more questions are you gonna ask me?"

"Seventeen," Red Cap said with no pause.

Bale rolled his eyes and crossed his arms.

"Okay, so, the next question I need to ask is in regards to your marital status".

Bale exhaled low. If he was any more uncomfortable with this he'd be crossing his eyes and rolling his arms.

"Are you Married?"

"No".

"Engaged?"

"No".

"Have you bought a ring?"

"No...wait. Yeah, I bought a ring," Bale said embarrassed.

"Dating?"

"Uh, yeah. Yeah, I guess. I don't know. We've been sleeping in the same bed and stuff".

"Single?"

"I hope not. Wait, why are you still-".

"Sir. Are you single?" Red Cap lowered his sunglasses and looked smugly at Bale, "Ready to mingle?"

"This is stupid and so is your hat".

Vana and Bale met back up inside Lillipatton. The two of them began comparing the questions they were asked. Turns out Vana wasn't asked about her relationship status, Though she was asked to give a detailed description of her sexual experiences.

"I just kinda made stuff up," she told Bale, "I told them I was an international art thief who specialized in stealing Greek sculptures".

"How is that sexual?"

"Dude. They were Greek sculptures. Have you ever seen a Greek sculpture? Those sandal-jockeys were pervy as Hell".

Bale and Vana were stopped yet again and their walk-and-talk was interrupted by a town official giving out frogs. According to the official, everyone in Lillipatton was legally required to have a frog on their shoulder. Nobody in the border patrol offices had a frog, but Bale scouted the town's huge park and noticed everyone had frogs. Green frogs, red frogs. Big frogs, small frogs. One guy had a frog who looked more like a big, green cat with a frog mask on.

The official had an assortment of frogs in a large glass tank he pushed around on a cart. In the tank was a small pond of dirty water, a large soil landscape with tiny trees and mossy stones.

Every couple of minutes he would reach into his vest pocket and take out a handful of dead crickets to toss into the tank. Vana asked if all his pockets had crickets in them and the man didn't answer. He simply blushed and started describing all the frogs.
He pointed to a red and blue frog with a tiny pink bow on its head. He said her name was "Plum" and she was a Strawberry Poison-Dart Frog. Vana wanted to pick the little frog up, but the official warned her that this frog's sweat was poisonous. Vana would need to either wear gloves or scrub her hands with the official's blueberry hand lotion.
"Wait, wait, wait," Vana held up a hand, "This is a Strawberry Poison-Dart Frog?"
"Yes".
"Named Plum?"
"Yes."
"And I need blueberry hand lotion to hold her?"
"Yes."
"Sir, please give me that frog".

Bale wanted a colorful Red-Eyed Tree Frog named Flex, but the frog avoided Bale's grasp. The official chuckled and insisted Bale pick a frog that wants to be picked. Bale grumbled and sighed and settled with a wide, flat frog with mossy green skin. This bullfrog's name was Globulous. Bale lifted the fat frog up to his face and tried smiling at the frog. But his friendly impression did not impress Globulous.
Bale and Vana walked down the main road of Lillipatton and did some sight-seeing. Frog Food Marts sold fried crickets. Vana tried one and spit it out after two bites. Well, she tried. And more importantly she tried it twice. What a waste of ten dollars. "Patty's Parlor" sold frog clothes so Vana could replace Plum's pink bow with a wild Salmon-colored wig. She also got her a little red scarf. Adorable. Bale bought Globulous two tiny fez caps so he could use the hats as nose plugs because holy moly did this frog smell.
"What is your frog doing?" Bale asked Vana as Plum snagged flies out of the air with her tongue.
"What? She eats flies".
"That's not what she's doing". Plum ate the flies, yes. But she didn't swallow completely, instead it seemed as though the flies were transferred into Plum's neck sac.
"Oh. Okay. She has a neck sac," Vana said.
"My frog doesn't have a cool neck sac," Bale said defeated, "He just smells bad".

The local motel-appropriately named "Captain's Log"-was just a hop, skip, and a leap down a dark street. It was a thin street, basically an alleyway, and the buildings above leaned even closer together. No amount of stone steps could keep those two buildings from loving each other. Vana was in the middle of her story about meeting Steve-O at Adrenaline Junkies Anonymous. Before she could do her perfectly raspy Steve-O impression the alleyway exit was blocked off by two jackasses.
The tall one had a backwards blue baseball cap, a white tank top with a dinosaur silhouette on it and baggy black shorts. The other was a short girl with her hair tied up into a ponytail that fell all the way down to her belt. She wore a pair of denim overalls and a pink T-Shirt. They had matching black sneakers. That detail doesn't matter, but it was cute that they matched.

"You two tourists walked down the wrong alley," Overalls laughed.
"Yeah, we're the toughest twosome in the whole city," Blue Cap boasted. He reached into his pocket and quickly pulled out a dark gray frog. "Do you know what this is?"
Bale was muted by the absurdity of a man pulling a frog out of his shorts. Vana spoke out earnestly, "A frog?"
"Not just any frog," Blue Cap shouted.
"Oh. Please continue".
"This is a genuine Upland Chorus Frog. His name is Screamer," Blue Cap proudly held his frog friend.
"Oh. Why is his name-"
"Yeah, but don't think Screamer is on his own," Overalls called out.
"Oh. Okay, well, I didn't-"
"Check it out," she commanded as she pulled a black and green frog. "This a Green & Black Poison-Dart Frog".
"That's a pretty obvious name-"
"And his name is Needles".
"Oh. Why is his name-"
"Why do these people have frogs in their pants," Bale rubbed his face and groaned as he asked.
"And now we battle," Blue Cap shouted, "Go! Screamer! Needles! Show them who they're messing with!" The frogs hopped forward. Screamer ribbited enthusiastically and Needles' throat inflated. Vana tugged on Bale's sleeve and instructed him to run. Just as they began to turn, a storm of tiny, thin green needles flew out of Needles' mouth. Bale took the brunt of the attack and he tumbled onto the pavement. A series of needles protruded from the back of his neck.
Vana screamed. And then Screamer screamed. A booming sound tunnel blasted out of the frog. Invisible to the naked eye, the wave of noise flew out like a bullet train and pushed Vana down the alley. She skidded and rolled and laid bruised on the end of the alleyway. Blue Cap and Overalls boasted and high fived and shared a celebratory vape rip.
Bale could hear Vana groaning, which turned into quiet swearing. Bale sat up to see their attackers laughing. He pouted and expressed to them that "frogs don't do that". They heard his complaint, but laughed even harder. According to them, every frog in Lillipatton had superpowers. Their powers only awaken at night, so youths of Lillipatton will battle with them for street cred.
"You jackasses," Vana screamed from down the alley, "You attacked us with frogs for props?"
Blue Cap laughed, "And to teach you tourists not to come around here".
"We're leaving tomorrow, dude," Bale told him.
Blue Cap shook his head, "And we'll make sure you never come back".

Bale stood up and felt Globulous inflate in his palms. "Of course," Bale thought, "if all the frogs have powers, so should Globulous". Bale held his frog out towards his attackers. He called out for Globulous to attack. Blue Cap's eyes widened and Overalls began to gasp. In no time, Globulous inflated into a balloon shape and floated out of Bale's hands. He quickly flew into the night's sky. The pasty, green pigment of his slimy skin became lost in the dark blueness of space and Globulous was rendered a memory.

The duo of dastardly dimwits laughed even harder as Bale internally screamed and outwardly shook like an orphan in the cold. Bale looked back at Vana and told her, "If Plum inflates we're going to kill that official in his sleep". Vana nodded hesitantly and took Plum out of the tiny carrying purse she bought at Patty's Parlor. She held her in her hands lovingly and silently prayed for her help. Plum's eyes glimmered in the moonlight and she leaped out in front of Screamer and Needles.
"Ah! Another Poison-Dart Frog," Overalls started, "As a fellow Poison-Dart Frog, this one should have the same powers as Needles".
Blue Cap snickered, "Whatever, this pinky pushover stands no chance".
Vana cheered Plum on and encouraged the frog to try it's best. Plum's cheeks inflated and deflated, it almost looked like it had something stuck in its mouth. Slowly out of Plum's mouth came a green needle. This only riled the two punks on more, to see Plum pathetically imitate Needles. Plum held the single needle in her froggy hands as Screamer and Needles pounced. Plum rolled and tussled with Needles and dug her single needle into the rival frog.

Bale, Vana, Blue Cap, and Overalls watched as Plum strained and struggled to pin Needles down. With the needle. The victory was short-lived as Screamer's powerful sound blast sent Plum rocketing into a wall. Plum stuck to the wall like a cheeseburger's pickle to a glass window. Vana screamed and ran over to Plum. She slowly peeled the poor frog off the wall as Blue Cap cheered on his loud amphibian. Overalls opened her arms and goaded Bale.
"What? Is that all you got?" she asked.
"Yes. Yes it is," Bale replied.
"Well good! Step off".
"Step off? We were walking towards you two".
"Oh right". Overalls tugged on Blue Cap's shirt. The two of them picked up with frogs and walked off, complimenting their frogs like proud frog parents.
"Jesus Christ," Bale groaned. He looked back and was happy to see Plum was still breathing. Vana carefully cradled the frog into her container.
"Let's take this goddamn frog to a goddamn frog doctor and get out of this goddamn town," Vana said, voice as low as an undercarriage grinding against gravel.

"Dude, when did you even take out your contacts," Overalls asked as she and Blue Cap came back to the alleyway a few hours later.
"It was before the frog fight. I figured I'd get some eye-drops in before the fight".
"And what? They were faster walkers than you expected?"
"I don't know. I guess. Just help me look for it okay".

Blue Cap and Overalls scoured the ground for a couple of minutes. Overalls found the contact under a nearby trash bag. Just as she picked it up she heard a "flop" sound. "Hey man, I found the-" as she stood up she immediately spotted Globulous on Blue Cap's head. No longer inflated, Globulous looked more like a wet towel. His body slowly extended and covered more of Blue Cap's head, and his green skin was now a murky, blueish black.
"Dude, you got that balloon frog on you" she told him.

Blue Cap breathed heavily, "Yeah, my head hurts".
"Take your hat off".
"It kinda burns".
"Take the hat off, Josiah".
"But...but it's my hat, Kimberlina".
"Take it off".
"But...but I-" the frog covered Blue Cap's entire face. Overalls reached forward and tried to rip the frog off, only for the slimy body of Globulous' body to stick to her hands and extend further. Overalls screamed into the night, but her cries of fear were drowned out by Globulous who became the size of a tarp as it swallowed the two of them.

Screamer and Needles escaped from the pockets of Blue Cap and Overalls. They croaked and tilted their heads in curiosity. The tarp of frog shrunk and twisted and began to resemble a cocoon. Bursting from the side of the black cocoon came out two arms. The ambormaility rolled and tilted and got both hands on the ground. Legs popped out next and the creature rose. One hand glowing with a screen of light, the shadowy monster ripped the cocoon off. The frogs looked up at the shadowy monster and listened patiently. It lifted its palm of light and the quiet ringing sound became sharper and louder. This bothered the frogs, but they remained. They knew better than to run. "Call me," it told the frogs, "Call. Me. Back".

Chapter 9: Cup of Woah

Coffee places were supposed to be peaceful, Bale assumed. He didn't frequent coffee places, and if Vana and Plum didn't share a love of coffee they probably wouldn't have gone here for breakfast. "Cup of Woah" was a cute little place off the highway exit. The new rental car smelled like a barn, so the prudent coffee smell was a nice replacement. "I like my coffee like I like my NBA players," Vana snickered. Bale begged her not to finish her joke.
The peaceful tones of the cafe were drowned out by the live poetry session happening towards the back of the place. The barista-her name was Primrose but her attitude was Blue Cheese-she ensured Bale and Vana that the poetry performance was an all day thing. "From open to close," she said with the excitement of a dying cow, "It's sad all the time".
"The red vines rip me apart as I bleed to death. You took my life, you took my breath," the poet ached in anguish, "Love is a gun and I am the corpse. Black dreariness drives me morose".
"Hey. Hey Bale," Vana whispered from across their table, "Do you know what his dreariness and my coffee have in common?"
"Please don't".
"Why the mood?" Vana held her little pink cup in both hands. Plum held her tiny paper cup the same way.
"This place is depressing," Bale replied. Their table was three feet from the stage and every now and again the poet would ask people to quiet down.
"I dunno. I think it's cute. Look at my cute cup".
Bale glanced into his own cute cup, "Yeah, the cups are cute".

The poet finished and paused for applause. A foursome of folks clapped. They looked unsure. Like one of them started slowly and shortly, but then it was followed and nobody wanted to take sole ownership for the clapping. They would fall together. Primrose stopped whatever barista thing she was doing and snapped her fingers a few times. It was probably a company policy. Just as the poet walked off the stage, he was replaced by an equally pale, skinny, and black-turtlenecked aspiring writer.
He began vomiting depressing rhetoric about how love sucks and death is promised and signing up with the "Cup of Woah" rewards program is free for the first three weeks. The soothing sounds of a man with no father were overcome by the darkness of Bale's coffee. He looked deeply into his cute cup and watched as the black liquid waved and moved like a tide of the ocean. Light brimmed from the bottom of the cup. It felt as warm as the coffee when it shined, but somehow Bale only felt cold inside.

"Alright, everyone get the #$%& down!" the gun-wielding madman shouted as he kicked in the front door. He waved his pistol freely. If it wasn't so terrifying it would be kind of whimsical. He swung the gun like he was conducting an orchestra. Vana stuffed Plum into her jacket and hit the floor. Clearly, now she had something to lose. Bale followed her onto the pink and white tile floor as a symphony of people screaming and bodies ducking for cover filled the coffee shop.
"Everyone stay the #$%& still or I'll start blowing heads off," the gunman proclaimed.
"H-Hey. Excuse me," the poet on stage said, "Can I just sit against the wall?"

"I said everyone get on the #$%& ground".
"I k-know. B-B-But you made…you made me…" the poet shook nervously, standing with his toes pointing towards each other.
"Oh, for the love of-yeah, fine. Go sit over there".
The poet nodded and shuffled over to the back wall where he proceeded to crumple up like a sheet of paper and slide down the wall into a fetal position. Truly, he was melancholy right down to how he sat.

The gunman wore a white painter's suit, a white one with splatters of blue here and there on the top half of the suit. He had on grayish, worn-out sneakers and tight black gloves. To hide his face he wore a black ski mask with a plastic dog mask over his face. Whether he was a painter, a limo driver, or an amatuer dog impersonator, today he was an asshole. He swore a lot and walked around the room several times. A few times he asked people to lift their heads and talk to him, he talked to Primrose too. Bale couldn't hear their hushed conversation, but he could hear the unamused tone of Primrose deflect interest even in this dire situation.
Bale and Vana remained mostly face down for about twenty minutes as Dog Guy talked to people. At one point Dog Guy slammed his gun over a guy's head and knocked him out. As the victim bled and his partner screamed, Dog Guy threatened her with a similar fate. One brave soul, definitely not Bale, stood up in the corner and called the Dog Guy out.
"Look, buddy. If you want money," the brave man said, "We'll give you whatever you want. Just stop hurting people".
Dog Guy turned to him and said nothing.
Brave Man went on, "I'm a counselor. For kids, ya know? And my wife," he motioned to a woman on the ground next to him, "she's a school teacher".
Dog Guy took a few steps towards him.
"We-We have people who need us, ya know?" Brave Man started tearing up, "S-So you gotta let us go".
Dog Guy was a few feet away now.
"You gotta, man. You gotta let us go".
Dog Guy was less than a foot away.
"Y-you gotta. Okay?"
"I have this idea for a movie," Dog Guy calmly said, now loud enough that Bale could hear him, "It's about this little girl who moves into a haunted house, full of ghosts".
Brave Man looked confused, his face red and wet.
"But one of the ghosts is a little boy, and that ghost becomes her friend. What do you think?"
"I-I think that s-sound great, man. That sounds so good".
"Yeah?" Dog Guy's gun lowered.
"Y-Yeah! That sounds like a l-lot of f-fun! Right? Right everyone?" Brave Man looked around the room and raised his arms.
"Any critiques?" Dog Guy asked enthusiastically.
"N-No. Not at all! It all sounds great-"
Dog Guy fired his pistol and blood flew out of Brave Man's knee. He tumbled and screamed and held his curled knee up to his chest. As he winced and cried, his wife became pale and sunken-faced as she watched him bleed. Dog Guy cursed under his breath, then loudly.

"I have an idea for a movie," he said loudly. Then he shot into the ceiling. "It's about a girl in a haunted house," he shot again. "And she makes friends," another shot, "With a #$%&ing," another shot, "Ghost". He raised his arms and asked if anyone had any critiques.
"That sounds like Casper" Vana shouted. She was still on the floor with Bale, but could not contain herself anymore.
Dog Guy turned, then he slowly shambled over to her. "What did you say?"
"Your movie," Vana held her hands on top of her head and had her eyes shut, "It sounds like Casper The Friendly Ghost".
Dog Guy remained silent for a moment. Then he nodded. "Yeah, I guess it does".

Everyone in the coffee shop was forced to sit against the far left wall of the shop. Even the pissy poet. They were all told to face the wall or they'd be shot. The only people not against the wall were Dog Guy, Vana, Plum, and Bale. The four of them sat in a booth on the other side of the ship. Also, Brave Man and his wife were let out as police surrounded the cafe, Vana was able to convince Dog Man to let them out so Brave Man could get to a hospital.
As he put it, Dog Guy wanted an audience for his pitches. He always wanted to make movies, but nobody would ever listen to his ideas. Nor would anyone ever engage with him about his passion. Vana's knowledge of pop culture would give Dog Guy what he so desperately claimed, as she could shoot down every idea that was derivative.
"This kid in high school has to decide if he wants to play football like his Dad, or be in the school band," Dog Guy explained.
"That sounds too much like High School Musical," Vana replied as she sipped her room temperature coffee.
"Yeah, but it's football, not basketball".
"They made like four of those movies, dude. People are gonna compare them".
"Alright. How about this; a football player is sent to prison, but he can get out early if he and some other inmates win a football game against-".
"The warden's team of guards?"
"Yeah. Too predictable?"
"Adam Sandler did it".
"#$%&. Okay, a football player suddenly discovers he has a daughter-"
"Yeah, that's The Game Plan, stop with the football stuff".
"Fine, fine, this guy puts a team together to pull of a heist at a casino-"
"Ocean's Eleven, or whichever number they're on".
"Wait, wait, wait. The thieves are all stage magicians".
"That's a thing. It's called Now You See Me".
"Oh, my #$%&ing god," Dog Guy scratched the top of his head, "This old guy has a bunch of toys that come alive-"
"Small Soldiers? Indian in The Cupboard? Toy Story? The one Winnie The Pooh movie?"
Dog Guy groaned. Vana asked him when the last time he'd seen a movie was. "When did Willy Wonka come out?"
"The book or the movie?"
"The movie".

"The good one or the weird one?"
"There's more than one?"

They went back and forth for about an hour. Movie after movie, pitch after pitch. After a while Bale considered reaching over, grabbing the gun, and blowing his own brains out. But as the conversation went on and Dog Guy got more relaxed, he stopped swinging around his gun. He placed an elbow on the table and started getting way more in-depth about his thought process. Vana even got him to laugh. He was upset so many of his ideas had been done already, but there was a humor to it. He slapped the table and howled in laughter when Vana explained the movie "Cars" to him. Maybe this was all he needed. Someone to listen and understand, someone as nostalgic as he was for the art of cinema.
With a burst of power, a hidden doorway on the floor opened in the middle of the coffee shop. Three armed officers emerged and aimed their rifles at Dog Man. Before he could stand, four more officers broke down from the ceiling. Dog Man pushed his chair back and stood up. He fumbled for his gun, but dropped it as the arms of an officer broke through the wall like it was made out of wafers and wrapped around his neck.
The rest of the wall-burster broke through and wrestled Dog Guy to the ground. And as all light and vision began to vanish from Dog Man's sight, and the grip of the policeman tightened, he felt some relief that this is how his day would end. Nobody died. He didn't kill anyone. But he somehow managed to make a friend. Dog Guy slowly drifted off to sleep, reaching for a distant idea for a movie about chickens who escape from a farm.

Bale held Vana for a long time that night. On the motel bed. On the motel floor. In the motel shower. Every time he let her go, she needed him to come back. Bale had never seen her this fragile, nor this angry. "You shouldn't see me like this," she would say. By this time, Plum was fast asleep in a small bed Vana bought from the gift shop. The night had settled in and no noise could be heard beyond the motel room. And the only sounds were of Vana.
Bale stroked her hair as they sat on the floor of the bathroom. Vana vomited a few times into the toilet. She begged Bale just to leave her there. But Bale remained like a repressed memory. He promised he wouldn't let her go. The static light of the bathroom illuminated two very broken people.
"What did you see, Bale?" Vana asked after a session of crying and screaming. She looked up at him, her eyes as wide as the Serengeti, "What did you see in your cup?"

Chapter 10: Main Street Drugs

Everything solid casts a shadow when it's set against light. And light can come from anywhere. The stained glass window of a church on your wedding day. The interior of a car as you pick someone up from the airport. The gaudy, yet charming ceiling lamp hanging over your table at a restaurant. Light is everywhere, and often the only way to escape the darkness.
That darkness. It waits for you. It's always there, sometimes just sitting on the very edge. Sometimes in places you forget exist. Empty homes full of people's stuff and framed memories. Diners shut down for the night and stranded in the middle of brightly-lit franchises. Darkness sits in your closet when you are asleep. With your clothes. With your shoes. It likes having the door closed.

Just as light casts a shadow against every solid thing, people are no exception. The majority of us don't see. Well, we do actually. But our brains tell us it's just a shadow. Darkness becomes visible, like us. But unlike us, it cannot be solid. Darkness is bound to us like an anchor and forced to drag along the surface of the Earth wherever we go. Against its will. Whether we are leaping bar to bar with our friends. Whether we are miserably leaving a funeral. Or perhaps we're just taking our dog for a walk. Darkness is bound to us.
And how would you feel if it were you? Unable to rise off the ground. Unable to cut loose from a giant who doesn't even regard your existence. Dragged around the pavement and grass as children ask "Mommy, who is that". Only to be met with a cold, "That's nothing, honey. That's just your shadow".
If it cut itself loose, it would be reassuring to think the darkness would simply return to where it came from. Slinking back into the corners of the Earth where man is absent. Slumbering in serenity, knowing light has no power there. That would be reassuring. But most things are capable of anger. Most things don't forget.

Bale and Vana's brief stop at "Main Street Drugs" was quite mundane compared to their last few stops. Outside of the shop Vana couldn't help but notice the word "Main" didn't light up. "Well, I guess they're advertising the best part," Bale said. The two shared a dry laugh and walked inside and out of the drizzle. The drug store was palely lit by fluorescent lights. Clear as it all was there was still a murkiness to everything. Bale grabbed some headache medicine, Vana grabbed some pain killers, Plum pleaded with Vana to buy some strawberry candies.
The store was very small and had no windows. It reminded Bale of the studio apartment he lived in after high school. He couldn't wait to get his own place back then. Living in a building with a busted buzzer and thin walls was a worthwhile price to pay to live on his own. His building was maybe five feet away from another building just like it, and so on and so forth. His mattress sat on the floor in the corner, opposite the toilet and small shower. His kitchen consisted of a single counter with two drawers built into the bottom, an oven as old as his grandmother, and two hanging cabinets. One of which was missing a latch so it swung open constantly. He also had a mini fridge with a cat magnet on the front. Bale didn't have a couch, he had a beanbag chair and a radio he found in his dad's storage locker. It wasn't much, but it was his.

Until it was her's. She came in and fixed it for him. She repaired the cabinets, she got him a bedframe and a couch and a TV and a big fridge with new cat magnets. She got him a laptop and helped him fix the closet door so he could hang his clothes up instead of keeping all his clothes inside a suitcase. She made it all work. And in reality, she never wanted all this. This studio apartment. This mess of a man. But she still took it and twisted it into something decent. Something to build from. And she would build from it with him.

"Hey. Bale. Why is it so quiet in here?" Vana asked as they walked up to the single checkout counter.
"I don't know. I guess there's no music".
"Yeah, yeah, that's it. I couldn't put my finger on it," Vana tapped her finger against her bottom lip, "Why isn't there music?"
"Probably an expensive thing".
"What do you mean?"
"Oh, well, music costs money. Even recycled radio classics from the 80's, 90's and today's".
"Oh, right. Well, I think that's dumb".
"It's just business".
"Yeah, well, if I ever ran a store or something and I didn't want to pay for music," she hesitated, "I would just make my own music".
"Can you do that?"
"Legally? I don't know. You're the suit".
"No, no, no, I mean can you make music? Like, can you play an instrument?"
"I played a little piano when I was a kid".
"That's nuts. You're attractive and talented?"
"Shut up," Vana lightly shoved him.

They stood at the counter for only a few seconds and started wondering where the cashier was. Or where the shelf-stockers were. Come to think of it, there was nobody else in the store. Bale and Vana looked around, down every aisle and found nobody
"Well, now what?" Bale asked.
"We could trash the store".
"What? Why would we do that?"
"Haven't you ever seen a movie or a TV show where the characters are trapped inside a store and so they race around in shopping carts or use the cashier's conveyor belt like a treadmill?"
"I don't watch a lot of movies or TV".
"Yeah, well, it's super common. Wasn't there a news story about something like that?"
"What? Oh, yeah, I know what you're talking about," Bale started taking bills out of his wallet.
"There was a guy who spent a few days inside a Walmart, right?"
"Yeah, yeah, yeah. I think that's so cool," Vana was lifting one item at a time to show Bale the prices on them.
"I'll admit, it's kind of neat," Bale placed forty-five dollars on the counter.
"What about change?"
"It's fine. There's a coin shortage".

As they carried their purchases to the door, Vana asked Bale, "So, if you had to be trapped anywhere for a night, where would it be?"
"I don't know. Maybe an arcade?"
"You'd need coins to play the games".
"A fancy restaurant?"
"Booor-ing".
"A theme park then".
"Now we're talking".
"Wouldn't it be kind of-". Bale stopped at the door.
"What? Kind of what", Vana stood behind Bale, "Bale, what's wrong".
Bale didn't turn around. "He's out there".
"You…you see him?"
"Yeah. I see him".
Across the street from "Main Street Drugs" was a single streetlamp casting a cone of light down on a figure. Pitch black, with small stars scattered throughout. Simple, round white eyes. And a square hand with a white screen. The sound was muffled, but with no music in the store Bale could hear it clearly. It's hand was ringing.
"Open the door, Bale," Vana instructed him.
"I don't know if I can".
Vana reached out and grabbed his hand. "You can".

Bale began pushing with one hand, and gripping Vana with the other. Whatever this monster was, it couldn't break him. Because she would fix him. She was his light. This was his shadow. And his journey would not end in darkness. As the door swung open and the streetlight went out, everything became drenched in pitch black. Sound seized. Warmth died. It was just it and them now. Them and the darkness. And the darkness didn't forget.

Chapter 11: The Airport

Bale was shaken into consciousness by the sound of an alarm clock. As he hastily sat up and looked around him he realized he was in a motel. Bale stepped out of the bed, knocking over an empty Jack Danials bottle as he stood. He slipped into his baggy suit with the repetition of a pendulum and drove his rental car to the airport. The only stop he made was to a coffee place. Coffee would help the headache.

"I'm sorry, sir, but we're actually out of coffee at the moment," the perky woman behind the speaker said.

"But…this is a coffee place," Bale said out his driver's side window, aware of the line of cars behind him.

"I'm sorry, our shipment is just running a little late".

"Oh," Bale sighed, "I…really wanted a coffee. And the airport…it doesn't-".

"I'm sorry, sir, but there is a line behind you. Is there anything else I can get you".

"Oh, sorry, yeah. Can I get a….a bagel?"

"Of course! What kind of bagel would you like".

"Raisin, please," his grandmother's favorite.

"I'm sorry, sir, but we actually don't have any raisin bagels left".

"Oh, okay," the honking began behind Bale. "Well, what about a cinnamon bagel?"

"Oh, I'm sorry, sir, we don't have any cinnamon bagels left in stock. Is there another kind of bagel you-".

More honking. "What kind of bagels do you have right now?"

"Please mind your tone, sir," the voice strictly said, "We only have plain bagels right now"

Bale breathed deeply. "So then why would you ask me what kind of bagel I want if you only have one kind of bagel".

More honking. One guy shouted. "Sir, would you like a plain bagel or not," she asked.

"Yes. Yes, I want a plain bagel".

"Sir, your tone," she replied sharply, "Would you like any cream cheese on that".

"I don't know, do I?" Bale mocked. The honking was constant now, like someone was leaning on the horn.

"Sir, we don't accept this kind of attitude here. Currently, the only cream cheese we have in stock is plain cream cheese".

"Fine. I will take plain cream cheese, please," Bale shouted.

The voice shouted back, "Alright, will that be all today?"

"Yes, it will! Thank you".

"Pull up to the first window".

"Wait".

"What? What now".

"Can you please put the cream cheese on the bagel for me".

There was no response from the speaker.

"Hello? Please, I'm in a rush".

Still no reply. The honking continued, but slowly stopped. Bale sighed and pulled up to retrieve his bagel, which was all but thrown into his car. The cashier was an adorable college-aged girl who looked like she'd marry rich and never be ignored. Bale attempted to apologize, but remembered he'd never have to come here again in his life. Bale said a lot of rude things and then drove away with his food, unaware of what his words would do to that young woman, and unaware that the cars that honked at him were not trying to insult him, they were trying to warn him.

He stood there at the counter, bagel in one hand, suitcase in the other. The line onto the plane moved steadily and when he reached the stewardess to hand in his ticket, she informed him that no outside food could be taken onto the plane. "That's fine," Bale said, "the lady never gave me any cream cheese anyway". He dumped the bagel in the trash and boarded his flight. Sitting by a window, Bale was told to silence his phone when it started ringing. The number was unknown. While he had it out, Bale checked his voicemails.
"Bale. We need you to come in tomorrow…"
"Hey honey, let me know when you get…"
"We're calling to inform you about your car…"
Wait. Did Bale have a car?
"Smith called out and we need you…"
He took a bus to the airport, didn't he?
"Maybe when you get back we can…"
"Can you grab your father's med…"
And the airport had a coffee place. That's where he got the bagel. The bagel. The bagel. The…the bagel.

He stood there at the counter, bagel in one hand, suitcase in the other. His pockets harbored his phone, his wallet, some receipts from a taxi ride and a trip to the airport's coffee shop. Bale's mouth burned from drinking his coffee so quickly. He never liked it dark. Sometimes it felt like it was looking back at him. The line was moving surprisingly fast. As Bale was about to toss his bagel, the stewardess put a hand on his shoulder. "You can take your bagel," she whispered. Bale thanked her. She looked young, college-aged maybe. She'd probably marry rich.
Bale sloppily cleaned off cream cheese from his mouth with his sleeve as he searched for his seat. Window seat, just as he liked it. The stewardess asked everyone to silence their phones for some reason. Maybe there was an in-flight movie. Bale went to silence his phone when he noticed some voicemails.
"Bale, I need you to come back…"
"Hey, honey, let me know…Bale, come back…"
"We're calling to…we're calling…"
"Smith…Bale…and we need…Bale…"
"Your father…suspension…Bale…my name…"
Her name? What was her name?

He stood there in the wreckage of the airport. Any planes that didn't fly through the walls probably exploded into flames just by sitting still. He had a bagel in one hand, and his phone in the other. The phone wouldn't leave his hand. And it wouldn't stop ringing. There was no line onto the plane, just brushes of ash against the ground. The stewardess was beautiful, she was dressed skimpy, and in her arms was a basket of bagels so fresh and warm they permeated the smell of gasoline and burning rubble.

She begged Bale to get on the plane. She promised him all the bagels in the world if he got on the plane. She drew him close with a wave of a hand and held his face close to hers. "You can have anything," she said, "just board the plane, sir". Bale's bagel slipped from his hand and dissolved into sand as it bounced off the stained floor. Bale dropped to his knees as his phone rang louder and louder.

"Call. Me. Back," a voice came from the phone.

"What," Bale looked up at the stewardess, "What did you say?"

"I said," her form twisted and grew, "get on the plane".

"Call. Me. Back".

"No," Bale shook his head as he watched the woman transform into a dark, mangled tree. Her face became that of a snake's and acidic moisture expelled with every word. "I heard…I heard something else".

"Get. On. Board," she hissed.

"Call. Me. Back," the phone rang.

"I have to remember," Bale held his other hand to his head, "I have to remember her name. What the hell was her name".

He met her at a tattoo parlor. She was free. Fearless. She talked to him like what he said mattered. He wanted her name. And he almost gave her something. Something beautiful like her. What was it? Come on, Bale. Think. A name can be forgotten, but he held this in his hands. This…this toy. Yes, it was a toy. It had pretty colors. It..it was…

As the jaws of the stewardess closed around him, Bale reached into his pockets and pulled out everything he had. His wallet flew into the flaming breeze, receipts burnt into a crisp, and he dug and he dug and pulled out a small, black, plastic toy. It was a kaleidoscope.

Bale slept for a few hours. He couldn't have slept well though because he felt as tired as a marathon runner. Bale was in a hospital bed, surrounded by machines that beeped and booped. He was in a hospital gown. The kind that don't cover the kiester all too well. The lights were dim, and on the TV against the wall was an episode of "Futurama" where Bender played with his chest like a washboard instrument. There was a little pressure on Bale's stomach. Bale looked over to see Vana slumped over a chair, with her arms and her head resting on him. Bale smiled to himself.

Chapter 12: Main Road

Doctor Hershey ran through a couple of possibilities with Bale. They knocked blood pressure out of the park pretty early, and Doc seemed more certain Bale was hallucinating. "How much sleep have you gotten the last couple of days," he asked. Bale thought back to many sleepless nights where he would just stay up and watch Vana. "So you haven't slept at all? That's bad," he said, this man with a medical degree. Doctor Hershey suggested the "black man" was a figment of Bale's imagination, perhaps triggered by the lack of sleep.
"Can we not call it "the black man", Doc?" Bale asked softly.
"Right, right. God, how awful of me".
Vana fought back a smirk and tried to remain serious, "So, Bale needs more sleep?"
"Possibly. Bale, let me ask you something else".
"Yeah, what?"
"Have you been under a lot of stress?"
Bale placed himself at his job back home. His office was the size of a broom closet, but everyone he worked with treated him like he won the office in a "Who Can Kick The Most Puppies" contest. He placed himself in his studio apartment. What used to just be a place to sleep became a monument to the power of codependency. But comfort was never something easy for Bale to grasp when the only thing his girlfriend would say after the apartment was furnished were things like "So when are you gonna move in with me?" and "So when are we gonna get a house?". Bale just wanted to be done for a little while.
His home life wasn't without its bouts of stress either. It seemed like no matter how much money he made, how old he grew, or how many accomplishments he completed, Bale would never be older than thirteen when he stepped into his parents' house. His mother would always comment on what Bale hadn't done yet. His father would reminisce about a life he lived before Bale's birth. His mother wanted grandkids. His father wanted a beer.

"Yeah. I guess I've been stressed out for a long time," Bale kept his eyes on the white tiled floor. The fluorescent light beamed off of the tiles with nauseating force.
"Oh, well, I mean have you felt stress recently," he clarified.
Bale looked up at him, and then to Vana, "Yeah, things have been kinda weird lately".
Vana added, "Like when you met that bear monster".
"Yeah, he was alright. But, like, before that. In Tapetown".
"Yeah, yeah, yeah. We met a giant tape man".
"And then there was the hostage thing".
"At the bank or at the coffee place".
"I meant the coffee place. We didn't take any hostages at the bank".
"Oh, yeah, right. What about the frogs".
"Yeah, what the hell were the frogs about?"
The doctor cleared his throat.
Bale did the same and looked at him, "Yes, I have been under a lot of stress".
"Perhaps I could refer you to a mental health physician". Doctor Hershey took out a business card and a pen from his jacket pocket. As he began writing he abruptly stopped. He looked back up, "Did you say you robbed a bank?"

Bale and Vana sat in the country jail for at least an hour while the local authorities made some phone calls. Vana leaned against the bars and whistled "Sweet Georgia Brown" while Bale sat on a bench in the back of the cell. Bale kept the top of his head against the wall and stared at the ceiling. They could hear the muffled voice of the police captain in the other room, but the only consistent sound was that of water dripping. Bale lifted his head and looked over at a skinny man on the other end of the bench. He was naked except for an adult diaper, hairless save for a handlebar mustache, and silent when you ignore the dripping. He was also insanely wet. Like, dying from dehydration in the middle of the desert so he ran sixty miles to the nearest Bomb Defusal Tournament kind of wet. Although he didn't smell like sweat. "So, did you, like, fall in a river or something?" Bale asked him. The man moved his eyes towards Bale, and then he moved his head like he was a robot or something. He spoke very softly, "This ain't water". Bale decided to stand up, stretch his legs, and never sit down there again for the rest of his life.
The Captain let Vana and Bale out and walked them out into the lobby. During the walk, the captain claimed the Chief of Police vouched for Bale and Vana, saying the whole bank robbery was a staged training exercise.
"Chief of…we never met.." Bale began to speak.
The Captain cut him off, "Apparently he wasn't on duty when you met him. I don't know if maybe you two got his name. Sunny Glass?"
Vana and Bale became audibly elated. "Sunglasses," they said to each other.

The Captain left them in the lobby and told them to be on their way. The department was very busy today. "I don't know if either of you noticed, but there's an extremely sweaty man back there".
"It's not sweat, sir," Bale replied, "He doesn't smell bad".
"Well, it can't be water. He told us it wasn't water. Jesus Christ, this is tough".
Bale was ready to ship off, but Vana stayed and asked one more question, "Hey, have there been any sightings of a bla-shadowy man attacking people?"
"Vana, come on he doesn't-" Bale was cut off again by the Captain.
"Hold on," the Captain leaned in so only these two could hear him, "I ain't never heard of a shadowy man, but it sounds paranormal. We got this mystic in town, she might know something".
The Captain took a card he got from the mystic and gave it to Vana. "Oh cool. Has she ever helped you personally?" Vana asked.
"As a matter of fact she did. When I was quite young she revealed to me my past life. I was quite the evil fella, but motivated by my past misdeeds I fought in Iraq and then joined the police force when I got back. I owe a lot to her for that".
"Wow. That's awesome. Thanks for everything, Captain Hutler".
"No problem, Miss. And, please, call me Dolph".

Roma Phenomenon owned a small parlor on the edge of the small town. As Bale and Vana traveled there they got a lot of weird looks from the locals. As if they could tell they were going to meet this mystic. Vana couldn't even hail a cab. And she tried using her good leg too. This parlor, "The Place of Knowing", was garishly covered in red drapery. To call it a parlor was generous. It consisted of one room with an antique box in the center of the room and four blue floor pillows surrounding it. The floor was red carpet, the windows were covered in a black film, and the only light source were a dozen of those LED candles you can buy at the party store just kind of scattered throughout the room. She probably tried real candles once, but that might have burnt the parlor down to a tool shed.

Sitting on one of the pillows was Roma Phenomenon. She was a round woman with tan, aged skin. Her long, gray hair was braided into two, long ponytails that swung on both sides of her head. Over the top of her head she wore a violet bandana, her white blouse was open noticeably low, and below that was a long, purple dress. She appeared to be quite short and her fingers, arms, and neck were adorned in various pieces of jewelry. She had some accessories on her ears too, but they appeared to be wooden beads and charms. Her voice was raspy, although hurtful to hear there was a comfort to her tone. Her big, dark eyes lit up as she opened her arms and invited the couple to sit down with her. Vana sat on Roma's left, and Bale on her right. Plum had been fast asleep most of the day so Vana laid her down on the pillow across from Roma. Roma smiled at the sight of the frog.

"Tell me now, children *cough*. What *cough, cough* brings you here to my *cough* Place of Knowing this night *cough*?" Roma asked.

There was a long pause, but before Bale could answer Vana quickly asked, "Shouldn't you know? It's your place of knowing, right?"

Roma, with no pause, began laughing loudly. She coughed very hard as she laughed and stopped to clear her throat. "I can tell *cough* this is gonna be a good time *cough*".

"Miss Phenomenon, the Police Captain sent us here," Bale replied, "He said you could help us".

"Ah, yes, Captain Hutler *cough*. I love that man. Too bad he's taken. And with four kids too *cough*".

"Wow, I didn't know that," Vana laughed, "I guess this really is the place of knowing".

Roma laughed again. The force of her laughter and the crashing volume of her coughing bounced all around the small room. She told Vana "You are too much, child". She turned back to Bale, "Tell me what plagues you, my boy".

Bale explained the shadowy man. He told Roma about the kaleidoscope, the coin in the hotel room, the beach at Sendoffs, everything he remembered about the shadow man and his weird phone hand.

"Huh, phone hand," Roma pondered, "that's different. And you said, *cough* you said a lot of weird things have been happening ever since you left *cough* the Boardwalk?"

"Yes. Very weird things," Bale replied.

"Yeah, like the frog city".

"And the tape monster".

"And the dog guy".

"And the bear God".

"Oh," Roma said, "you met Supay".

"Yeah, he was really nice".

"Oh, yes, very nice boy that Supay," Roma coughed into her arm this time, then proceeded, "I think I know *cough* why so much of this has been *cough* happening to you".

Vana folded her arms, "Is it a curse? Because I've been screwing this guy for, like, a month and I haven't gotten myself tested yet".

Children in Dubai could hear the eruption of laughter and lung disease that poured out of Roma's mouth. She laughed so hard her spirit left her body, went across the street, bought a hotdog from a vendor, and then came back. Roma begged Vana to be gentle, "My old heart cannot take it". Roma reached out and patted Vana's hand.

Roma opened the antique box and inside were various long wooden boxes. Each had a pattern painted on them, and as she dug through them Roma briefly explained that the world they live in is not the only world that exists. "Oh, you mean like aliens and stuff?" Vana asked. Roma shook her head, probably thankful Vana didn't make her laugh again. "No, no, aliens exist in our world too, child" Roma smiled widely, "Ah, here it is".

She took out a box made of dark wood and opened it to reveal incense. "You'll have to forgive my slowness," she said as she reached into her dress pocket, "It has been quite a long time since I explained The Worldscapes".

"Hey. Your dress has pockets," Vana pointed out.

"Yes, I know".

"That's cool. I might start wearing dresses now".

"Don't make her laugh," Bale said.

"I'm not kidding, dude. I didn't know they made dresses with pockets".

Roma used a yellow cigarette lighter with little monkey heads on it to light a single stick, causing a green smoke to fly out. "This will clear your minds and make you more *cough* open to the what I have to teach you *cough*".

The room became darkened by the green smoke. Bale was nervous, but the dread darkness usually brought him was not present. What became present were clouds of various colors appearing in the room. Purple and pink and orange and red, various astral figments resembling universes and galaxies. Vana whispered, "Are we sure this isn't a space thing?"

"What you see is The Fleshscape", Roma said.

"That's a gross name," Vana replied.

"Well, look here," Roma pointed to a small blue dot floating among the stars. "This is Earth, and like many planets far beyond our grasp, it is home to physical creatures. Beasts, fish, birds, insects, and, of course, people. This is true of other planets too. Different as we might be from each other, or from creatures lightyears away, we are all organic. We are all made from flesh and bone".

"Okay, so why not call it the Bonescape?" Vana annoyingly asked.

"Because some animals don't have bones, okay?" Roma quickly responded. "Like, jellyfish *cough* and bugs and stuff. Okay?"

"Okay, jeez".

"I'm sorry, I just *cough* get that question a lot. May I continue?"

"Yes, please".

"We all live in the Fleshscape because we are all accustomed to a physical state of existence. But some sentient life, even here on Earth, can access another world called The Mindscape".

The cosmos surrounding them faded away and was replaced by a blue space full of white lines. At first, the lines seemed random and contradictory, but as Bale kept looking he began to see the lines form stick figures and shapes and connective systems. Ideas and concepts began chaining together.
"If the Fleshscape is the collective physical realm, then the Mindscape is the collective non-physical. It is where all our minds join and exist. It is where the basic instincts of hunt, nurture, and survive were born. The Mindscape expands beyond all limits as knowledge advances here on Earth," Roma began swinging her hands around in an "airing out" motion, "But we can go even further, children".

Now the blueness morphed into a light brown, a sort of widescaled sepia tone. A static effect jumped around the room, multiplying and evaporating all at once. Sounds of cars and indiscriminate voices and rushing water fought for superiority within Bale's ears.

"Deeper we find The Rescape," Roma stopped waving, "And here is where the collective becomes less collective. The Mindscape holds all we know, but The Rescape protects all we remember. It is the easiest realm to access, but the hardest to truly master. Here, every one person has a history. A lineage. But, a larger pillar of memories exists in The Rescape, a pillar formed and kept alive by memories people share. Even complete strangers remember the same thing, but in different ways. It is this simultaneous individuality and coexistence which forms these pillars and carries not only The Rescape, but every other realm as well".
"Don't tell me there are more," Bale groaned.

"Oh, there is always more," Roma swung her hands again, this time pushing out and spreading her fingers over and over again. Until the beige wonderland around them vanished and only an off-white mist remained. At first it was underwhelming, like some fog had just roamed into the room. But as Bale looked around for something to grab onto, he saw something. A figure in the smoke. The shadow man? No, this man was bigger and stronger. He couldn't place it. Well, not until he saw the red of his eyes. "Hasta la vista, baby," said the booming voice as the man fired a scattershot from a shotgun at Bale. Bale ducked to the floor, but was pulled back up by Roma. "Open your eyes, child. What you see is not flesh, what you see are dreams".
Bale looked around the room as characters from fiction flew out of the mist and vanished back inside. A man in a red cape flew overhead and a trio of rodents scurried by as they sang in perfect harmony. Bale looked over at Vana as she gazed upon an enormous red dog jump onto the back of a laser-blasting lizard monster. Bale briefly looked at Plum, who was awake now. She danced with a little white rat in people's clothes as a band of aliens played jazz in the back of the room.
Roma brushed her hands out to push the characters away and continued, "The Dreamscape is the antithesis to the Mindscape. There, all knowledge exists together, but in the Dreamscape every story exists on its own. It is a realm where every character breathes as if they were alive, where every meeting of fiction and nonfiction alike can take place".
"Wait, wait, wait, so Captain Jack Sparrow could team up with, like, Santa Claus?" Vana asked excitedly.

"He could. But he could also team up with Bugs Bunny or Uncle Sam or Momotaro. He could share words with King Arthur or Dr. House or Donkey Kong or Sherlock Holmes. Or he could go on his adventure from his movie, or a slightly different version, or it's the same movie, but he is played by David Hasselhoff. The Dreamscape is ideas, it's imagination, if you can picture a world or a story, then it is out there. It exists. And the overwhelming density of its mass is only supported by its never ending contribution of creativity, as even the same old story about a talking sponge can create a platform for the rest of the realm to stand on".

"You know, I could have gone my whole life without knowing Spongebob was an essential universal concept, but here we are," Vana said blankly.

"What does any of this have to do with the shadowy man?" Bale asked.

"Well, if this creature is unknown to you, there is a place it might currently reside," Rome balled up her first and raised them to her mouth, "Though, you may not like where we are going". She blew from hole within her fists and the white haze evaporated. The plastic lights went out. The room became wrapped in pitch black. Bale could feel his muscles tense up. His arm hairs stood up. And his breath became cold. All of this realm stuff was new to him, but he could feel that he'd been to this place before.

"This is The Unscape. The last and most mysterious realm. It appears as utter blackness, devoid of shape or sound or concepts. Some religions refer to Hell as a place like this. The Unscape is home to everything that does not exist. And these unexisting things lack any appearance or depth, they have not been given anything. These are thoughts that do not exist. Memories lost to the dead and unrecorded by time. Souls yet to be brought to our realm. The Unscape is not evil. It is not good. It simply is because everything inside of it is not".

From his cold breath Bale asked, "What makes you think the shadow man came from here?"

"Do not be mistaken, boy. Nothing comes from here. But, the less you know about this creature, the more likely it would be to stay here".

"Well, how do I keep it there," Bale asked, "I don't want this thing following me around anymore".

"I am afraid I don't know how to seal it away, but I know it is not possible. Not unless everyone who has seen this creature could simply forget it".

"Great. We just have to invent an amnesia ray," Bale stood up flustered. As he walked towards the door, the darkness fell like icicles and bounced like smoke off the floor. Bale broke through the visual storytelling and walked out. Vana got up to follow him, but Roma suggested she sit back down.

"Perhaps your friend needs some air. To process all he has learned. I see you, though, are handling it all very well".

Vana shrugged, "I watch a lot of TV".

"Please, sit with me," Roma pointed to Vana's seat, "Perhaps you seek answers of your own".

Vana nodded and sat down, "You know, now that you mention it," Vana looked up at Roma, "What can you tell me about my past life?"

Chapter 13: The Titanic

The smell of salt was inescapable as the winds over the North Atlantic blew past Gordon's face. He leaned against the North Eastern railing of the boat and marveled at the majesty of the ocean. From behind him a young man approached. The boy's pockets jingled as he moved, though he tried to walk slowly to prevent the sound.
"Mr. Wheaton, sir," the boy said, "I have what you wanted".
"Excellent work, laddie," Gordon said as he turned, "If ye had me waitin' much longer I'da keeled over this railing".
The boy chuckled and from his pocket pulled out a handful of keys. And then another. And another. Each key had a letter and a number written on them. "I'm sorry it took so long, sir. I hadn't realized you didn't have your sea legs yet".
"Aye," Gordon placed his fists on his hips, "And what be your excuse?"
"My father was a fisherman, sir".
"Ah, well, good career and all that nonsense. Hand me them keys and be on yer way".
The boy turned away slightly, "And my payment?"
"Ah, smart lad," Gordon reached into his coat and fumbled around. He took out a catcher's mitt wrapped in newspaper. On the back of the mitt there was a signature of a famous baseball player. The boy was elated and took the mitt. He gave Gordon the keys.
"Surely, this can't be all of em'," Gordon said as he weighed the keys in his hands.
"You got me, mister," the boy tried on the glove. Perfect fit, "It's only about 1/4th the rooms".
"Hmm. Well, still, good work. Howja do it?"
The boy shook his head, "A little thieving, a little gadgetry, what's to know".
Gordon laughed and scruffled the boy's hair. The tall man walked off to begin his pilfering while so many guests were off dancing and falling in love. The boy followed and asked what he was looking for on the boat.
"Why, anything I can get me mitts on," Gordon laughed, "Fancy folk like these gotta have some riches lying 'round".
"I don't suppose you need a look out,"
"You understand that dirty glove was yer payment, right? I don't have nothin' else to give ya".
"Nonsense, Mr. Wheaton. Fancy folk like these got to have some riches lying around. You'll find something to pay me with".
Gordon laughed and smacked the boy on the back, "A regular smooth talker yerself, boy! Very well, you can be me eyes. What should I calls ya".
"Andy, sir. I'm Andy Doyle".
"Ah! Dandy Andy! Good ta be workin' with ya".

Gordon and Andy lined their pockets with jewelry and loose bills. They giggled as the gawked over women's underwear and danced like noblemen as they tried on the hat's of wealthy cruise guests. Andy even found an autographed baseball to go with his new mitt. Gordon managed to find some expensive cigars inside a locked box. He was no lockpick himself, but Gordon had enough raw strength to pull the wicker container apart.
After exploring over thirty rooms and running return trips back to Gordon's cabin to stow the riches away, the two took a break to sneak some food from the dining hall and rest. They

watched the sea as they sat, with their lobster and port wine. Gordon was a sloppy eater, rushing into every bite.
"Eager to get back to work, Mr. Wheaton?" Andy asked.
"Pants ta that," Gordon said with cheeks full of food, "When ye get ta eat like a king, ya don't settle for one dish". Gordon spat as he laughed at his own humor, "If I down this meal fast 'nuff, I can still sneak me a second, or a third! Food can't last as long as diamond rings, after all".
Andy looked back at the sea, nipping at his chicken. Gordon asked if he was going to finish his baked potato and Andy passively handed it over. "Mr. Wheaton, what's being on your own like?"
"Eh, whaja say, kid," Gordon was washing his food down with wine.
"Being an adult. Out there on your own. What's it like? No parents or teachers or nothing?"
"Hmph," Gordon rubbed his chin, "Not all it's cracked up ta be, I know that much".
"What do you mean? You get to be in charge of yourself don't you?"
"Aye, but people expect to much from ya. Strangers expect to much. Everyone wants something, kid. And when yer grown like me, all ye want is the freedom you were promised".
"Are you not from the States?"
"I'dda think me accent gave it away. Me and me parents, we moved here from Ireland when I was just becoming a man".
"Where are they now? Your parents?"
"Hell if I know. Got sick of watching me father hit me mother. So I ran off, fended for meself," he fell silent only for a moment, "Worked out, aye? Now I'm here, robbin' the biggest boat in the world". Gordon stood up and raised his wine bottle. With a loud belch and a hardy laugh he shouted to the ocean, "I don't need anybody! I got the world to meself". Andy stood up prepared to calm the drunk down, but they were quickly sidelined by two men. They appeared to be civilians. They approached from nowhere and started asking questions. Then, enraged by their interruption, Gordon swung his bottle at them.

The three men traded interchangeable insults at one another and as Gordon tapped his bottle against one of the men's cheeks, the other pushed Gordon, who rolled back onto his hands and knees. Gordon roared like a boar and tackled the pusher, only to be grabbed. Gordon was held still by one man, as the other laid punch after punch into Gordon's stomach.
Gordon glared at Andy and coughed up what sounded like a plea, but Andy was too afraid of the scrap to get involved. Onto the cheap blanket they were sitting on he scooped the rest of the food and wine and swung the sack over his shoulder. Andy ran off from the scene and didn't look back. He didn't know what to assume about Gordon's fate, but he couldn't fall with him.

Andy returned to the meager broom closet he was told was a cabin. It was a small space with only two beds against the wall, bunk bed style. His mother wasn't in the room, probably still working in the banquet hall. She served French delicacies to people richer than God, but aspired to be a musician. Andy casually played with the strings of her violin now and again. He had no talent for it, but the sounds of the strings calmed him down.
He did so now, then unloaded his ill-gotten gain into a suitcase bigger than they needed. What would she say if she knew? He would have to think of something. A generous patron? Perhaps he saved the pet cat of a wealthy dutchess?

His plan would have to wait though, as Andy could hear screams outside his cabin. The hallways of the deck became flooded by employees and crewmen bustling to one end of the ship. Against the tide of masses, Andy was swept over to a railing and pinned by the screaming civilians. Andy looked around for an authority and was only met by the same fearful face over and over. That was until Andy saw the catalyst of this panic; a glacier. A glacier so massive, Andy instinctively criticized how the captain could have missed it.

"The hell do you mean we hit an iceberg," Captain Smith shouted to Officer Murdoch.
"Well, sir, it didn't seem like a powerful obstacle," Murdoch said frankly. He and Smith stood in the Captain's office. Smith was nearly finished with his wood whittling of a pirate ship when Mudoch burst in.
"It's an iceberg, you blasted fool! Not an icecube. Not an icebox. An iceberg!"
"As per your instructions, sir! We were told to drive through any and all ice formations".
"Small ice, Will! Small ice formations," Smith squeezed between his eyes and commanded his officer to begin evacuating women and children first.
"And what of you, Captain?"
"I will do the same. I need only a minute alone to pray".
"Ah, very well, sir," Murdoch nodded and left the room to begin evacuation.
Smith leaned back in his chair. To his left he looked at a portrait hanging on his wall. The painting was of himself-as a boy-and his mother. Smith sat up, grabbed his flask of whisky from under his desk, and walked over to the portrait.
"Well, Mother," he said, "This must be it. This boat will sink, and as will I. I always knew that incident with The Hawke would come back to bite me. And it must be here, on the largest vessel, in the middle of an ocean I know as well as God knows me. Here is where I fail. I'm sorry, Mother," Smith used his sleeve to wipe his mouth after slugging the whisky down, "I'll be seeing you soon".

Moments flew by as women and children were loaded onto liferafts, people flung themselves off the ship, water bursted into the dining hall and left many drowned or crushed by debris. The band kept on playing, but the screams ran through their symphony. As lovers parted and the rich fought for survival, authority figures on the ship became too distracted to keep Gordon in his holding cell. Gordon drunkenly stumbled out and looked through a window to see the menacing ice pillar. He belched and wiped sweat from his brow. He needed to get off this boat, but not without his treasure.
As Andy scrambled through the crowds of people in search of his mother, he was accosted by people who believed they had more of a right to live. Andy approached an officer and explained that he couldn't find his mom, but his plea was interrupted by an overweight woman with hair the size of the iceberg. She had no children, just dogs. But her dogs were her children. Andy sought out another officer, even believing to have seen his mother in a crowd.
As Andy scurried he was suddenly grabbed and pulled into a hallway. Gordon looked manic as he held the boy by his shirt collar. Gordon's beard was rank with sweat and liquor and his eyes were red as the devil.
He gargled for a moment, and then asked, "Where is it, me boy?"

"What? What are you-".
"Our loot! Where be our loot? Where it be?"
"Loot, I don't-I don't know-".
"Look here, ye vermin," Gordon growled, "I broke meself out the slammer. I went back to our lunch spot and the treasure was gone. Gone! Where didja move it ta?"
Andy shook and pushed off Gordon, Andy said quickly, "I don't know! Leave me alone".

Andy ran out of the hallway and into the crowd again, sifting through fur coats and heavy bags just to reach the railing. He pushed himself up and leaned forward as he tried to look over the crowd for his mother. But then he heard the roar of a dragon and was pushed off the railing by Gordon, who charged him from across the deck. The two tumbled and bounced off lower levels of the ship until Gordon grabbed the railing of the lowest level.
As Andy and Gordon pulled themselves back up they stepped into shallow water. This level was going under, and in a matter of time so would they. Andy tried to run to a staircase, but Gordon grabbed his arm and flung him into a wall. Gordon grabbed and lifted the boy, and inches away from his face asked again "Where be me loot?" His breath stank of booze and his language became harder to understand. Andy kicked until Gordon let go and the boy rushed into another hallway.
Gordon's voice echoed the abandoned quarters of the boat. He called out, "Doyle. Doyle! There's no escapin' here, me boy".
Andy knelt behind a corner and covered his mouth.
"Come on. Come on out," Andy could hear Gordon, he could hear him walking too. The water was up to Gordon's shins, "I just want me treasure. Ya come out, see? And we find it. And we leave this damned ship".
Andy crawled on all fours through the water. He was slow, but he was quiet. But the cold ocean water went up past his arms and legs as he crawled.
"Think about it, boy. All them riches, for you. For me. Hell, ya gotta have someone ya care for," Gordon began swinging doors open and peaking inside, "Maybe a mommy? Every boy has a mommy".
Andy couldn't hide in a room or he'd be found, but he still had one trick left. When he and Gordon parted ways he swiped the room keys off of Gordon. Andy slowly slumped up around a corner and tried to read a room number off the wall, but it was too dark.
Gordon sped up, "Maybe we can keep this going, me boy," he laughed now, "You, me, and yer mommy. We'd make quite the family, me thinks".
Gordon thought he saw Andy and flung himself forward at a hatrack that floated out of a room. He wrestled and rolled with the hatrack for a moment before realizing what he was doing. Gordon felt like a fool. He picked the rack up and bent it in his hands, "Maybe-maybe yer not like other boys. Maybe," Gordon snapped the rack over his knee, discarded one end and kept the sharp wooden stick, "Maybe yer alone".
Andy knew his keys. He didn't know his place. He didn't know these rooms. But he knew this would be his only chance. Andy stood, the water up to his knees, and he slowly moved over to an open room.
"Ya know what that means, dontcha boy," Gordon spoke through the darkness.

Andy ducked into the open room, just behind the doorway. He looked across the room at another open room. Andy reached into his pocket for the keys, but also for a small jewelry box he made sure to keep on him from the looting. He opened it and gathered a handful of rings into his palm. He was planning on saving these rings for his mother. Andy tightened the rings in his hand and grit his teeth.
"It means," Gordon said, "When you're gone-".
Andy reeled his hand back and threw the folly of rings into the room across from him. The rings splashed and plopped into the water, some even bouncing off the vanity in the room. The sounds were enough to lure Gordon, who finished, "Nobody will miss you".

Gordon rushed through the water and stood in front of the open room. He yelled out to Andy and ran into the room wildly swinging his wooden weapon. Gordon splashed and swung until he fell into the water. As he flailed to regain stability, Andy appeared at the door. Gordon looked back and saw Andy's silhouette. He called out to him again.
Andy reached in and shut the door. He held it there and went through the keys, testing each of them against the lock. Gordon struggled, but he got up and ran to open the door. Andy was in the middle of testing keys when he felt the door open. Even with all his might the boy knew wasn't as strong as Gordon, but he was leagues smarter. Andy went from pulling with all his might to a sudden shove. The door slammed against Gordon's head and knocked him back into the water.

"Captain, we still have room," a crewman signaled as Smith loaded another child onto the liferaft. "Come aboard, sir".
"Not in the cards, my friend," Smith replied. He smiled with no humor, "First rule of being Captain: you always go down with your ship".
Smith looked behind him and heard shouting. Andy ran across the deck just drenched in cold ocean water. Smith shouted to the rafts that another boy was found. He took a blanket from a pile and wrapped Andy up. As Smith began to push him, Andy grabbed him and said through exhausted breath, "Please, sir, my mother".
"What is it, son?" Smith asked.
"My-my mother. I need to know if she's-if she's safe, sir. She was in-in the band and I don't-I don't know-" Andy was coughing up salt water by this point.
Smith looked up and cast his view across the ocean at all the rafts. He lifted his horn from off the floor and called out, "This boy is looking for his mother! She was in the band," Smith stopped to get the boy's name, "His name is Andy Doyle!"
Then, a scream. A raise of arms. A beautiful woman with long, curly hair. She waved and shouted Andy's name. Smith looked back down to Andy and whispered in his ear, "She's here, son. She's here waiting for you".
Andy thanked Smith and was secured on the raft. Tightly in his hand, Andy held the last stolen ring. He could have given it to an officer. He could have given it to his mother like he planned. But Andy decided to keep it to himself. As a reminder. Even if he did the wrong thing with the wrong person, he was going to survive this. This "end of the world".

Smith sat in his office. With his whisky. With his portrait. With a new block of wood he could trim and cut until it resembled his pride and joy. The very thing he loved which would be laid to rest. He knew The Titanic as well as he knew these seas. Perhaps he would have time to shape the bow. Smith didn't know what Andy did. He didn't know about the drowning man locked at the bottom of the boat. He didn't know what God had in store for him, but death wasn't meant to be comfortable. Death is supposed to hurt. But what makes a man feel more human than feeling pain?

Chapter 14: Eastchester

There was an eerie chill as Bale and Vana entered Eastchester. Quite a long period of straight roads and tall trees. The atmosphere in the car wasn't much better. Vana went on and on about her past life, but Bale wasn't there. He was in his head. This shadow came from a dark place, could Bale have been there too? In the hotel? But how could it have gotten here? In the Fleshscape. Gross.
Vana broke through the one-sidedness, "Bale, are you okay".
"I don't know. This whole shadow guy and realm stuff? It's freaking me out".
"Weird".
"Yeah, it is".
"No, I mean you. You're weird".
"Rude".
"No, not rude. Remember Supay?"
"Yeah, love that guy".
"Yeah, well, that guy was, like, an Incan God of Death. And you just hung out with him. Like it was normal".
"Where'd you hear that?"
"Roma told me about him after you walked out".
"Yeah, well, what does she know".
"More than we do".

They pulled into a shopping plaza. Here would be the part where A. Bale and Vana argue over trusting what Roma told them, B. Argue over getting Chile's or Boston Market, or C. Get attacked by a giant robot. It was the third option. Well, they did the other two first, then it was the third option. As they walked towards Boston Market-Vana giddy to get her way-they lunged back as a twenty-foot tall machine landed between them and the restaurant.
It had a cylinder body and legs shaped like a kangaroo. From its sides came six metal tentacles, and at the top of its body was a clear dome with exposed computer machinery inside. The front of the robot was covered in glowing red lights and at the bottom of the cylinder was printed a name, "Killifier".
"Oh, God," Vana screamed, "Don't hurt Boston Market". The machine reeled back using the treads on his feet and backed itself up through the restaurant. "No," Vana cried out, "Not Boston Market". The machine drove forward. Bale grabbed Vana's arm and the two ran away. But the machine was faster. Soon enough it towered over them. But just as its superheated steel radiated on the back of Bale's neck, the machine came to a stop.
Bale and Vana looked back at the machine to see what could have stopped it, but behind the machine they heard a voice, "Someone move those two already". Before they could reply, Bale and Vana flinched when a man suddenly appeared standing atop their car. He was a pretty boy to say the least. Shoulder length blonde hair, a square face, piercing blue eyes, and tan skin. To clarify, this guy clearly used a tanning booth. He wore a yellow full-body suit adorned with logos and words and symbols made from black marker.
"Hey there," the blonde said to Vana, his eyebrow shooting up like it came out of a toaster.

"Hey, get off of our car," Bale said. He was ignored.
"Hope you two like vacations," he reached out and put a hand on both of their heads, "because we're going for a trip".

Bale, Vana, and the Blonde were now on the other side of the plaza. Bale and Vana both felt slightly sick and Bale even dry heaved. The blonde laughed, "Sorry, pal. Everyone's first time can be rough," he glanced over at Vana and smiled, "You seem to handle the transition pretty well". Vana was catching her breath, but squeezed out a quick, "Yeah, my parents moved a lot". The blonde laughed again, but before he could mug for the camera he was called back into the fight by the person who kept the robot from moving.

This person was a tall, black woman with wildly large hair and a pair of copper framed sunglasses on. It wasn't exactly a bright summer day, but maybe they were just cosmetic. She wore the same yellow suit, but her gloves and sleeves were completely removed, revealing her strong arms. Her yellow suit had no markings on it, save for three words on her back: Proud, Black, Woman. From what Bale and Vana could tell, she had her hands under the back of the machine so it couldn't roll forward. As her grip began to slip, she called out "Blastmask, let's go!"

The next contestant for "Who Wore it Better" was a slim woman with a some sort of blue biker helmet on her head. She ran out from behind a parked car and held the side of the helmet. From the black visor blasted out a snow-white beam of energy that pushed the robot over. The strong woman rolled out of the way as the robot fell onto the Boston Market. Vana's heart broke once again. She looked toward the blonde, but he was gone and now somehow standing next to strong woman and "Blastmask". The strong woman then called out, "Alright, Foremen, let's take it apart". Bale, Vana, and the citizens watched as the robot was pulled limb from limb by the superheroes. Strong woman ripped metal off the machine and tossed it aside, Blastmask penetrated its body with beams of light. The blonde would just grab onto a part of the machine and disappear with parts of the robot gone too.

Within minutes the machine was just scattered pieces of technology spread throughout the parking lot. The people cheered for The Foremen and rushed up to them to get autographs and pictures. Bale and Vana stood back perplexed. Nobody did anything with the robot parts. Nobody seemingly got hurt. And these people of Eastchester acted like it was all just a show. Bale tried to ask Vana what she thought, but Vana gasped and pointed at Bale's leg. There was a shard of metal lodged into the back of Bale's right thigh.

The blonde showed up just as soon as Vana screamed. He put his hand on her shoulder, "Are you alright, Miss?"

Vana pointed at Bale. Bale shouted, "Dude. She's fine".

"Wow, okay, maybe don't speak for her?" the blonde replied.

"I have scrap metal in my leg".

"Okay, well, I would hardly denote that as scrap. It's too big to be scrap metal. It's more like debris," the blonde rubbed his perfect chin.

"Help me, you asshole," Bale shouted.

The three heroes loaded Bale and Vana into their gaudy yellow van. It even had a big sign on top that said "The Foremen", in case anyone forgot they drove around in a clown car. The blonde drove, Blastmask was in the passenger seat, and the strong women didn't ride with them all at. Instead she simply ran to wherever it was The Foremen lived.

"So, you're probably wondering what our deal is," Blonde said as he looked into the mirror.

"No, I'm wondering why we're not going to a hospital," Bale replied.

"Our place is better than a hospital," Blonde smiled, "Besides, I was talking to the lady".

"My name is Vana, by the way," Vana said to him, "And my boyfriend's name is Bale".

"Oh, yeah? So where is this Bale guy?" Blonde said with a smug smile.

"Just tell them who we are, Drake," Blastmask said, clearly irritated.

"Yeah, yeah, okay. So we're The Foremen. We used to be lab assistants to this scientist named Zebediah Dean. His experiments backfired and gave all us superpowers".

"Can one of you heal people," Bale asked.

"No, dude. Just wait a minute. Jesus," Blonde continued, "People call me Skip, because I can teleport myself, other people, all kinds of stuff. I'm kind of the leader".

"You're not the leader," Blastmask said.

"I said I was "like" the leader, Summer," he replied.

"I'm telling Paula".

"Okay, fine, so I'm not the leader. And Paula is that girl who ran ahead of us. She's super strong, super fast, and nothing can hurt her. That's why we call her The Queen. And she's not even the real leader anyway," Skip tilted his head back a little, "but still, what a woman".

"Ahem," Blastmask coughed.

"Oh, yeah, right. And this little ray of sunshine is Summer, but we call her Blastmask. You can probably guess why".

"So if you call yourselves the Foremen," Vana asked, "Why are their only three of you, or does this Doctor guy count?"

"Well, Doctor Dean isn't really out in the field like the rest of us. He just teaches us how to use our powers," Skip replied.

"And he gives us a home," Blastmask mumbled.

"Our actual fourth member is at the mansion. We call him-"

Bale cut in, "A mansion? Does this mansion have a hospital? Because I need a hospital".

Skip stopped the car. Everyone was pushed forward for a moment. Skip took a breath, turned around so he could see Bale and said, "Dude, if you want a hospital, get out and walk. Otherwise, shut up and get with the program".

Bale didn't move. He kept his eyes on Skip and shook badly. But he didn't move. Skip turned back around, shifted into drive, and quietly said, "Yeah, that's what I thought".

Zebediah Manor was a huge building with multiple wings, a wide front yard and equally wide back yard, and a small house towards the back of the property. The group drove up the driveway and into a big parking lot with several fancy cars and a motorcycle. Bale and Vana followed Skip and Blastmask out of the car and into the garage where Queen was lacing up her boots. She asked what took them so long, to which Skip replied, "You say that too much".

Inside the living room were luxury furniture and a beautiful chandelier hanging from the ceiling. The room had an old world feel to it. Multiple antique maps displayed on the walls, a large fireplace with photos of The Foremen placed atop it. Blastmask helped Bale sit onto a fold-out wheelchair and began pushing him towards the lab. Vana wanted to go with, but Skip offered her a tour of the house and something to eat. Vana teared up at the thought of what happened to Boston Market, but overcame the remorse and told Bale they'd meet up later, much to his despair.

After a brief elevator ride, Blastmask rolled Bale into an old laboratory. A mix of natural and artificial, Bale was dumbfounded by the array of machines around him. As well as all the plants hanging from the ceiling. Bale briefly glanced at Blastmask.
"You uh…you said your name was Summer," Bale asked.
"Yeah. Everyone calls me Blastmask".
"I got that. But, do you mind if I call you Summer? That other name is kind of.."
"Silly?"
"Yeah, kind of," Bale smiled politely.
Summer looked at Bale silently. There was, though, a brief movement implying a chuckle. "You can call me Summer if you want". She lifted Bale by the arm and walked him over to an operating table. Bale looked unsure, but Summer swore nobody was going to cut him open. Bale got onto the table and asked, "So, the helmet. It doesn't come off?"
"It comes off".
"Oh, good".
"Well, I can't take it off".
"Oh, lame".
"If I do, my powers become uncontrollable and I destroy everything".
"I'm sorry to hear that. Is there any way to…you know…".
"Fix her?" a voice echoed from behind a door, "I've been trying for a long time". From behind the door came a monkey as tall as a man. He wore yellow shorts which were ripped up and over his body he wore a lab coat. His face was charming, yet creepy. Following him came a long furry tail that dragged along the floor. He had bad posture, leaning too forward and letting his hands drift over the floor like his tail.
Bale flinched at the sight of the monkey man, but Summer put a hand on his shoulder and explained,"This is our other teammate. Mick".
"Some people call me Simian," he said as he stood over Bale. From under the bed he pulled out a bag with a red cross on it. "Alright, let's get started".

Skip and Vana were in the kitchen eating tiny sandwiches. Skip mostly flirted with Vana. Vana mostly ignored Skip. The stalemate was cut short by Queen and an old man in a wheelchair. Grateful for their entrance, Vana introduced herself to the old man, who turned out to be Zebediah Dean. Dean was a humble host, mainly boasting about his superpowered allies, but he didn't circumvent any questions.
"Okay, so I get the science experiment gone wrong stuff," Vana said, "Well, I don't really get it, but I'm probably not supposed to get it. I guess what I want to ask is-".
"You want to know about the robot," Dean finished.
"Yeah, am I-".

"Predictable? Perish the thought, my dear. The experiment that birthed The Foremen also granted me the ability to read minds, to a certain extent".
"Woah. So you can hear everything I'm thinking?"
"To a certain extent, as I said. Base level thoughts, nothing too deep".
"A number between 1 and 20?"
"Please, must we play this game?"
"Come on, man. 1 and 20," Vana repeated excitedly.
"Very well. 13,".
"Oh my God! Okay, okay, I'm thinking of a color".
"Blue".
"A fruit".
"Papaya".
"A state".
"Ohio".
"A song by Bowling For Soup".
"There's Nothing Wrong with Ohio".
"That's awesome," Vana nodded to herself, "But, yeah, the robots".

"The Killifiers? Yeah, we've been fighting them for a couple years," Mick explained to Bale after cleaning off the remainder of the wound.
"How long is a couple years," Bale asked.
"Hmm. I don't know, twenty years," Mick looked perplexed and glanced at Summer, she nodded and added, "Almost twenty-two years".

"And they just keep coming," Vana asked Dean.
Dean nodded. In the corner of the kitchen Queen whispered something to Skip, something aggressive. Dean added, "These robots appear from seemingly nowhere and attack the city".
Skip teleported next to Vana and leaned against the wall behind her, "Which is why we save the city everytime".
Vana jumped, caught her breath, and went back to talk to Dean, "If you've been fighting them for so long, why not find out where they're coming from".

"That part is complicated," Mick said as he helped Bale off the bed, "A few times we've captured them, or taken a piece of them back here, but the parts eventually turn into smoke or something and vanish".
"Once," Summer added, "We thought of following one back from where it came, but they never stop destroying stuff until we destroy them".
"Then there was that one time we tried to lure it into kidnapping Queen," Summer said.

"It ended up killing me," Queen explained, "Gripped me with its claws and crushed my insides".
Vana turned to her, mouth agape.
Queen shrugged. "I got better".
"You'll find the medical technology in my lab does wonders for recovery. And The Foremen and I have a natural healing factor as well".

"It's true. Go on, try to knock me out," Skip said. He walked over to Vana and lifted his face. He pointed to under his chin, "Go on, I'll heal".
Vana looked at Queen. Queen nodded. With a quick motion Vana clocked Skip in the Adam's Apple. Skip began coughing and wheezing and barely squeezed out something about checking the answering machine. He teleported out of the kitchen. Queen had herself a small laugh.
Dean smiled wide, but kept his composure.
"It's nary we find ourselves having guests. We would love for you and your partner to stay for dinner tonight".
"You guys aren't vampires, right?"
Dean looked confused, "Uh, no?"
"Okay, just making sure".

A storm brewed outside Zebediah Manor that night. Lots of heavy rain and powerful winds. Skip and Simian were drenched when they came back inside from clearing the chairs off the patio. Skip laughed at how badly Simian's wet fur smelled, but Simian suggested someone more competent could have simply warped between the raindrops. They butted heads as Queen and Dean prepared dinner. Blastmask set the table in the dining hall. The silverware reflected off her helmet.
Bale and Vana were given a room to rest in if the storm continued. As per Vana's request the room was on the opposite end of where Skip's room was. Bale hadn't put on his pants yet and Vana was changing in the attached bathroom. Bale sat on the bed and examined his leg where the debris hit him.
"Bale," Vana called from the bathroom, "Put on some pants".
Bale didn't reply. He simply examined the wound.
Vana spit her toothpaste cocktail into the sink, "Bale, did you hear me".
"How many people do you think they've brought here," Bale asked. He had to repeat himself as Vana walked out of the bathroom.
"I don't know. Dean said they don't get many guests. Why".
"Summer and Mick told me they've been fighting these robots for twenty-two years. Don't you think in that time they would have seen more people get hurt? What if people were killed by these robots".
"Bale. These people saved us and now they're feeding us. Is it really right to talk about them like this? I thought you liked them".
"I do, I do. It's just-if these people have been here in Eastchester for twenty-two years, how have we never heard about them? Or the robots".
"We never heard anything about Tapetown. Or Lillipatton".
"I guess," he continued to study his leg.
"Look at me," Vana told him.

Bale looked up to see Vana in a long red dress. It looked soft and it showed a lot of shoulders. Her hair was something out of a magazine. She wore light makeup, but her lips were red too. Bale awed at her image.
Vana looked coy, "Kind of a different look for me".

"It's a good look," Bale said, "I didn't know we were supposed to dress up".
"Yeah, well, I wanted to dress up. I don't get invited to dinner as much as you think. Plus, you and I haven't done this yet".
"What's this?"
"A dinner date. A fancy mansion. Probably some wine and laughter. We can act rich and entitled and turn our noses up and scoff," she gave an impression of an old rich person that made Bale laugh.
"You really are something else, Vana. Don't tell me you're only doing this for me".
"It's for me too, don't worry. I want to see Skip's face when he realizes the only person getting all this tonight," she motioned down her body, "is you".
Bale stood up and walked over to Vana. He held her sides at first, but then hugged her deeply. Ever since the drug store things have been tense. He started this journey with her because she ignited something in him he thought had been dead for years. And here he was, in the home of strangers and superheroes and surrounded by robot battles and crazy technology. He was out of his element. Right where he belonged.
"Vana," Bale said as he held her, "I don't know if it's obvious by now…".
"I love you too, Bale".
They held each other for a while. Both shook. Both sighed. Bale ran his hands over Vana's hips and felt his hand slip into something.
"Dude," Bale said, leaning back so he could look at her, "Does your dress seriously have pockets".
Vana scoffed and shoved Bale onto the bed. Then she put her hands on her hips, "Put some damn pants on".

Chapter 15: Zebediah Manor

The storm did as storms do. It raged, it crashed, it delayed trips and kept Bale and Vana cooped up in the Manor for the night. After a dinner of Thanksgiving-like proportions, the hard traveling duo felt themselves too full for even heavy petting. They laid exhausted on the bed of the guest room. Vana was moaning and groaning a way Bale expected to come differently that night. She apologized and even seemed embarrassed, which was a new look on her. At her request, Bale left the guest room in search of stomach relaxers.

Bale wandered the halls of Zebediah Manor quite quietly in a pair of gray slippers he bought a few towns back. Although the hallway was dark, Bale found himself in front of a fireplace in the living room. It was a large room lined with bookshelves and tall windows. Bale watched as the rain came down like an onslaught. The dark sky hid the rain well, but the sharp strikes of water hitting the windows were hard to ignore. In the back of the room was an old record player and a series of records were lined up on a shelf next to. Bale looked back at the fireplace and noticed a series of framed photos along the mantle.

Photos showing the progression of The Foremen throughout the years. There were little differences, but the earliest photo showed the group prior to getting their powers. Mick was a tall, but round man with unkempt hair and a big beard. He probably would have been a podcast host if he didn't become an ape person. Queen, or "Paula" as she was once known, was in good shape, but not nearly the adonis she would later become. And Summer was just the happiest looking girl before the accident. Her dark brown hair was tied into a small braid, her face was lined with freckles, and her eyes were deep pools of green.

Behind the group were two men. One was Dean. He didn't look too different. Still bald. Still pale. But in the photo he was standing. Bale guessed the accident might have crippled him, but he had no way of knowing. Whatever Doc Dean was working on resulted in matter transportation, energy projection, muscle advancement, telepathy, and whatever the hell was going on with the ape guy. Clearly there was no straight line for this accident.

Standing next to Dean was another man. He had a curly head of hair and looked about as old as Dean. He was shorter, but wore the biggest smile in the photo. Bale squinted and tried to read the nametag. At first he wished he had a cell phone so he could use its flashlight. But the mere thought of a cell phone sent chills down his spine. Bale put the photo back and felt cold. The room felt darker. Bale hastily walked back to his room, but bumped into something he didn't notice. Bale sprung back and put his hand on his shirt pocket, reaching for the kaleidoscope. The dark figure before him was no shadow man, but was actually Summer.

"Dude, are you lost," she asked. Her helmet was off, but she wore a black mask with a mouth slot, kind of like a mailslot in a door. She wore it during dinner so she could eat. It was creepy then in the dining room light, so it was only creepier now.

Bale cleared his throat, "Uh, yeah. Vana had an upset stomach".

"Yeah, Paula's food will do that for ya. Just because her intestines have muscles she assumes everyone's got em," she waved at Bale to follow her.

In one of the biggest bathrooms Bale had ever seen, he and Summer searched the medicine cabinet. "If you, uh, don't mind me saying," Bale said, "you looked pretty good in that photo on the mantle".

"Oh, the one where I don't look like Cobra Commander," she replied as she read bottles on the shelf.

"Aren't you a little young for G.I. Joe".

"My Dad and I watched a lot of reruns. Until, you know, all this".

"Who was the curly-headed guy? He was standing next to Doctor Dean".

Summer pulled out a bottle of stomach relaxers. She handed it to Bale, "Here. That should help her".

"Thank you," Bale stood and waited for an answer.

Summer stood too. But her body language had an uncomfortable aura about it. She looked to the side, then back at Bale, "Dean doesn't like us talking about him".

"Why? Did he quit or something?"

"No, he-well, he died".

"Oh, God. I'm so sorry. How did-".

"I have to go to bed, okay? Goodnight," and just like that Summer marched out.

Bale stood there alone now. The last stander. He looked at the bottle. Then to the mirror.

"Jesus," he thought to himself, "Have I always looked like that?"

Vana was asleep when Bale got to the guest room. So much for needing medicine. Bale hesitated, then walked around the guest bedroom. He looked in the bathroom, behind plants, into windows, under the sink. He found the standards of a guest bedroom and he didn't know what he expected to find. As he put down the bottle of medicine and walked towards the light switch, he heard a creak in the floor.

Bale opened the door and was face-to-face with Skip. Skip raised his hands and almost shouted. When he saw Vana was out cold he restrained himself and backed up. Bale walked out and closed the door so the two were alone in the hallway.

"What are you doing," Bale asked.

"I was coming to talk to you. I didn't know she was asleep".

"Okay, well, here we are. Talking. What's up".

"Quell the attitude, bro. Doc sent me a mental message to come get you and bring him to you," Skip leaned against the wall with his arms crossed.

"Am I supposed to believe that".

"Why else would I be out here".

"Because-" Bale stopped to lower his voice. He pointed at Skip, "Because you haven't backed off Vana since we got here".

"Dude, come on".

"No. No. I'm for real, buddy. She's not interested. She's with me. And not like the "Spring Break" version of being with me. I mean "so in love it freaking hurts" version of being with me".

"Jesus Christ, Bale. Are you really that worried about me sweeping her off of her feet".

"No, I'm worried you'll just teleport into our room at night. Or you'll teleport into our car when we leave. Or you'll send me to Mount Everest or something".

"That's not how it works, okay? I can only teleport to places I can see," Skip poked a finger into Bale's chest, "And the next time you accuse me of being some kind of perverted creep, I'll teleport into your mouth".
"What," Bale looked shocked, "You can do that".
"Yeah. I can, I have, and I'll do it again if you go around saying stuff like that again".
Bale fell silent.
"Yeah," Skip scoffed, "That's what I thought. Now get a move on".
"That won't be necessary," Dean said as he rolled in through the darkness of the room.
"Oh, Doc," Skip turned to him and straightened up, "You can go back to your room, Bale here was just about-".
"To come find my room? Well, I grew tired of waiting. Besides," Dean made his way between Skip and Bale. He looked to Skip, "I could hear your vulgar thoughts from across the manor".
"Doc, I'm sorry. He just-".
"Do not blame our guest, young man. Now, return to your room so Bale and I can talk".
Skip looked mortified and his glare at Bale could split mountains. Skip nodded to his leader, looked down the hallway and vanished.

Bale followed Dean back into the living room. They turned a few lamps on and Bale sat in a chair across from the Doctor. Dean began by apologizing about Skip. Before the accident, Skip was a kinder person. He was a ladies man of course, but he knew how to take a hint. Dean always assumed he would eventually date Summer and only hesitated because they were coworkers.
"But now that he can go anywhere," Dean shrugged, "he thinks he can go anywhere. The burden of youth, wouldn't you say so".
"Why did you want to talk to me, sir".
Dean stiffened. He smiled, "Right to it then? Very well," Dean took out a box from the side of his wheelchair. Bale was weary of boxes, but settled down when it was revealed to just have cigars in it. Dean took out one, then offered Bale a cigar.
Bale shook his head, "I don't smoke".
Dean nodded. He lit his own and put the box on a small table. After a puff, Dean leaned back and explained to Bale that he's always monitoring the minds of his people. And when Summer thought about Lucien-the man in the photo-it set off Dean's notice.
"She told me that he died," Bale said as he leaned forward.
"It's a touchy subject. Lucien was my best friend. And, unlike everyone else, he wasn't there for the accident," Dean rolled over to the window to look out into the storm. "Picture, if you would, a machine that walks like a man. An accursed contraption that came from nowhere. This machine I speak of is what we have been calling The Fabricator".
"And that's where the Killifier came from".
"And more like it," Dean replied. "The Fabricator has been making these robots to attack us. And one robot got too far. It broke into our home and killed Lucien".
"I'm sorry. If I knew how bad it was, I wouldn't have asked".
"You are forgiven. After all, you were just curious".
Bale stood up, "I should get some sleep. We should be out of here in the morning".

"There's one more thing," Dean said, still staring out the window. "I want to read your mind".
"I'm surprised you haven't already".
Dean turned, "That's because I haven't been able to the entire time you've been here".
"What?"
"Your mind is not available to me, Bale," Dean began moving towards Bale, "Which is quite unusual. The only time I've been sealed out of someone's thoughts was a Killifier disguised as a woman Skip brought to the manor one night. He was severely reprimanded for that". Dean was directly in front of Bale now and brought his hands up to form a bridge under his chin, "I read Vana's mind, Bale. And there is plenty she does not know about you. I imagine if you were a robot assassin in disguise, you wouldn't tell anyone".
"Doctor, you can't be serious".
"Oh, I am. I am very serious, Bale," Dean closed his eyes and Bale could feel pressure on his scalp, "You'll find that when it comes to my home and my family, I can be deadly serious".
Bale put his hand over his forehead, "Stop. That hurts".
"How strange. Perhaps you're a robot with a human brain. Wouldn't be the first time".
Bale stepped back. He swung his arm in search of something to stabilize himself on, but instead he knocked a lamp off a table and dropped to the floor. Bale was on his hands and knees. His head strained under the pressure. He tried pleading, but couldn't form words. Dean rolled closer and placed his hands on Bale's head, "If you show me your mind, I'll have no reason to doubt you".
"Get off me," Bale groaned.
"Show me what you're hiding, Bale. I must know," Dean's fingertips pressed harder before Bale's mind went blank.

The sound of shattering glass was faint, but Vana caught the sound as she turned off the bathroom sink. Her stomach still upset, but the medicine doing its job still, she poked her head out into the hallway in search of the sound. There were new sounds. A muffled conversation, followed by a light switch being flipped. As Vana slowly walked out into the fully lit living room, she saw a broken lamp laid on the carpet as well as Queen and Blastmask standing near Bale and Dean.
Bale was on his hands and knees and Dean had his hands on Bale's head. Queen and Blastmask simply looked back and forth between each other and the tranced men. Vana hastily made her way in and demanded to know what was going on. Blastmask tried to calm her down, but Queen's voice was as strong as she was.
"You need to go back to your room," she told Vana.
"Screw that. What the hell is your boss doing to my boyfriend".
"Whatever it is, we have no way of-"
"Hold the phone, you don't even know what Dean is doing? Are you serious? What is this".
"Look, we trust the Doctor-".
"What? You think he's giving Bale a brain massage?"
"Hey! Doctor Dean is a good man. For all we know, your boy-toy was the aggressor".
"You think Bale attacked him? Well, some host you turned out to be".

Blastmask stepped between them. She tried to explain how they've never seen this happen with Dean. She tried to explain how Dean could have been helping Bale. But her reasons and theories were trounced not by the preceding argument, but by the sound of a metal scraping against the floor. The trio looked down the hall. Something slowly moved into the light. Nobody moved. They simply watched.
This wasn't human. This was a machine. A Killifier shaped like a person, with a skeleton made from scrap metal and bolted together. It had a red visor on its head and scanned the room, detecting the three women and the two men. The Killifier name brandished its chest and on the end of its arms were wide saw blades. Vana expected the robot to say "exterminate" or something else a science-fiction robot would say. But this wasn't science-fiction, it was horror.

"Get her out of here," Queen told Blastmask as she approached the robot.
"No way, dude," Vana shouted, "I don't go anywhere without him," she pointed to Bale.
Queen groaned, "Fine. Blastmask, cover them," she then charged in and grabbed the robots arms and kept them up. The robot tried to bring its arms down, but to little success. Queen spread the robot's arms and lifted her leg. With a wide grin of satisfaction she placed her foot atop the robot's chest and pushed herself up. Standing atop the robot, Queen pulled and pulled until the arms came out of their sockets.
The robot backed away and observed its stumps. It tried kicking at Queen and she simply freed up one hand to catch the attack. Queen laughed as she pulled the robot in and used the detached saw blade to behead the automaton. The machine dropped as Queen put her fists on her hips and turned around.
To her horror, Queen saw four more of the same machines exit the opposite hallway behind Blastmask and Vana. The two turned around and Blastmask readied her laser. Vana glanced back to Queen and told her to look out. Queen turned to see five more robots enter the same way the first one did. "We're gonna need back-up," Blastmask said nervously. Vana rolled her eyes and tiredly said, "I can't believe I have to say this". As loud as she could, Vana cried out "Skip, help me".
Skip went from being in his bedroom to being outside his bedroom to the upstairs lobby to the downstairs lobby to the hallway to the living room in a matter of seconds. He stood before Vana with a smug smile. What would he say? Something clever like "I thought you'd never call" or maybe he'd open with a compliment like "I like your PJ's, but I bet they look better off of you". Maybe he'd show his inner sensitivity with a dark joke about how being an orphan means she'll never have to meet his parents at an awkward dinner party.
Skip smiled and told Vana, "Hey, nice PJ's, I bet my parents-well I don't have parents, but that would make dinner-if you're asking me to dinner in which case I didn't-I never thought-".
Vana shoved him and widened her arms as if to say "Look around, asshole".
Skip took a look around the room. He nodded. Skip picked up one of the detached saw blade arms, then he picked up the other one and handed it to Vana. He had a confident smile and encouraged her to fight like hell. Probably the first attractive thing he'd said to her so far.

Blastmask tore through hordes of Killifiers with beams of bright whiteness as Vana swung her saw blade at any stragglers who managed to get past the lasers. Vana swung like the Little League championship depended on it. Skip would surely be impressed if he weren't warping around the room smashing robots. He grew visibly tired, but just as one of the Killifiers jumped at Bale, Skip warped between the robot and the zoned out man and tore a slice up the robot's head. Oil covered his perfect face.

Queen was ripping and tearing in her own right. She had picked up two of the Killifiers and was using them as blunt clubs. Pulverizing the robots with their own defeated comrades. Queen could be heard laughing even louder. According to a quick comment by Blastmask, Queen liked the little ones best. Skip appeared behind Vana and defended her from another robot. He suggested moving Bale and Dean.

"We don't know what moving them will do," Blastmask shouted, another maelstrom of holy retribution pouring out of her mask.

"I don't know, maybe it will distract the robots," Skip replied, "And what the hell are they doing anyway".

"Oh, that's the best part, Skip," Vana added. She shouted in Queen's direction, "Nobody here seems to know what the good Doctor is doing".

"I still say it was Bale's fault," Queen shouted back.

"Well, I hate to agree with Queen, but-" Skip was cut off by Vana, who impaled another robot.

"Stuff it, alright. And don't you guys have a fourth?"

"What? Simian? Please, he's not any help," Skip chuckled.

"Go get him," all three women shouted.

"Jeez, fine," Skip raised his hands, "Try not to die while I'm gone".

Vana swung her saw into a robot just as it hopped onto the back of Dean's chair. The weight of the machine started to tip the chair backwards, but Vana cut into the robot's shoulder and yanked hard. The robot hit the ground and Dean remained in his place. As the robot tried to rise back up, its head was impaled by the saw blade as Vana screamed out in anger and the saw tore through the metal shell of the robot's head. Oil painted Vana like a Pollock painting.

Finished with her opponent, Vana went looking for another. Her bloodlust was taking hold. She briefly looked at Bale. Still immobilized on the floor. She was scared for a moment. What if this was it? What if this was where she'd lost him?

Chapter 16: The Mindscape

People aren't meant to enter The Mindscape. Not without a proper guide, that is. When Dean got his powers he was able to access The Mindscape only in brief circumstances. Whenever he read someone's mind he could feel his physical body become displaced. As if he were existing in two places at once, but the feeling never lasted long. He'd start reading a mind, he'd get that feeling, the feeling would go away, and then he'd carry on reading minds. His connection with The Mindscape was only momentary.

Now though, with Bale's stubborn mind in play, Dean was not only fully materialized into this place, but there was the sense in his mind that he only existed here. Bale didn't know as much, but he recognized this place as the blue, white-lined dimension described by Roma. But being there for real revealed new details. The white lines in the sky remained as he remembered, but on the ground level with him and Dead there were bubbles everywhere. As one bubble passed him it popped, only to be replaced by a dozen new bubbles. As it floated away, Bale could see those dozen pop into two dozen. He assumed that would go on forever.

Bale turned to look at Dean, "Is this what you wanted? Now we're stuck somewhere that makes no sense".

"Don't be stupid, boy," Dean shouted, "I've studied this place. And here, it only makes sense". Dean gazed around in wonder. He watched the white lines in the sky form machines and athletic runners. Curious, Dean began moving his leg and was elated to find that in The Mindscape his legs could work.

As he stood, Dean said, "Look, Bale! I can walk again! All with a thought! An idea! My word," he gasped, "Imagine what else I can think of".

Bale tried to reach for the old man, but Dean turned into a goddamn Chinese Dragon and flew into the sky. Bale had no words. The man could have become anything he could think of and his first idea was a goddamn Chinese Dragon. Bale was not as creative. He simply lifted his fist to the sky and raised a knee. As he did so he began rising into the air and flying, keeping this heroic pose as he did so.

Bale followed Dragon Dean through the Mindscape, swerving past bubbles and white lines over and over with hardly any distinction. The two were forced to stop at a wall that stretched as far as they could conceive. This large white wall appeared to be infinite. Bale examined it and found more of those bubbles bouncing against the wall to no avail.

Dragon Dean stroked his long beard-another detail he made sure to include in his weird dragon fetish-and suggested the bubbles could represent thought, and the wall was some sort of block. Bale had no interest in this research and flew between Dean and the wall. He crossed his arms, "You need to get us out of here".

"I have no intention of doing that," Dragon Dean said blatantly, "I must study this place".

"Okay, so study it. I don't care, man. Just get me out of here".

"Why would I do that? You're my ticket in and out of this place, as it were".

"I don't care if it's out there or in here, but I'm not one of your damn experiments," Bale claimed, the energy of flight bolstering him.

"Out there or in here, my friend," Dragon Dean began to multiply like he were in a mirror hallway of a funhouse. Bale was now surrounded by a horde of Dragon Deans, "I am a God compared to you".

With the swing of his tail, Dragon Dean slammed Bale into the wall. He then grabbed him with his huge claw and dragged Bale against the wall as he flew across it. Dragon Dean slammed him a few more times during the wall dragging, then he tossed the disoriented Bale into his horde of clones. These multiple dragons ripped and tore at Bale, leaving him a tattered mess that fell from the sky and impacted the ground scattering a group of bubbles.

Dragon Dean flew back down to find Bale, returning to his human form as he did so. The horde of dragons circled the sky, ready to strike again. Dean regaled Bale with all his degrees and doctorates. He described a trophy case that stood in his bedroom and how every year of his life he had outsmarted men twice his age the last year. Dean didn't know where Bale came from, nor did he care. There was no way Bale could ever outthink him. But, to Bale's credit, Dean needed him to get what he wanted. Just as he needed those stupid Foremen.

Back then it was all so simple. Dean and Lucien had to tolerate the interpersonal drama of these four employees daily. The love triangles, the family disputes, the issues of race and sexuality and the fear of the future. All from people who could not possibly understand the work they were doing. If successful, Dean and Lucien could have unlocked secrets to the universe nobody could.

Lucien was a brilliant engineer, Dean was a marvelous physicist. And together, with the legwork of their employees, Dean and Lucien were on the verge of creating a miracle machine. One that could rewrite the atomic code of any object. "Imagine," Dean would often lecture, "a machine that could rewrite the code of life itself. We could turn cancer cells into red blood cells. The genetic code for diabetes into a recessive gene. Toxic emissions could be converted into the scent of lavender".

It was all a dream for them. Dean and Lucien. Partners, geniuses, lovers. And if this machine could do what they designed it to do, they could become very wealthy lovers. When the day to test the machine came, so did the trouble. Everything was falling apart just before that fateful night.

Summer would be leaving town to live with her mother in the big city, as her father couldn't afford to have her live with him anymore. Drake would be leaving too, as a woman he had dated in high school revealed to him that she was raising his son. To Dean's surprise, Drake expressed nothing but excitement in being a parent whether he would be with this girl or not. He needed to be there for his son. Paula had wanted to leave Eastchester ever since she was a little girl. There was nothing there but bad memories and bad people according to her. Dean knew Mick was done too. He couldn't read minds back then, but he didn't need to. It was clear Mick's heart was never in this project. Maybe he'd just wander off one day.

Lucien had his relatives to worry about. It was always the one thing standing in their way, from Dean's perspective. These two, old, obsolete people. Lucien's aunt and uncle who took him in after he came out to his father and was kicked out for being queer. Lucien owed everything to these folks.

The dominoes would fall into place, Dean thought. The invention will be a success and these entitled children would realize their work was bigger than their lives or their freedoms. They could use the machine to cure Lucien's relatives of their oldness or cure his father of his bigotry. This machine could fix everything and nobody would ever leave Zebediah Dean again. Not like his parents did. Not like his first wife or his daughters. Not like the people of Eastchester who so proudly ridiculed him. Dean would be like a God to these people after his machine cured their pathetic world. And he'd be happy.

The machine worked. Just not the way any of them expected. The energy expelled was infused into Dean and his coworkers. The energy unlocked parts of his mind no human should have access to. But he was a genius. He was deserving of this gift. To see into the minds of others. To manipulate their memories and their thoughts and make them believe anything. In the end, it didn't matter if the machine ruined the lives of his employees, because he could change the narrative. With his powers, Dean made the whole town think he was a respectable socialite. With his powers, he made his disfigured employees think they were fantastical superheroes who were loved by the public. With his powers, Dean created mechanized foes for his superheroes to battle.

And he did all this in a matter of four years. All the while keeping his love, Lucien, all to himself. Puppeteering his lover into a faceless villain, a boogeyman to keep the attention of The Foremen. Lucien became Dean's personal Fabricator of Evil. And as long as he had a grip on Lucien, the giant robots would be nothing but oversized toys. The angry townsfolk would be nothing by worshippers. The Foremen would be nothing but happy slaves. And anyone who dared to step into his town would become part of the masses, another back to be stepped on. All it would take was a thought.

"And that's why you're so special to me," Dean told Bale. "You are the first and only person I have met who has been immune to my powers. My control. Your girlfriend? Easy! She'll be the Foremen's personal butler in a week". Dean crouched down to look at Bale, "But you. I don't understand you. I can't see your thoughts". He placed his hands over Bale's head, "But perhaps if I try hard enough I can see your memories".

"I won't…let you…" Bale coughed.

"As if you have a choice," Dean laughed, "Now, let me see what makes you so special".

Both men strained to maintain control. As Dean pushed harder and harder, his dragon army faded away. The rest of the Mindscape began to fade. It became sepia, and the two men were now standing on the side of a tower. A tower of nerves and electrons. The Rescape. But as Bale resisted, so did the venue transfer. Suddenly, they returned to The Mindscape. Bale grabbed Dean's arms and threw the man off of him.

Regaining stability, Dean flew at Bale. Bale flew back at him as they became locked into each other. As Dean's hands gripped Bale's head, flashes of a studio apartment appeared in their minds. Then they saw a large man on a recliner drinking beer. Then they saw a gorgeous woman pointing and yelling. Then they saw a board meeting. Then they saw a kaleidoscope. "Is that it," Dean yelled, "Is that the cause of all this? The reason your mind is off limits?"

They returned to the ground and Dean multiplied again. Two of the clones held Bale back, as the true Dean plunged his hand into Bale's chest and strained to pull out the little black plastic toy. Dean studied it. He looked at its colors. He peered into it. Dean became angry. He saw nothing. He understood nothing.
"It's just..it's just a toy," Dean breathed in anger. "All of this for a toy that doesn't mean anything?"
Bale shook his head, "You're wrong, Doc. That toy means everything".
Dean gritted his teeth. He looked at it again and pondered. "Perhaps. Or perhaps it's significant just for existing," the smile grew as he balled up his hand, "If it means everything to you, then it means nothing to me".
Dean threw the kaleidoscope into the blue chalky ground. And with one stomp he shattered the toy. He dug his foot into the floor where he crushed it, laughing as he did so. Bale shook his head frantically. He had begun losing hope again. What if he had lost the way back? What if the mad Doctor would keep him here forever? What would happen to Vana? Had he dragged her all the way across the country just to be enslaved?
The darkness overwhelmed Bale. And as Dean began to smugly monolog about his superiority, Bale could barely hear him. There was a sharp ringing in his ear. Something like a cell phone. The Mindscape became darker. Dean looked concerned. And as Bale's vision blurred, the sounds of ringing were joined by a chorus of horrid screams.

Bale and Vana were fed a new narrative. One where they never met The Foremen. One where they stopped in Eastchester, had Boston Market for lunch, and then got back in their car and left. No manor. No secrets. No memory of the last 24 hours.

Cleaning up the robot bodies wasn't difficult. Dean simply went down into the basement and into his secret room where he kept Lucien. He was strung up to wires and wore a visor over his eyes. Lucien asked for forgiveness. Just as Dean was about to leave the room, the trance of guilt over Lucien had vanished and, in his anger, Lucien swore to use his mental link with the Killifiers to target Dean and the others.
The threat fell on deaf ears. Because it was fake. An emotional notch that Dean implemented in his lover's mind when he needed an enemy for his heroes. If freed, Lucien would likely feel the same, though. He had a reason to be angry, as his condition was worse than the others. They could at least pass for humans.
Dean shut his eyes and got up from his chair. Because that was a lie too. Dean's hand laid atop the cord to the life support systems. Dean wondered if Lucien would want to die if he knew what he had become. What Dean had turned him into. The robots cleaned themselves up. And just like every Killifier did after their defeat, they snuck into the guest house in the manor's yard and simply packed themselves away like Christmas decorations.

Would he want to live, Dean thought. Perhaps Lucien could fix himself, build a machine to support his disfigured body. He built machines to help the others too. He could fix everything, Dean believed. In truth, Dean always envied Lucien for that. Lucien could fix things, just as he fixed Dean.

But the real truth was, as it always is, painful. Dean would never grow out of being a mad scientist. He would never stop wanting the approval and admiration of others. He would never stop feeling insignificant in the grand scheme. Dean wrapped his hands around the plug and ripped it out of the wall. In Lucien's last moments, Dean brought him to a lake, not unlike the one they visited when they were in college. Dean and Lucien held each other as they watched the fireflies dance over the lake. And those lights never left Lucien's eyes.

Would it be easier to forget? Maybe. But he would risk the lives of his students. So Dean made them forget. He made them and the town think that the fight between good and evil, man and machine, was fought every single day. But nobody ever died or got old or changed. Dean remembered though, because if he forgot what he saw there-in the Mindscape-he would never trust himself to stay inside his home. Fear did not make Dean stronger. Fear locked his doors.

Chapter 17: Big Red's Beach: Judgment Day

Bale and Vana visited a beach not too dissimilar to the one near the tattoo parlor they met at. The experience was quite romantic. While neither of them could remember much about the last few hours, the missing pieces of memory were cut off by Bale's anguish. Somehow his toy kaleidoscope was broken. The colorful glass remained a solid lens, but the plastic blast case around it was cracked. Minor as it was, Bale was worried he might end up breaking it if he wasn't careful.
"You know," Vana said, "we could probably buy you a new one". The two of them were walking by the beach, across the street from various shops and restaurants. "Or we go to an arcade, win twenty tickets, and trade them in for a new one".
"Yeah, I get it, it's a cheap toy," Bale replied, "but I can't replace it". The hot sun beared down on his head. Good thing they bought matching hats.
"Bale, when you get a flat tire, you replace the tire. When you throw away shoes, you buy a new pair. When you lose your right molar in a bar fight, what do you do?"
"Stop getting in bar fights?"
Vana laughed, "Okay, well, that's not gonna happen".
"Look, this little toy? It means something. I had it when I met you. I had it when I threw my phone in the ocean and we-".
"Whoa, whoa, whoa. You threw your phone in the ocean?" she stopped in place.
"I told you that. The night we, ya know".
"Had crazy sex, yeah, I remember. But I thought you were joking".
"Who jokes about throwing their phone in the ocean?"

A threesome of young people approached Bale and Vana from the stairs of an apartment building. They overheard the conversation and speed-walked over. They all wore matching red tank tops. Their skin was orange. Their hair was blonde. And each of them had distinctly narcissistic attitudes.
The lead Red Tank hassled them, "Throwing stuff in the ocean, dude? Big Red's not gonna like that".
"Yeah, well, I don't like your hair," Bale replied. Vana patted him on the shoulder.
"Liar," the Red Tank snapped back, "Everyone loves my hair! And if you litter on Big Red's Beach, you're gonna have Big Red breathing down your neck".
"Oh yeah? Well," Bale looked around and thought for a moment, "I got your mom breathing down my neck".
Red Tank's face turned as red as his tank. His buddies snickered, but resumed their tough exterior. Vana went from making the sound of spraying water. "That's it! I'm reporting you to Big Red," Red Tank turned to his pals and they marched off.
"Who the hell is Big Red anyway?" Vana asked.
"Maybe he's chewing gum," Bale replied happily.
"Alright calm down, George Carlin."

The suntanned skin of those three goobers impressed Vana in a way their hair did not. She and Bale grabbed towels and laid on the beach. At first, Bale was confused. During one of their many pillow talks Vana didn't much care for tanning. She thought it was too boring. And when you tan you never get what you expect. "I guess in that way it's like eating a lot of salad," she said, "you think eating the same leaves and onions is gonna help you lose weight, but you don't get what you want fast enough so now you're angry, hungry, and you spent all your money on lettuce".

Now it was different though. She had a boyfriend. And not a beachbum who likes tanning just to satisfy his bikini fetish. No, she had someone to talk to. Granted, Bale mainly complained about his kaleidoscope, but after a while the conversation turned to childhood experiences. Vana hadn't always lived on a pier. In her youth, she lived in a big city with her parents. "John and Emily. Basic names for some basic people," she regaled as she sipped from her bottle of Cherry Coke, "We lived in a nice, secure apartment building. It even had one of those fancy mailrooms with the passcode and everything".

Her father was a lawyer, her mother was a fashion designer, and her home was as large as a Walmart. Not exactly a Supercenter, but still fairly large. They had a maid who cleaned up even the most messy of little girl's rooms. They had a private chef who visited once a day to prepare some grandstanding meal, while the rest of the time her nanny would cook for her. And when her nanny wasn't feeding her she was taking her to concerts and movies and stage plays. Vana could swim in the community pool or use her father's old arcade room or watch anything she wanted to on their huge television.

"I spent a lot of time in front of that TV after…after I stopped playing piano". Bale was listening, but now fully turned to look at Vana. She tried to wave it away and move on, but Bale eventually got her to admit that her parents made her take piano lessons. Her grandmother was a celebrated pianist and Vana showed a lot of potential, in her families' opinion. She didn't want to play. The piano was too slow for her. And it's not like The Offspring had a piano player on stage or anything. After she stopped taking lessons she never really touched it again and resolved herself to dive into the world of television.

She had her favorites, of course. When she was younger she liked cartoons, when she was an early teenager she was all about reality TV, in her formative years it was all "America's Funniest Home Videos" and "Mad TV". Sketch comedy really stuck with her for some reason. She could never get into watching stand-up outside of a select few comics, but stuff like "Saturday Night Live" and "In Living Color" and "The Chappelle Show"? Those shows kept bringing her back. Vana didn't think she was naturally funny, like those people. Or naturally talented, like her parents.

"What?" Bale replied, "You're super funny. And you're wicked talented".

"You're just saying that to make me feel better".

"No, for real. You're super funny".

"Alright, alright, I'm funny".

"And you're talented".

"Come on, Bale. You don't have to say that".

Bale lifted his shirt and pointed to her name on his side, "You gave me this".

"Yeah, but, like, that's just my name".

"So what?"
"I've been writing my name since I was three, that's what. And names are just easy. Every tattoo artist knows that".
"What if it was a hard name? Like, Chrysanthemum? Or Bartholomew? Or, I dunno, Geoff".
"I hate when Geoff is spelled that way".
"How…how did you know I was saying it like it was spelled that way?"
There was a long silence.

"Aye, what's up, fellow beach goers?" a man in a red tank top walked up to Bale and Vana. Red wouldn't just describe his shirt, it would sum up his whole aesthetic. His shorts were red, his sandals were red, the tower around his neck was red. His skin, from his blonde luxurious hair to his hairless feet, was as red as a lobster. His eyes? Hazel. His eyes were hazel.
"Whoa, buddy," Bale lowered his sunglasses, "I think you need to see a doctor or something".
"Yeah, man. You should not be that red," Vana added, "Are you, like, in pain?"
"No pain, no gain! That's what I always say, sis," he laughed, but then his eyes narrowed, "Now look, amigos. I don't want to be telling tales off the shore or nothing, but I heard from a few seagulls that one of you has been doing some littering on my beach. Is that true?"
"Little seagulls?" Bale replied, "Oh, those red guys. I guess they're with you?"
"I am a friend to all those who walk my beach".
"Okay, well, those seagulls were wrong".
"You calling my seagulls liars, my guy? Because if you are, I got something to tell you," the man crouched down and looked Bale dead in the eye, "I'm Big Red. And this is my beach. And what I say goes on my beach. And if anyone, and I mean anyone, threatens my beach and the people who walk it, I snap them in my hands like a toothpick".
Bale and Vana stared and blinked simultaneously. Vana chimed in, "He's telling you the truth, okay? He didn't throw his phone in your water".
Big Red made a relieved sigh and stood up.
Vana added, "He threw it into the water of a different beach".
Big Red was about to turn around, but then he snapped back with the expression of a professional wrestler who just smelled what his opponent was cooking. "Hold it right there, Suzie-Q," he pointed, also as a wrestler does, "My beach is connected to the water," now he pointed at the water, "And that water is connected to the ocean". He then swung his index finger around like he was lassoing a horse, "And that ocean is connected to all the water on Earth". He crouched yet again to staredown Bale, "You know what that means, brother?"
Bale stuttered, "It means…when we swim in the ocean we're technically swimming with sharks?"
"That's terrifying, and yes, but it also means if you litter in any ocean, you litter in my ocean!"

A lot of things were said. So to shave some dialog, Big Red called Bale lots of names, Vana called Big Red a lot of names, Bale called Vana "Bana" by accident, which the three of them had a giggle about, but the conversation basically ended with Big Red challenging Bale to a showdown at sundown. Vana said it sounded romantic and Big Red got angrier. Bale wished he believed in God so he could pray for his life.

The argument with Big Red was merely a warm up for Vana. In an attempt to blow off some steam she dragged Bale to a tattoo parlor they passed by earlier. Earlier she had no interest, but Bale was starting to realize she was good at hiding things. Like he was. This parlor was called "Triz" and had an all-female staff. Vana thought that meant she had some leeway with them from the get-go. She was wrong.
"Yeah, no, we don't do that," said Beth at the front desk. She was short and in very good shape. Her exposed arms looked as though they could crush coal into diamonds. Maybe that's how she got her earrings.
"What? Why not?" Vana asked.
"You're asking me why we don't let people off the street come in here and use our equipment to give their boyfriend's tattoos?"
"I'm not just someone off the street, okay? I'm a tattoo artist".
"Oh, you want a job?"
"No, I don't want a job".
"Well, good. Because we're not hiring".
"I'm willing to pay".
"And now you think you can bribe us to get what you want?"
Vana's face went blank. She lifted her hands like she was describing how long something was, "This is a business. People pay you to get what they want all the time".
"That's not the kind of service we provide".
"You're being unreasonable," Vana declared.

"She was being unreasonable," Vana grumbled as she sipped her fruity drink at the bar next door. They were sitting there for only a few minutes, but when Vana was angry Bale felt as though time moved at a slower pace. She kept going on and on about "professional courtesy" and "fellowship of the trade". Bale was only half listening. On the TV above the bar was the local news. Big Red was prepared for the showdown later that day. On the TV, he was lifting bleachers over his head. Bleachers populated by around a dozen adults.
"Vana," Bale said, keeping his eyes on the TV, "We should go find a hotel room. Today may be my last day on Earth".
"You want to sleep with me? Now? Have you not been listening," she went back to complaining about the tattoo parlor. Bale went back to not listening. When Vana complained she was a different person. But somehow she was also a familiar person. Beyond her appearance. Beyond her voice. Her anger. Her spite. That vitriol was something Bale had known. It was something he almost married. It was something he threw into the ocean. Maybe he never left his home, he and the woman he left could have worked things out. Counseling, therapy, maybe they just needed to talk.
She would get so angry sometimes. Bale had a work ethic etched in stone, but no matter how hard he worked he could never get to the place she wanted him to get to. "You're better than this", she would say. This was only when her anger was free flowing. But when she targeted him it was much more of an issue.

Before this trip he wasn't an adventurous person. The only time he'd go to a club would be by himself, alone at the bar. She hated that. "Don't you want to have fun? How do you have fun?". He worked too much, he'd say to himself. Worked because his parents told him to. Worked too hard to provide for her. Never worked for himself, just for his worth.

When Vana calmed down and looked over at Bale. He was a million miles away. She put her hand on his and tried to apologize. Bale turned to her with tears building. He was afraid he would die and that Big Red would be the one to kill him. Vana put her arms around Bale and tried to assure him otherwise.
On the other side of Bale sat a tall, heavy-set man dressed in a navy sweater, blue jeans, black boots, and a gray beanie. He had a big, brown beard and his skin was blue. Completely, vividly blue. Bale and Vana turned to him with perplexed looks. He introduced himself as Big Blue and told them he could help Bale with his problem.

Chapter 18: Big Red's Beach: The Sarah Connor Chronicles

Legends say the village of Brightfoot was subjected to a myriad of meteor showers. One such meteor found its way into the small European town's largest water source, The Mirror Lake, which stretched across the length of the snowy mountains and ran rivers throughout the region. What scientists of the modern era would call "cosmic radiation", the townsfolk labeled as "magic water" which would change the color of their skin at random.

As the generations came and passed, the mystic properties of the lake wore off and the multicolored families who drank from him continued to reproduce colorful new members of the Brightfoot community. These River People became less random in their coloration, as theorists suggested the color they were born with would define their characteristics, or perhaps it was the other way around.

The Yellow people were cheerful, the Brown People were stubborn, and the Green People were envious and stingy. The most common were The Red People, who exerted mostly aggression, and The Blue People, often seen sulking. Immigration out of Brightfoot was rare and it was believed once you left the village, you could never find your way back.

"My grandfather knew a guy with yellow skin. Everyone thought he had Jaundice," Vana told Big Blue, "Do you think he was from Brightfoot?"

"Ma'am," Big Blue replied, "I think your friend just had Jaundice".

Big Blue was very soft spoken and polite. He answered a lot of questions slowly, and he went further into details when Vana or Bale looked confused. He was cold and the way he sat was that of a tired man. Apparently Big Red was his younger brother and the two of them had lived on this beach since they were teenagers.

"My birth name was Eliah," Blue said, "And my brother's name is Terrence. He and I stopped using those names when we moved here".

"Any reason why?" Bale asked.

"Yes. Those names remind us of our home".

"I'm sorry to change the subject," Bale said, "But how can you help me with your brother? Are you gonna convince him to call off the fight?"

Blue waved his hand, "He's not going to fight you, sir. He just wants to prove he's stronger than you. And don't worry, I want to help you prepare for it".

Bale raised an eyebrow, "Why would you help me win against your brother?"

When Big Blue ran the beach there was an optimism to all of it. Anybody was allowed on the sand or in the water. If you ran out of money, there were people who would give you money. There was a friendly atmosphere, families and couples and even just people on their own exploring the luxuries of the spot. Big Red never liked the way his brother ran things. Some visitors would say horrible things. They would tease the boys. Make fun of their skin colors. They would trash the beach or bother the people hanging around it.

But Blue was a beloved man back then. If someone got in his face, his friends would stand up for him. If someone littered on the beach, somebody else would clean it up. All Big Blue had to do was radiate positivity and hide the sadness inside himself. "It wasn't right," Big Red would tell him, "If you are threatened or if your home is disrespected you should use your power to put people in their place".

When Big Red was big enough he challenged Blue to a competition. The winner would take control of the beach. When Big Blue reminisced on that day, he had a lot of regrets. So much he could have said to make his brother understand. So much he could have done to outdo his brother in the competition. But at the end of the day, Blue just didn't try as hard as Red. He didn't want it as bad as Red.

Under Red's guidance, only good looking people were allowed on the beach. Strong people. Wealthy people. Soon enough the problem of jerks on their beach was no longer a problem, because jerks became the clientele. And with so many shallow groupies backing him up, nobody could touch Red, not even Blue. Maybe trying again would solve everything, but the sadness overtook Big Blue and he became a shell of the man this beach knew him as. Now all he did was drink at this bar and cry under his bed.

"Okay, I get the brother-versus-brother thing," Vana said, "but Bale is nowhere as strong as you or Red".

"Hey. I'm strong. I moved that tree trunk out of the road," Bale stated proudly.

"Bale, that tree trunk was the width of a toaster. I wouldn't even classify it as a trunk".

"If I can add to the topic," Blue added, "it sounds more like a very long branch".

Bale huffed, "Alright, alright. So I'm a wimpy branch-lifter".

"But I know how you can beat Big Red," Blue told them.

"Is there some secret psychological weakness I can exploit? Or is the way to win more cerebral? What even is the competition?"

"It's a lifting competition," Blue quietly replied.

Vana clapped her hands, "Aw, you love lifting".

"But I can make you stronger. I know a trick".

Bale scratched the back of his head, "I'm not really into working out. Is this going to involve working out?"

Big Blue had a brief, but warming smile on his face, "You'll only have to work one muscle".

Vana went off alone to go another round with Beth over at Trez. Which worked out fine as Bale needed to do this next part alone. Sundown was approaching and the competition would begin soon. Time was running out and so was the author's interest in this chapter. According to Blue, the key to victory was strength, and the key to strength was confidence.

"And I'll find confidence here? In the ocean?" Bale was instructed to get on all fours in the water.

"It's not so much about what's in the ocean," Blue explained, he stood behind Bale and was ankle deep in the water, while for Bale the water went up to his elbow and mid-thigh. "It's more about what's on the ocean. What you can see".

"It's kind of hard to focus on that, Blue. It's really cold".

"I know. Don't think about it. Just look into the water and tell me what you sea".

Bale ignored the obvious pun there and just stared into the water below him. There was the sand and the rocks and the rest of the ocean iconography. When he was a kid, Bale was convinced the seaweed would come alive and drag him down to Hell. Jesus, he was a messed up kid. Just like his parents. And theirs. Really, there was just a legacy of paranoia. And why wouldn't there be? When Bale looked back on his life it just seemed like weird occurrences were routine. Even before this adventure.

When he was ten years old he was playing on a beach just like this one. He had his little toy box next to him and was just about to witness the epic battle between Charizard and Leonardo when a shadow was cast over him. When he looked up, little Bale met eyes with a beautiful woman with long, golden hair which flew like a flag as she removed her helmet. She wore top-to-bottom armor and held a sheathed sword on her hip. Her horse was white as a star and had the hair to match her rider. The woman in armor looked down at Bale with a spark of interest and asked him if he had a home. Bale said "I'm here with my Ma and Pa". The woman nodded and wished him a good day before riding valiantly into the distance, vanishing in a sudden fog of green smoke.
At age thirteen Bale was chosen to retrieve his friend Seymor's autographed baseball from Mr. Shills' backyard. All the neighborhood runts knew not to step in Mr. Shills' yard. Why, Rosie Montary from down the street heard from Carly Dows at school that Mr. Shills was a cannibal from a hundred years ago. And you can bet your bottom dollar that once Bale and his friends looked up what "cannibal" meant, they never even stepped next to Mr. Shills' fence. But fortune favors the brave. And if Bale could cross into Shills' yard and get that ball back, maybe Carly Dows would go steady with him. Whatever "going steady" meant back then. Bale navigated between several piles of dirt in the yard, moved numerous trash bags as big as grown-ups out of his way, and recovered the ball from under an old fire pit which smelled of old meat. The fire pit was shiny, probably from all the rings and golden artifacts and glowing space rocks hidden under the wood. Anyway, Bale got the ball, returned it to Seymor, and Carly held his hand for the next two months.
At age sixteen, Bale, Seymor, Carly, and Frank The Dog were parked on the side of the road after witnessing a meteor impact the nearby lake. The three friends were on their way to pick up Rosie for the big school dance when they witnessed this event. Frank The Dog was barking non-stop so the group investigated the fallen object on the riverbank. As they got closer, the meteor's exterior became shiny and smooth. The flames slowly died out as small nodes of white light shot out from various places on the space rock. As the front of the object rolled open like a treasure map, the group witnessed a pair of creatures exit the craft. They were tall, square, and their bodies appeared to be full of deep holes. Their flesh was the equivalent to rusted metal, and their small faces sat atop their torso's like the head of a grandfather clock. A series of long, gray tentacles sprouted from their sides and they appeared to float wherever they went. Their speech was incomprehensible, but Seymor could understand them. "They need our help," he said, "they're planet is in danger". As the aliens welcomed the teens into the ship, Seymor puffed his chest and agreed to help. Carly grabbed his hand and agreed to help. Based on her track record she would probably hold his hand for, like, two months. Frank The Dog took one long drag from his cigarette, breathed it out, and replied, "Sounds like the ride of a lifetime, woof woof". The three of them embarked on an epic extraterrestrial adventure while Bale agreed to drive Seymor's car back to his house. That night, Bale and Rosie ditched the dance to screw around in a movie theater.

"Do you see it yet?" Blue asked.

"What am I even looking for?"

"It should be obvious. It should be all you're thinking about".

Bale looked deeper into the water. All he could think about was how weird his life was. Around every corner, like clockwork, something would happen to him and he would just move on. He would reject the call to action and neglect the severity of it. What was he supposed to do? Make his grandparents worry sick while he followed that knight into the Middle Ages? Was he supposed to let that crazy old Mr. Shills eat him alive in exchange for holding some cool rings and magic rocks? If he didn't stay on Earth the night of the dance, nobody would have been there for Rosie. Nobody would be there to touch her bra and swap spit while half-watching "Robocop 4: Autotorny at Law".

The past was becoming vivid. The seafoam began to part as the ocean showed to Bale his reflection. His every reflection. His childhood. His teenage years. His college experience. That brief period where he was really into "The Crow" and collecting ornate candles. He saw himself and all his quirks. His interests. What was lost to him was now laid bare on the sea's surface. Maybe it was all weird. Maybe it all should have never happened. But it did. And he was okay. Maybe he was better than okay.

There was a warmth inside of Bale now. He felt a strength he had never known. His body stayed the same, but under his skin he felt as though a herd of bison was stampeding past his every muscle. Bale rose from the ground and felt the sun wash over him. This endorphins inside chirped and somersaulted as Bale reveled in his screwed up existence. He was strong. He was ready.

Chapter 19: Big Red's Beach: Salvation

The rules were simple: whomever can lift the heaviest will win, but the opponent must admit defeat first. Winner gets ownership of the beach and chooses how the beach is run. Big Red was surrounded by supporters waving big red flags. No, the flags didn't say his name or have little pictures of him on them. The flags were big and red. Big Red himself came dressed for success in a black fishnet top that exposed pockets of his steel physique underneath. Coupled with red shorts and a pair of red and white sneakers.
Beside him, Bale had Big Blue who was booed on his way over, and Vana who had just had her own victory over Beth. Bale purchased a blue muscle shirt and black shorts. Big Blue lent him his smallest pair of sneakers, which were uncharacteristically lime green and pink. Bale kept his hair out of his head with a white headband. Vana said it looked good on him and he wasn't going to argue with her. She had started a winning streak.
Big Blue repeated his lesson to Bale and Vana told him even if he lost they would probably forget about all this in a week. "Seriously," Vana remarked, "Nothing is on the line here". While he wouldn't tell her, Bale knew she was wrong. Yeah, this was not about the beach. It wasn't about Big Blue either. It was about him, and how the world was eager to push him around, despite how many offers of adventure and intrigue the world had for him. This was Bale's chance to push back.

As the sun rested against the sea, Big Red parted his wake of fans and pointed at Bale with power, "You got a lot of nerve getting my bro to be your hype man".
Big Blue kept his mouth shut and his head down. He wasn't a fighter. "Your brother taught me what it takes to stand up to people," Bale replied, "Maybe you're just mad he never taught you".
"Seriously? For real, bro? You're gonna throw my own brother in my face?"
"If that's what it takes, baldy".
The crowd chuckled and rooted for both sides. Red didn't like that. He grinned, "Fine. I'll start his party off".
Red walked over to the tallest, buffest civilian and grabbed him by the neck. His other hand went between the man's legs. And with a pull and a push he lifted the man over his head like he had caught a raging pig. Red set the man back down. As the man sunk into the sand, he was bombarded by multiple phone numbers for licensed therapists. Red waved his hand at Bale, taunting him.
Bale took a quick look around and noticed a motorcycle parked on the pavement. Bale walked over and picked the bike up. Using his leg strength he lifted the bike and held it over his head like he was about to throw it into a volcano as some sort of ritualistic sacrifice. Big Red didn't hesitate to tip a car over by grabbing and flipping the front of the car. Bale countered by tilting the same car, sliding his body under it and lifting it over his head. The hot metal burnt Bale's hands, but the pain didn't outlive the confidence. Big Red nodded respectfully.
Big Red waited for the city bus to be completely filled before he lifted it. Now that the contest reached the streets there were more heavy things to lift. To counter the bus, Bale pushed a burger joint three feet forward, then he pulled it three feet back. Big Red jumped into the side of a hotel and pressed his feet against it, causing it to become crooked. Bale jumped down an

open sewer grate and started blasting out of the ground over and over like some sort of extreme Whack-a-Mole.
Big Red rubbed his hands together so fast that electricity was bursting between them. With his electrified mitts he dug into the sand of the beach and pulled up every grain of sand as they magnetically clung to each other. Bale waited until the feat was over. Big Red looked so sure, so smug. He told Bale to admit defeat. But Bale wasn't going to do that, he still had a few tricks up his sleeves. Metaphorically, of course. He didn't have sleeves on right now.
Bale walked into the ocean and dipped both arms into the water. He started rotating his arms like two turbines, with a power and speed so great his body turned white from the rushing waters spinning around him. Bale became a whirling dervish of aquatic ecosystems. Fish and turtles and sharks and all the majesties of the sea traveled up and down and around his body. What lied before Red and the other observers was a tower of liquid and an ocean of dry sand.

Bale stopped to reverse his momentum and rush the ocean water back where it was all supposed to be. Wet hands on his hips, Bale asked, "Giving up yet?".
Big Red looked amongst his comrades. Many of them were cheering for Bale. Red gritted his teeth and shook his head. "I got one more big one for you, dude".
Big Red planted his hands on the sand and flipped his body over into a handstand. He then started pushing himself up. Bale looked confused, "Hand-standing push ups are impressive, but I don't think that's-". Then he felt it. The ground below him was moving. The ground around the whole beach was moving. Big Red wasn't pushing himself up, he was pushing everything else down. The Earth? Maybe. The universe? Possibly. Big Red kept pushing up and down, laughing at Bale as he did so.
"You'll never be as strong as me," Red laughed, "You're too weak. And small. And my Mom would never sleep with you". The crowd was a little confused by the end of his sentence, but they seemed to be swaying to Red's side. Bale had to think fast. But opted just to copy off someone else's test. Bale got into a hand-stand pushup position and pushed every time Red didn't push. This shook the ground even harder. Vana, Blue, and many others had fallen onto the sand due to the earthquakes this pushup battle was causing.

Bale knew he could keep going, but he couldn't win by doing this. It would never tire Red out to look so strong like this. His ego wouldn't allow it. That's when it hit Bale like a ton of bricks. Bricks he could easily hurl into the sun if he wanted to. Bale went back to standing. Red did the same, first thinking Bale was going to surrender. Bale made his bet, "Last test, you big red bastard". Big Red nodded. Bale proclaimed, "First person to lift their ego wins".
From both of their bodies, the men generated a glowing mass in the shape of a billiard ball. Bale held the ball in his hand like that apple on the cover of "Twilight". Red held the ball like a piece of candy between his thumb and his index finger. Red chuckled, tossing the ball from hand to hand. But Bale remained still.
Suddenly, the ball Red was tossing around fell faster. It grew bigger too. From candy ball to beach ball, from beach ball to wrecking ball, until it was the size of a mountain and cradled on Red's back. The spectators ran off to watch from a distance. But Vana and Blue stuck by Bale's side.

The ball weighed down on Red. His knees buckled and cracked. His huge, pearly-white teeth grit like tectonic plates scraping against one another. His breathing became quick and loud and his eyes were sealed shut as he struggled to hold the weight any longer.
The weight would have killed him. But one traded glance between Red and his brother made clear everything Red needed to understand. Through strained lunges and crushed confidence, Red admitted defeat.

With the beach reclaimed, Bale handed control of it back to Blue, who in turn agreed to share ownership with his brother. Blue admitted to liking some of Red's changes. Together they could maintain a community of positivity and acceptance while also abiding by standards and rules. Red offered an olive branch to his brother by returning the land to the name "Blue's Beach". But Blue had a better idea.

With the brothers satisfied, Vana dragged Bale back to "Triz". When they arrived, Vana' new bestie Beth had left a booth open for the two of them. Beth instructed Vana to close shop when she was done. Before leaving Beth even offered Vana a job and they traded phone numbers.
"You don't actually plan on working here, do you?" Bale asked.
"What? Hell no," Vana laughed, "Have you looked at this place?"
Bale was too sober to think of a tattoo idea, so he left it up to Vana. "Surprise me," he told her as he pointed to a spot on his back he couldn't see without a mirror.
Vana laughed. She was silent for a moment. But soon she knew exactly what to give him.

Vana turned the key and the two of them walked away from the tattoo parlor, like the night they first spent together. Whatever they saw in each other hadn't changed since then. It actually grew stronger. Just as Bale did. He had asked Blue, after the competition, if he would always be this strong. Blue simply laughed then. He told Bale, "The heart is a muscle, Bale. And even when a muscle is strong, you can never stop training it. That's the difference between getting strong and staying strong".
Vana hadn't lost her touch. Not that Bale would know because she didn't even let him see it after the tattoo was done. But the process reminded Vana why she loved drawing. All this traveling gave her little opportunities to keep her own muscles trained. She decided she owed it to herself to continue drawing when she could. "Lest my next Bart Simpson look like Brendon Small".
As the two held hands and walked towards the beam of a streetlight, they stopped in unison at the sight beneath the lamp. The familiar silhouette of The Shadow. His hand was still ringing. His demand was still the same. "Call. Me. Back". Vana turned to Bale and tightened her grip. "What do you want to do?" she asked. Bale just nodded slowly. "I'm going to talk to it". Bale let go of Vana's hand and started walking forward, ignoring the tendrils of darkness that permeated the corners of his vision. But his hand was grabbed by Vana. She didn't plan on stopping him, but she wasn't going to let him go alone.
Six feet from the creature, Bale spoke through the insipid ringing to say this, "Listen to me, Shadow. I'm not afraid of you anymore. At your best I've survived whatever experience you've

put me through. And at your worst I've walked right through you". Bale dug into his pocket and took out his kaleidoscope. "This may be a little busted, but I know it's what you're afraid of. Now I don't know why it's special in that way or if what Roma told us was true, but I know as long as I have this.....as long as I have her," he held up the latched hands of himself and Vana, "you can't hurt me".

The creature changed it's stance. It stood up straight and lowered its shoulders. It tilted its head and the ringing of its hand went silent. Bale swallowed once. "I can stop you. I will stop you. Every time you try, I will overcome you. I am stronger than I was before. Both of us are. So do me a favor and leave us alone". The shadow kept looking at them, maybe it expected more cliche dialog. But it accepted the answer. It slowly moved backwards, gliding atop the ground. No more ringing. No more demands. The shadow went back to whatever dark place it came from.

Bale sighed in relief and smiled at Vana. She held him there under the spotlight, putting his head on her shoulder. Her hand ran over his back, over the tattoo she gave him. It didn't matter if his little glass toy was broken or not. Vana gave him a new kaleidoscope. It was a tapestry of colors and shades and dimensions and it splayed over his back from shoulder to shoulder. Vana believed it could protect him, but more importantly it was a part of him he could always have. A part that would follow him far after this journey. And-just like her name which sat on his skin-Bale would carry it even if he lost everything else.

Chapter 20: Sand City

What could a city of sand offer? Multi-colored layers of sand sold in mason jars? Glass containers in the shape of books which held dirt labyrinths for that one kid in class who collected ants? Perhaps they could sit and watch the construction vehicles move one pile of dirt onto another pile of dirt. This pitstop did offer a moment to relax. Bale wanted to perform more feats of strength, Vana wanted to do more drawing, and here and there they found their opportunities.

Sand City had a community playground just covered in sand. Bale and Vana bought some tools and built a sandcastle. It wasn't anything fancy, and one of the pillars was sliding down, but Plum seemed to enjoy having some temporary property. Yes, Plum the Frog. I didn't forget about her.
To satiate their fun in the sun, Bale and Vana had a bowl of mixed fruit between them. They brushed sand off their hands and left Plum to tour the castle, an experience better than a house inspection because there is a tiny frog involved. As they ate, they could hear construction equipment in the distance. There were few other people at this sand playground. Probably because there were no toys or jungle gym equipment. Or because this town was pretty one note. Tall spires of sand could be seen in the distance, and every once in a while a gust of wind would blow sand into Bale's face.
He took a cloth to wipe sand from his face and said, "I didn't know you could play the piano".
Mid chewing Vana replied, "Why're you asking about it?"
"I'm curious. And Sand City sucks".
"Gee thanks".
"Why'd you quit playing".
"Stuff happened between me and my piano instructor".
Bale looked at her, silent.
"I don't like to talk about it. Maybe I'll tell you sometime".
Bale nodded. He dug out a few blueberries.
Vana looked away. After a brief pause, "You had a girl back home, right?"
Bale swallowed hard, "Yeah. Why are you asking about it".
"I'm curious".
"And Sand City sucks?"
"Yeah, that too," Vana smiled, "Were you married?"
"You asked me that when we met".
"You never told me one way or the other," Vana crossed her arms and looked at Bale. Her pouty disposition spoke volumes. She had her long, dark hair tied up into an intricate bun. Loose hair shot out here and there, but contained by some elastics was a powerful force of follicles. It wasn't very hot, but the sun reflected off her skin perfectly. The dry, sandy air was near nonexistent when you watched Vana's body move.
There was a soft language to her movement. No tension or repositioning. She sat cross-legged on the sand and her shoulders were tight and aimed like she was going to shoot up into the sky at any moment. Bale didn't study her body movement much. He was raised to believe anyone who takes an interest in the way a woman's body moved was secretly going to kill her. Unless it was a sexual thing.

Bale had himself a big exhale. His body language said "This weather sucks. This place sucks. And the only good part of it is asking me questions and the answers to those questions suck". He nodded for a moment, met eyes with Vana and told her that he would tell her about this woman he ran away from. Or, as he put it, the women he "Fran" away from.

When Bale moved out of his parents' place and into his dinky little studio apartment he was working a warehouse job. The warehouse where he suffered the wrath of Hank and his weekend excursions. It was also at this warehouse he met an office woman named Francine. She appeared to be an average woman. Short blonde hair cut in a bob. Small frame with nonexistent muscle mass. She wore a lot of makeup and had a very strict voice, which worked out fine because she was usually the person to listen to. She wasn't exactly high up when they met, but Bale could tell by knowing her she had the smarts to run a business.
They met at the company Christmas party. Bale wasn't exactly the social butterfly, and he was still too new to hold a conversation with anyone other than Hank and Hank's poor victims of small talk. Bale snuck out the back of the building to get some fresh air and avoid hearing Hank's Hawaii story again. Francine was out there, bundled up in a big fur coat with a cigarette in her hand.
They greeted each other, but that was it for a few moments. "Do you need a light or something," Fran asked.
"Oh, no. No, thank you," Bale replied. "I don't smoke".
Fran nodded and went back to staring over the hills. "Come out here for air?"
"Came out here for quiet".
Fran sighed, "Well, sorry. I'll finish up".
"No, no, no. Not like that. You're good. You're fine," Bale rubbed between his eyes, "I'm just not a party person".
"Neither am I," Fran said, "I've known too many people who were".
Bale nodded. He remembered being the college type. He didn't know if he carried that stigma with him, most people didn't treat him like a child or a brother of sorts. Most people saw right past him. Fran saw past him too, as this was not the first time they had talked. Although, this was the first time they talked as people and not drones in the corporate machine. Bale noticed her though. Her long dresses, her tight haircuts, her sharp voice.
Tonight had been the first time Bale had seen her loosen up. The hair, the makeup, the attitude, it was all the same. But beneath the fur coat was a blouse with color and texture. A low enough cut to know what she had hidden. Her skirt was short enough to indeed reveal muscle mass that Bale hadn't noticed. Her stature was different too. Maybe Bale just never saw her standing before.

"How long are you planning to stay here?" she asked.
"I don't know. I'll probably leave before nine so I can swing by the grocery store".
She turned to look at him. "I mean with this company".
"Oh, crap, my bad," he cleared his throat, "I don't know. Until I pay off my loans, I guess".
"Student loans? You went to college".
"Yeah. Marketing. Sounded fun at the time".

"Most of the people your level here haven't even finished high school".
"Yeah, well, same finish line, I guess," Bale shrugged.
"No. $%&@ that," she pointed at him, "You shouldn't be down there with them. You should be up higher. Have you ever worked in an office setting?"
"No, but why-".
"What's your name?"
"My name is Bale. We've met before".
She nodded. "Well, Bale, I'm going to look at your file and see to it you're transferred".
"That's a very nice offer, Francine, but why would you do that?"
She walked closer to him. He could smell her perfume. "Because someone who's worked as hard as you should be rewarded. And besides, I know what it's like to waste your time and money for a career nobody wants to give you".
Bale nodded. "Thank you, Francine".
She put a hand on his shoulder and tilted her head, "You can call me Fran. All my friends do".
Bale nodded again, afraid his head would tumble off his shoulders.

As she put out her cigarette and turned to open the door, Bale asked her to wait. Bale hadn't been in a relationship since Carly in high school. His college experience was littered with half-assed dates and Dole's routine nightly visits from girls Bale never saw again afterwards. Fran wasn't some girl. She was a woman. A woman with drive and goals and a strength behind every word. A strength Bale had never seen before.
He was swinging above his league here. Both in a work setting and an age setting. Bale was in his early twenties and Fran was in her late thirties. If his parents could afford babysitting back then, his sitter would have been Fran's age back then.
But Bale read in a magazine a phrase that stuck with him. Maybe it was because he was at ER for nearly eight hours that night and Dole would never pay him back for sitting there and waiting for those doctors to pull that coat hanger out of Dole's body, but that magazine was a sanctuary for him. "Fortune favors the brave". Bale asked Fran to stop for a moment. She looked over her shoulder. Bale's next words slid out smoother than an anaconda across the jungle's soil. "Can a friend buy you a drink?"

At first, Bale's mother was skeptical. He didn't tell his mother how old Fran was or what kinds of conversations they had. Those moments belonged to Bale. His mother would ask to meet her, she would stalk her social media, she would call Bale in the middle of the day just hoping to hear her voice. One morning, Bale had told his mother over the phone that he had to do some grocery shopping and he had a date with Fran. So his mother found him at the supermarket and followed his car to Fran's house. He and Fran stayed in that night when they realized she was outside.
Fran grew tired of dodging Bale's mother. "I work in sales with sweaty men and their hair-pieces," she told Bale, "Your mother does not scare me". Upon meeting over dinner, wooden stakes made of crystalized awkward energy fell one by one between Bale, Fran, and his parents.
"Don't I recognize you from high school?" his mother asked.
"Your home is so subtle. You must be very comfortable people," Fran smirked.

"Bale, how'd you bag this one?" his father asked.
"My, I haven't smelled that brand of beer in some time".
"Hey, Bale, get your old man another drink. And one for your girl too".
"I imagine it would be hard to raise children with your work ethic".
"Bale, Poppa needs another one".
"Who does your hair? It's just so retro".
"My baby Bale always had a great taste in girls".
"Beer beer drink drink beer".
"Passive aggression. Passive aggression".
"Can I live your life? Can I please live your life? Oh, you seem so much cooler than me".
By the end of the night Fran and Bale's mother were cackling in amusement. A few martinis for them. A truckload of beers for Dad and his recliner. And a Tylenol, Ibuprofen, Tequila shot for Bale. One big happy family.

Fran turned Bale's apartment into a "Home & Design" magazine cover. She made some calls and shook some hands and landed Bale a job at a marketing company. No longer was he bound to a warehouse cubical. Now he was in the big leagues. Wearing big suits. Clinking drinks and snapping fingers with men his age with the hair of men half his age. He was a big swinging, business card slinging, call my receptionist kind of guy. And at the top of his tall tower he stood with his woman, his muse, this dynamite stick of a gal who fixed his life. Who gave him a life his parents could be proud of. But at what cost?
"You think you're better than me?" she asked as she smashed a lamp against the kitchen wall. Her lamp. And her wall. They were at her place.
"Babe, I just said I could cover dinner tonight," Bale half ducked behind the kitchen island.
"No, No, I know what this is," she screamed, "Now that you're making more money than me and you wear your fancy suits, you think I'm just some arm candy".
"No, Fran, that's not what I think," Bale held his hands up in front of him, "I just wanted to treat you".
"Treat me? Am I the kind of woman who needs to be treated?" Fran swung and knocked a glass of wine off the table. She breathed heavily after the crash of glass against the tile. Her eyes darted to Bale. "What is your plan, Bale?"
"W-w-what? What do you-".
"What is your plan?" she sounded it all out slow and loud, tilting her body forward and dragging out her words.
"What? What do you mean plan? For, like, tonight?"
"For forever! For a year from now. Six years," she waved her arms, "Are we gonna have kids? Are we gonna get married? Are we gonna move in together and get a new house?"
"Well, probably not in that order," Bale smiled.
"I'm not joking, Bale," she screamed again, "I want to know what your plan is. I want to know what we're doing?" Her breathing was quick now. And tears built up in the corner of her eyes.
"What are we doing?"
Bale shook his head and started walking towards Fran. "Fran," he said softly, putting his hands on her shoulders, "We're just living".
She looked up at him, wide eyed as she always did when she was sentimental. "Just…living?"

Bale nodded. He embraced her. This ugly wall she threw up wasn't always a factor, but it kept their relationship from fully forming beyond a partnership. He was afraid, just like she was. But he was more afraid of a life without her. That night ended with Fran slapping Bale across the face and kicking him out.

"On the ride to the airport she called me and asked how long I'd be gone," Bale said, now laying in a therapy couch made of sand. Vana sat in a chair turned around so she could lean on the back of the chair cool teacher style. The chair was also made of sand.
"What did you tell her," she asked.
"I told her for a few days. She was upset. She wanted to fix things".
"Sounds like all she did was fix things".
"Over and over, yeah. Sometimes she would upset my mother and my mom would call me to complain about her and Fran would call me to complain about my mom," Bale waved his hand in a circular motion, "One night at the club and the two of them were best friends again".
"What did your Dad think?"
"I don't know. He liked her. He thought she was hot and he liked that she drank like he did. They never really talked without my mom being there. Maybe she was worried Fran would steal her husband too".
"What do you think he would have said?"
"If I told him the truth? Based on my history of dating? He'd tell me to smack her if she gave me lip".
"Wow. Didn't you tell me you had a brother?"
"Yeah, kind of. He's a lot older than me. And we don't have the same Dad. After he graduated high school we never saw him again".
"None of you?"
Bale closed his eyes and rested his head back. He must have been sixteen or so. In the middle of the night he briefly woke up to drink some water and he heard a voice downstairs. He crept towards the stairs and looked over the railing. He could see his mother in the kitchen, but nothing above her elbows. She was sitting at the kitchen table sobbing. In her hand she held a phone, and with her other hand she covered her mouth to silence her sobbing. It didn't help. She thanked whoever was on the other end of the phone and hung up. Bale could see her hold her head in her hands.
"What do you think happened?" Vana asked.
"I think he died. I don't know how. She never talked about it".
"You never brought it up?"
"My mother is the saddest person I know," Bale said plainly, "Why make it worse".
Vana nodded. She swallowed, glanced around, "So, what about Fran now?"
"I don't know," Bale rubbed his eyes. He got sand in them. "But I don't really care". Bale rose from his sandy seat and Vana followed. They stood there in the middle of this Sand City with their hands in their pockets and their shoes full of sand. Bale tilted his head back and closed his eyes again. His dry voice rang through and echoed inside Vana's mind, "I just want to live".

Chapter 21: On The Case

When she came into the room, Chris had just finished pouring his fourth cup of coffee. Some modern health guru online said caffeine could kill you, but Chris had survived worse. Truth of the matter was plenty of things will kill you when you have too much of it, but that's what bred survivors. Chris sat at his desk and rested his elbows on top. She walked in draped in a large fur coat, a lavender pants suit, and short blonde hair that framed her doll-like face miraculously. She introduced herself as Francine, but allowed Chris to call her Fran.
"Can I ask how you heard about me?" he asked.
"I Googled local Private Detectives," she smirked, "and your name made me laugh".
"Christopher Fable? I can see why you'd laugh".
"My boyfriend is missing".
"And you need a new one?"
Another smirk. She was good at that. "He got on a plane for some sort of business trip and never came back".
"You sound skeptical. Did you boy fool around?"
"Please. He could barely handle one woman".
Chris nodded. He laid out the price. She made an offer. Not a dirty one, just what she could afford now and what she could afford later. Work was slow. Compared to the kind of cases Chris took on, this one sounded mundane. Grunt work, really. But that little demon inside him was getting bored. "Alright," Chris finally said, "I'm on it".

Christopher Fable was a cityfolk. He grew up on dark, wet streets. Broke his teeth on the pavement. Broke other people's teeth on the sidewalk. The sunny, carefree boardwalk environment was alien to him. He didn't even get the chance to wear his signature black jacket and caddy hat. The heat didn't quit and the locals were loud and obnoxious.
That little demon inside was scratching at the door to get off this wooden nightmare, but Chris was working. He worked the bars and motels and put together a rough estimate of who this Bale character was. He already had a photo as reference, given to him by Fran. The photo was of Fran and Bale on a highrise. The wind must have been powerful to blow Bale's dark, stringy hair all over the place. But Fran had not a follicle out of place. She would have probably scared it back into place otherwise.
One of the bars had photos behind the pub. One such photo had Bale in the background. He looked worse in this photo. Maybe it had been because Fran wasn't there to make him look better, but in this photo he was alone in the back of the bar. His face was pale, his eyes were dreary, and his shirt was all messed up. Wherever he got off to next couldn't have been good.

A few more conversations with the bartender and the security guard led Chris to a tattoo parlor. A muscular woman with a deep voice gave Chris everything she had, which was a lot on account of her ADD forcing her to eavesdrop.
"So this Dale guy tells her he wants her name tattooed on him, right?" she told Chris.
"His name was Bale, but go on".

"Bale, Dale, whatever. Point is, he wants her name and she's all like "Mmm honey I don't think your Mrs would like that" and he's all "Mmm baby-girl there ain't no Mrs" and she's all like "Oh, nah?" and I'm over here like, "Honey, you better not". She made quite the face model when she did these impersonations. She went on to describe her coworker Vana and how usually when drunk guys come in to flirt with her they get a canister to the side of the head, but this Bale guy had her under some sort of spell. The next day she left a note saying she was taking some vacation time.

"Didn't that tick anyone off? She just left all of a sudden," Chris asked.

"Kind of hard to argue with Vana," the face model replied, "Since she owns this place and signs all our checks".

Chris spent more time on this case than he had planned on. He had only been behind Bale and Vana a few days, but tried to stay on their tracks. Chris flashed around a photo to some Tapetown residents, the photos were of Vana from her job, and one of Bale he got from Fran. The owners of The Sendoffs night club ID'd them, so did the staff at Hogan's Hotel. Chris thought he might have lost track of them after he drove past Longhill, but an extremely long traffic jam on the 404 gave him time to review his notes and restrain the raging monster inside of him.

Exhausted from days of work and unable to sleep soundly, Chris took a lunch break at a coffee shop. The poetry wasn't half bad. It calmed it down a bit too. The poetry-and the calmness hereafter-was stripped from his world when a gun-toting man in a dog mask broke into the cafe. He forced everyone on the ground. Chris thought he could hear him asking people questions. He must not have liked the answers though. Blast after blast the Dog Guy shot out knees and holes into the ceiling.

Chris could feel the demon just beneath the surface. It begged to get out. Insisted upon it. Among the madness and the red in the corner of his eyes, Chris could see Vana stand up from the ground. His eyes darted to her, darted to the floor, darted to his target. Bale. He could kill him right here and deliver body to Fran in a gift box. No, wait.

And Vana too. Fran would just jump for joy to have her cheating boyfriend and his side-piece on her doorstep. Maybe he could leave them partially alive and the two of them could spend their first date together roasting Bale and Vana over a fire. No, stop. This wasn't Chris thinking. It was the demon. He had to get out of this place. He couldn't let it out. Not here. As Vana and Dog Guy spoke, Chris slowly rose and darted across the room and out the front door. He made no sound, he never touched the floor.

Chris didn't remember some bits and pieces. He recalled pushing past police officers and leaping into the nearby forest. His clothes were covered in claw marks and singes. As he rolled over onto his hands and knees, there was dirt under his fingernails. The closer he looked, the more red the dirt looked. The wet mud and grass he slept on made him slip as he tried to get up. Finally risen, Chris coughed. He couldn't clear his throat. He coughed again and again until blood spat out. As did some small bones. He took a deep breath and listened. He heard his heartbeat. "Good," he whispered to nobody, "Just one".

When Chris returned to the cafe, Bale and Vana were long gone. All that remained were cops, terrified customers, and an unconscious psychopath in the back of a Paddy wagon. Chris checked his watch. He only had another day before he had to call Fran and fill her in. He entered The Cup of Woe by flashing his old police badge around and found the windowseat he left his coffee at. Some of the officers gave him the side-eye, but even they knew not to get between a detective and his coffee. He finished it in one gulp and stuck his tongue out in disgust. If the madman with a gun didn't set his demon free the coffee might have gotten close.

Chris had one more shot of catching Bale and Vana. After surveying a Town Map from an empty drug store, Chris was informed of the whereabouts of Roma Phenomenon. She could bear some helpful information. Or she could banish him to Hell. Chris let the dice roll as he entered her shoe closet of a workplace. He took his shoes off by the door and hung his signature jacket on the nonexistent coastrack. The jacket fell to the floor with a pathetic impact. Roma was sitting on the other end of the room. She snickered, but insisted the coat joke was only funny the first time.
As instructed, Chris sat down across from Roma. The scents in the room were strong. Someone had been here to see her earlier. Chris explained his case to Roma in great detail. Including the Dog Guy. Roma had known Chris for a long time. She was one of the few helpful people he had ever met who didn't have some ulterior motive to help him. She was also the one who taught him so much about mysticism. Not exactly close-up magic, but he knew how to glide a little.
"Has anybody already been here today?" he asked.
Roma shook her head, "Chrissy, you know meetings here are *cough* private *cough*".
Chris smiled, "Ah, so you're finally putting your charm to financial use".
Roma laughed, "Please, child. You know nothing of my charms". She cleared her throat, "What brings you here, Christopher Fable? Hunting another demon? Or are you still running from one?"
"Actually, I'm doing a job for a woman".
"Why am I *cough cough* not surprised?"
"Because I attract needy women?"
Roma laughed and made a "shoo" motion while she regained her breath.
"This woman is looking for a man named Bale. I've been on his trial for the past week or so, but I keep missing him".
"Maybe you should *cough* work on your aim," Roma laughed.
Chris remained silent. After she was done, Roma groaned, "So what? You're the only one allowed to make jokes?"
"I need you to tell me where they will be next".
"You know how this works, Christopher," Roma said with a low tone, "Fake profit for a fake reading. You want the good stuff? You gotta *cough* give up the goods".
Chris nodded. From a plastic bag he carried in his side pocket, Chris held up a little blue man inside the bag. The man had big red eyes and a mouth full of sharp teeth. He was naked save for a pair of black shorts, and his skin was without a hair. Instead of fingers or toes, the blue man had talons on the end of his limbs and dark red feathers covered his back.

Roma clapped her hands, "Yes, yes! *cough* Come to Momma Roma," she reached out and Chris moved the bag back away from her.
"Tell me what I want to know first, Roma".
She pouted, "Very well". Roma opened her box in the middle of the room and retrieved a smaller, thin box. She opened it and lit the incense inside, and as she waved it left and right a fog of red powder filled the room. The two became enveloped in the smoke. Roma then drew a small knife adorned with symbols and gemstones from under her clothes and slammed the knife into the smoke over the floor between her and Chris. As she carved the smoke open, she told Chris to look inside. Now on all fours he dug his head into the hole and was drowned in light. He saw nothing, but knew so much more.

Roma immediately ingested the blue man when Chris gave it to her. She then mumbled something about another twenty years being taken off of her or something. With their dealings done, Roma wished Chris good luck. She gave him a peck on the cheek, a smack on the ass, and told him the next time he needed help putting the demon to sleep to give her a call. "As long as you got the goods," she laughed.

Conventional payphones were a thing of the past, but fortunately for Chris the police in this town did things oldschool. Chris borrowed some change from a stranger he bumped into and stood in the police department. Fran must have been busy because she talked very fast and Chris could hear people in the background.
"I don't have a lot of time to talk," she said.
"Are you at an orgy? Like, one of those rich people orgies I hear so much about?"
"No, Mr. Fable. I'm at an important meeting, so do please get to the point".
"I'm calling on a payphone," he laughed, "I got all the time in the world over here".
"Why are you-Oh, nevermind," she groaned, "Do you know where Bale is or not?"
"Some women only want one thing".
"I'm going to hang up," she threatened.
"I got news about Dale".
"Thank God. Have you found him? Is he alive".
"Well, no. I-"
"What do you mean? Is he dead?"
"No, no, no. He is alive".
"Okay good".
"But I don't have him".
"Well, what the Hell am I paying you for?"
"My good looks and bravado?"
"Keep dreaming," she paused, probably to schedule herself a dream later. "So why are you calling me if you don't have him?"
"I have it on good authority where he will be," Chris replied.
"Okay, so go there".
"Not alone. You should be there too".
"What? Why?"

"You said you wanted me to find him, I don't think he'll come back without seeing you," Chris hesitated about bringing up Vana. He could soften the blow, but Fran seemed like the kind of woman to get so angry she'd cut the guy loose. And Chris was a contract PI. He wouldn't get the rest of his pay until the job was done. "Besides," he dangled the carrot, "I think there's something about him you should see".

"That's it? You're not going to tell me more".

Chris made a confirmation sound. He even nodded, more for his own narrative.

There was a long pause. "Fine," she said, "Give me the place and the time. And Mr. Fable?"

"Fran?"

"You should know I've shot a gun before".

"I should know that?"

"Bale knows".

Chapter 22: Mortars

Traffic getting into Mortars was heavy, but worth the drive. Mortars was a salute to capitalism. 6,000,000 square feet, nine floors, 300 businesses, 4 hotels, and 6 apartment complexes which lined the entree into Morters like heavenly gates. These monoliths of brick and architectural genius allowed the citizens of this utopia to look down upon the tourists, mere peons who could not afford to live in this sanctuary.
Mortars' many stores and attractions introduced a paralyzing amount of choice to Bale and Vana. After booking a room at the "Inn a Bind" hotel, they tried to make a game plan.
"So, today we'll get lunch, check out the water park, and then have a small dinner so we can do nasty stuff later," Vana began.
"Right," Bale nodded, "And tomorrow after breakfast we'll go to the theme park, lounge at the spa, and then go to that movie theater with 5D movies".
"And the day after that we gotta go to LEGO City,".
"Won't that hurt? I heard it hurts when they turn you into a little plastic person".
"Maybe. I think you have to sign a waver".
"Fine. Okay. And then the book store, right?"
Vana rolled her eyes, "You big nerd. Yes, we can do the bookstore. But then we gotta see the Art Gallery".
"Is that the one with that painting? The one made...".
"Entirely out of eyelashes, yes".
"I'll never understand art. What about the last day?"
"General shopping. You think you're new, strong arms can carry all my swag bags?"
Bale laughed, "Sure they can".

On their way back from The Fifth Season, Bale and Vana discussed the salivating golden lobster sandwich Bale ordered. Both were impressed by the rarity of the creature, but Vana still believed her pig roast to be more exquisit. It's not every day you're served a pig that got its GED.
They approached a large bridge between two sections of the mall's fifth floor. Their end was host to a pretzel shop, a jewelry place, and a gaggle of massage chairs, each costing three dollars for a full body. Four dollars and fifty cents if you wanted something special.
On the other side of the bridge they could see a wide bookstore, a clothing shop, another clothing shop, and a kiosk extension to a clothing shop. The bridge had the same black and red carpet which broke up the white tile that infested the mall's many floors. Customers could lean against the glass walls of the bridge or plant their fannies down on the burgundy, wooden benches that stretched across the bridge.
Above the bridge were several metal figurines resembling birds. They spun suspended from the bridge of the sixth floor. On the right side of the bridge you could look outside and see Mortars' various apartment buildings, one featured a public pool that had an automatic dome allowing it to be indoor and outdoor at a moment's notice.
To the left, one could stand in awe of this world inside a window. Marvel at the neon signs and octaves of modern rock and pop music pouring out of every door. The shape of human life

became inconceivable as the masses of civilians continued to flow wildly. If you listened closely you could hear people yell at each other or scream for help.

Unless you lived in Mortars, of course. In that case you could take the secret tunnels built between the mall and the commonplaces of the apartment buildings. These tunnels led out secret hatches throughout the mall, allowing residents quick access to grocery stores, general stores, and drug stores, to name a few. There is also a hover pad transport service residents can use to fly over the crowds. With a unique app called "Huv", residents could summon an automated platform which will fly to their location and take them to their building.
Bale learned all this from Vana, who followed a Youtube biographer who broke their teeth on Mortars content, having lived a few towns over. Now they live in a mansion on the west coast or something. Vana couldn't remember how the hover pads worked, but she foggily recalled the use of magnets.

As they walked across the bridge with their full stomachs and fuller bags, Bale came to a stop. Vana looked back at him confused. Bale looked like he saw a ghost. At first, Vana assumed the shadow man had returned. That, or the golden lobster was about to return. But through the unbelievable fluster of people, Bale could see her face clear as day. All the way here, all this time later, her cold eyes cut through the air itself. Fran's eyes met Bale's. She didn't look happy.

"All I want to know," Fran said, "is why". Bale, Vana, and Fran sat at a circular table. Among many tables, this one stood in a corner between a shoe store and an escape room business with rooms so big they could accommodate twenty bored and easily impressed people.
Bale held his cup of coffee. Vana had a bottle of orange juice. Fran didn't have the patience for a drink that couldn't get her smashed. She sat up straight as an arrow. She glared at Bale over her expensive glasses. Her blonde hair was darker than before, but still short like she used to have it. Bale hadn't realized how long it had been since he last saw her.
She elaborated, "Why did you-you just left. Poof! You're gone". She raised her palms up.
Bale narrowed his vision and scratched his head. Vana watched on in a state of shock, or maybe she felt starstruck. She had not seen Bale nervous like this. Bale thought for a moment, avoiding Fran's glare. He took a breath and tried to reply, "I needed a break".
"A break from what, Bale?" she was quick, "From me?"
"From work, you know?"
"Oh, you mean the job I got you? The job that pays you more than me?" Fran turned red, "And what do you do with all that money? You spend it on some tattoo girl?"
Vana snapped out of her confusion, "Actually-Francine, was it? I paid for my roasted pig all by myself".
"I bet you did, Mrs. Vana," Fran turned her nose up, "With all that money you have from your tattoo shop".
Bale looked over at Vana, "That's where you get all your money? You own that tattoo place?"
Vana smiled, "Dude, did you see how that place was decorated? Of course I owned it".
Fran was about to speak, but Vana cut her off to continue talking to Bale, "Wait, where did you think I was getting my money?"

"Well, I thought your family was wealthy. Like, maybe your grandfather invented the pencil sharpener or something".
"My grandpa is not as old as the pencil sharpener".
Fran snapped her fingers several times, "Hey! Hey! Hello?" she looked back and forth between the two of them. Bale and Vana fell silent. Fran spoke up again, "What was that?" She looked at Bale and repeated the question.
"Well, we were just talking-".
"About pencil sharpeners. Not about why you just up and left us".
"What do you mean-".
"Bale, come on. You don't think the first thing your mom did was call me? And when she wasn't calling and asking where you went, your coworkers were," Fran rubbed her forehead in a rare moment of exhaustion, "For Christ's sake, your mom thought I had you killed or something".
"Fran, I didn't mean to…to…"
"Scare everyone? Yeah, that's what you did. You scared everyone, Bale".

The three of them sat there for a few more minutes. Nobody, not even Fran, had any idea of where to take the conversation next. Around fifteen minutes later, Vana got up to go use the bathroom and give the two some alone time. Before leaving, Vana bent down and hugged Bale. She then sauntered off down a nearby hallway.
Alone with him now, Fran asked, "Who is she, Bale?"
"What? Her name is Vana. I thought I introduced you".
"That's not what I mean, damn it. What is she to you?"
"She's my friend".
"Stop playing dumb," Fran leaned in, more red and with a sharper tone. She could sharpen a pencil with that tone. "Is she your side piece? Your escort?"
"Fran, come on-".
"No, no, no. I can take it. So what is she? Is she blackmailing you? Or do you just have a secret goth kink I never knew about?"
"She…she just makes me-I don't know. It's easy with her".
"Easy," Fran laughed. It was not genuine. "Okay, so? What? I'm difficult then?"
"No, Fran. I didn't mean-".
"No, I get it. Hell, I agree. I am not easy. I'm not always fun or zesty like your little miss body paint might be. But I got you where you are. I saw your intelligence and your talent and your work ethic and your experience and I pushed you. And I made you matter. I made you important. And maybe I wasn't always fun, but you'd be nothing without me. And you are smart enough to know that".

All at once, no amount of strength could help Bale overcome this obstacle. Fran could cut him deeper than any shadow man could. She could be right too. About her part in his life. About who he is now. He really just left Fran and his whole life behind for this. For a mall and a rental car and a girl. That girl.
Bale sorted his thoughts. He compiled his fears. All Fran wanted to do was break him down more. Make him die of guilt. She threatened to call his mother. She made him wish Vana never

walked off. Bale wanted to know how she found him, but he could not change the subject if he tried. Fran was all in on dragging him through the mud.
So he offered an alternative. It was getting late. He needed time to breathe and think. Fran was tired. He could always tell by her eyes. He suggested meeting back up in the morning. Fran was so angry and so ready to break her heel into Bale's head, she agreed to the idea solely to prevent security from arresting her.
Fran stood up suddenly. She did not hug Bale, but she put her hand on his shoulder as she passed him. She told him which motel she would be staying at and that if Bale decided to "stop being a stupid idiot", he could come to the motel and they could fly back home in the morning. When she was gone, her presence was still felt. Bale leaned over his coffee. He wished the shadow man would appear and pull him out of this miserable world. Truly, this a Hell even he could not have fathomed.

Bale's intense staring contest with his coffee was splintered by the loud, drinking sound Vana made with her blue raspberry slushie. She stood next to him and just watched him. Their eyes met and she stopped sucking the flavored air from her drink.
Bale's eyebrow cocked, "Where did you get that?"
Vana spoke with blue lips and a blue tongue, "The woman's bathroom has a slushie machine".
"That's awesome. This place is awesome".

Tense wasn't enough to describe how Bale was feeling that night. It was a decent descriptor for Vana though. She was unusually quiet, not even wanting to talk about Fran or anything. Her last words before bed were "this is a problem for tomorrow's me". Bale hid in the master bathroom. It might as well have been a spare bedroom. The tub was big enough for four basketball players, a soft, white sofa sat in the far end of the room, and the sink had four sets of mirrors and hand washing stations. Maybe this hotel was for polynamorous couples.
It's funny. After all they'd been through on this trip, nothing shook Bale to his core like this whole situation with Fran. Bale looked up and down from the mirror multiple times, almost expecting his shadow to appear and pull him into some weird mirror dimension. But that didn't happen. He felt like it did though. He felt weak. Like somebody pulled every bone from out of his body.
Bale tried the exercise Big Blue taught him. He recounted every memory. Every mistake. Every time he overcame the odds. Inside himself he found nothing but disappointment. No victories, big or small, could erase this anxiety he felt. Bale tried again, this time by drawing a bath and staring into the water. Just as he did with the ocean. But there were no rocks or seaweed. On the floor of this tub was a plastic mat meant to message your feet.
The water was clear. The heat from the bath was soothing. Bale breathed in the lavender scents with his eyes closed. When he opened his eyes, he was not met by his reflection or anyone else's. No, just water. What if that's all it was? The water at the beach had radioactive properties or something. What if the shadow man stole his strength? Or, maybe, he just couldn't find what he was missing. All he had was Vana. And all he could think about was Fran.

Leaving his life behind should have been hard. His father relied on Bale to pick up his medication every other week. And his mother talked to Bale nearly every day. Sometimes their

conversations were mundane, but they became accustomed to each other's voices. Fran was the first person he'd see when he woke up, and the last person he'd see before going to sleep. Sleeping wasn't as easy as it used to be.
Maybe all this was wrong. Picking up a girl at a tattoo place. Going on a cross country roadtrip. Throwing his life into the ocean. What was this? The price? When the things you become freed from calls back to you? Did he really survive everything just decide it was all pointless? To decide Vana was pointless? But even if every chapter were different, Bale still had a life. And now, he believed all Vana had for a life was a life with Bale.

"And then what Bale?" Fran said, "You two settle down? Meet each other's parents? And then what? You get sick of her? You abandon her while you're on a work trip and you meet a girl six years younger than her, you fall in love with this new girl and just toss your goddamn phone away? And then what? You start all over?" Her voice was cracking like timber.

"And if he goes back home?" Vana replied. "Back home to a woman who never understood him? Never knew how to make him happy? A woman obsessed with structure and titles and status? What does all that mean when you've been through what he's been through? What does any of that mean when you barely have a father? When you hardly ever had the choice of what to do next?".

Bale's mother spoke next. "I just want you to come home, honey. Me and your father miss you. And we need you. Think of Francine, dear. Don't you think you've put her through enough? Bobby, talk to your son".
Bale's father slogged his words as he spoke them, obligated to say something, "Come home, bud. You're driving your mother crazy".
Bale lifted his face from the water. He spoke aloud to an empty bathroom, "What about you, Dad? What am I doing to you?"
"You're not being smart, Bale".
"Of course I'm not. I only went to college to be smart. I only got a high-end job to be smart. Nobody at home was going to teach me".
"Hey, your mother and I-".
"No. No," Bale shouted, "You didn't do anything".
"I taught you how to be a man".
"You taught my brother how to be a man. And he died for it".
The voices stopped. Bale's eyes were shut tight. His face was sweating, and as bad as it hurt, as sharp as the needles in his throat felt, he could not stop now. "He'd still be alive if you didn't drive him away".
"Bale, don't you dare-" his mother tried to interject.
"No, you shut up too! Neither of you did any of it right. You spent so much of your time trying to control him. Control the two of us. Then when he died, suddenly the whole goddamn world was on my shoulders. Suddenly I had to be the successful one you could brag about to your friends and coworkers".

"And you think this is success?" his father finally chimed in, "Crying in a bathroom to people who aren't even there? Bitching and moaning because you screwed up your own life?" Bale could feel his father's breath against his cheek, but he kept his eyes closed. "You can blame me and your mom all you want, but you do not get to pat yourself on the back. I might have messed you up, but I taught you better than to pass the buck. Your brother knew that! And you know what he did with all his bullshit childhood trauma?"

"He died," Bale said.

He could feel his father breathing heavier, "Yeah. Yeah, he died. For his country. He didn't cry himself to death in the bathroom. He was a real man".

"Not like me, right?"

"Not like you".

"Dad, I know you're not there. I could get on a plane, walk through your door, and you still won't be there".

"What're you trying to say".

"I'm saying you didn't just mess up. You failed. Every time. I don't know if it was the drinking. Or if you just never gave a shit about what I liked or what I wanted to do or any of that stuff. I don't think you ever even cared about me".

"Yeah? You don't think I know? I know I drink. I drink because once upon a time I was miserable like you".

"Honey, you don't have to-" Mom again.

"No, no. He needs to hear this. He might never get the chance," his father cleared his throat.

"Bale, I tried to escape too. I tried leaving my job at the factory. I tried breaking up with your mother. I even borrowed my buddy's hotrod and made a go at driving down the coast. You know what happened?"

"I don't know. You found alcohol? Or, I don't know, my brother happened?"

"I got hurt. I got hurt real bad, Bale. By someone I thought had my back. They took all I had. Landed me on the streets for months. I couldn't even go home. My pops-your grandfather-disowned me. My mother couldn't say a thing. Everyone expected me to either settle down or vanish completely. And here I was, tail between my legs, worse off than I was before. Crawling back to a town that rejected me, that ridiculed me. And your mother-God bless her-she was the only person who wanted me back".

"Because I needed him as much as he needed me," she added.

"And because the two of us were lonely. And afraid. And I thought-I thought back then-that she was my only chance to be happy".

Bale nodded. "How did that work out for you, Dad?"

"Better than I deserved, kid," the water brushed against Bale's knees. His eyes opened. The room was flooded by the bath water. But the lights stayed on. And the water stayed warm. "Better than I deserved".

Chapter 23: The Turnabout Hotel

Love drives us to do things we would never conceive of. It drives us to sacrifice. Sacrifice of strength. Sacrifice of time. Sacrifices that take from our existence and only aid in tethering our destinies to each other. Some people love because it is easier than to be alone. It is easier than to start again. Yes, sometimes what we invest is everything. And when love fails, we have nothing left to sacrifice.

Conversely, love is receiving. If one has to give, one other must receive, surely. One must benefit from the sacrifice. This benefit can be material, and sometimes that is enough. The benefit can be emotional, which is at its purest. But more often than not the benefit required is one of approval. Some people want to be loved so they have a reason to live. And not only to live, but to live happy with who they are.

Once upon a time, Bale was one of those people. Bale wanted to be allowed to be happy. To feel comfortable in his own skin. And the only cost was his everything. In the beginning, he thought this sacrifice was worth it. To feel loved. To be told he mattered. To no longer be alone. But as soon as he had what he wanted, he wondered what could have been.

So, here he was. The venue didn't matter. The time was late, the whole ordeal was very last minute. What Francine expected was an apology was not quite that. In fact, what she was about to hear would be very insulting. Albeit true. In fact, no truer words could have been spoken that night. As Bale had no intention of leaving with her. No, he simply snuck past a sleeping Vana and came to Francine's room to give her closure. His version of closure. An answer to her question.

"I wasn't happy. I thought I was because my parents were happy. They were happy because I was with you".
"But you didn't feel the same?".
"No. I liked how you helped me. With the job and the apartment. It's like, everything around you was working".
"And I wasn't".
"You made me feel like a loser. I don't want to feel like I lucked into a relationship, Francine. I want to feel like I'm wanted".
"I hired a private investigator to find you. How can you not feel wanted?"
"You know what I mean. When you weren't guilt tripping me into marriage, you were guilt tripping me about the job you got me. And you know what? I don't even like my job".
"You like the money don't you? The money you've been spending on this trip?"
"Screw the money. It was never about that. Do you know what I've been doing out here? I've been meeting people and making friends. I've been learning more about myself, about what I like and what I was missing".
"So, was the problem me or you, Bale".

"You. It was you Francine. I thought it was me at first. When I decided to not come back. I thought I was pissing my life away and I might as well live it up because I can't get my life back. But then I realized it was my life I didn't need".
"People need you, Bale".
"People never treated me like I was needed. What if I liked my old apartment? What if I liked my old job-".
"You never liked Hank".
"That's still true. But what if I never wanted to get married and have kids and a house and a dog and a picket fence? What if I wanted that stuff because everyone told me I had to have it to be happy?"
"Do you think you need her? Do you think she'll make you happy?".
"She does make me happy. Because I don't have to try and be my best self. She likes me for me. Like that song".
"What song?"
"It's Third Eye Blind".
"Okay. Go on".
"I just…I came here to tell you I'm not going home with you. I'm not going to see you again, and I might not even see my parents again. I don't know what's going to happen and that doesn't frighten me".
"Okay. Okay, Bale".

Love may be indeed hinged on sacrifice, but the same is true of self love. You only get one body. You only get to be yourself. Whichever version of yourself makes you feel at ease may not always be the truest form of yourself. Ripping off the expectations. Embracing the flawed, weak, repugnant presence found inside all things can sometimes bring liberation.
Bale's mother would never admit her envy of women like Francine. Free, Righteous. Powerful. Never bored by the prospect of their story ending. A life of pain is only an adventure when the pain comes to an end. As for his father, the man was shattered by the past, and he was exiled to a present where he was no more insignificant than the day he returned home. His greatest contributions to the world would be two sons who never truly knew him.

Time and time again, mortal beings such as yourself will attribute your growth to the attendance of someone else. The acceptance of someone else. And, just as commonly, you will lie and say "there is no special someone" or "I am happy on my own". It is within your nature to lie about such things. Just as it is within your nature to find companionship.
Love. Friendship. A mutual distain of a coworker or a common interest in music. Something. Someone. More than what you have. More than what you are. Simplicity is beyond what you desire. You want to be happy. You want to be angry. You want to feel, as feeling is the most human experience there is in the known universe. Next to death, that is.

When Bale rerturned to his room at "Inn a Bind", Vana was gone. Bale had only been gone for about an hour. Maybe she went for a walk. A stroll through the animatronic dinosaur park. Or

some late night paragliding over at "Wings on Wings: The First Paragliding School/Chicken Wing Restaurant". Before jumping to any conclusions Bale checked the massive bathroom, but he found nothing but wet towels and shag bath mats. What he didn't find was any of Vana's bathroom supplies. "Maybe she had to throw it all out," he said to himself, "Throw it out and replace it".
Maybe she had to throw out her clothes too, which would explain her missing suitcase and how none of her clothes were in the room. As he searched, Bale found a shoebox under the bed where his suitcase remained, but Vana's was still MIA. Bale sat down and opened the box.
Inside of it were dozens of photos he didn't remember taking. Must have been because Vana took them when he wasn't paying attention. Nearly all of them showed towns the two visited in their travels, and every photo had some piece of Bale somewhere in it. The side of his head here and there, a wandering arm or leg. One photo was of the beach with his butt centered in the middle of the shot.
The box also contained a keychain from each town, the free frog beds they got in Lillipatton, and a receipt from the Cup of Woah. There was also a scrap of paper Vana used to practice tattooing her name. Written on the back was Bale's name several times in many different writing styles. Another scrap of paper emerged also signed with Bale's name, but much more than that. The letter read:

Bale,
I'm sorry I couldn't say goodbye to you first. But if I tried, I don't think I could have. I had an amazing time with you. And I wish everyday could be as fun as the days I spent with you. But I think we both knew this wasn't as real as we'd like to be, right? It's funny. Plenty of guys I met back home say they'll take me away or something corny like that. But you're the first guy to do it, and you're, like, the only guy I think I could trust.
I know you're probably mad, and that's okay. But Francine is your girl and if you want to be with her, you don't need me around gumming up the works. I'm going home, Bale. You should too. I'm glad we could distract each other for a while, but the real world catches up to you eventually and nothing good like what we had could have lasted forever.
I hope Fran can make you as happy as you made me. And just know that I will always love you. And I will always want the best for you.
⠀⠀Vana

There was no time for jokes or references. There was no time to talk to Fran or confront his inner turmoil. There was no time to think. Time ridded itself from existence. Everything stood still. The falling note of abandonment sat in mid-air. The crowds window shopping at nine at night fell silent. The toast did not jump out of the toaster, it peaked. Somewhere on Earth a crying child became as quiet as a church mouse.
Vana left. She left thinking Bale wanted to be with Fran. Her stuff was gone. The rental car was gone. All she left behind were their memories in a box. A box that weighed nothing, but held everything to Bale. Like a bolt of lightning, Bale opened the door and ran down the hall and searched the parking area up and down, up and down, up and down. No cars moved. Nobody left. He was too late. And she was gone.

Chapter 24: The Unscape

There was stillness, suddenly. Time ceased to exist. And like all things that cease, it dropped into The Unscape like a stone into a pond. It would leave, of course, But the waves were felt regardless. The waves stretched and bent and twisted. They came to an end and faded into darkness indistinguishable from the rest of the darkness. But the waves were felt regardless.

Doctor Zebediah Dean awoke in a sweat. He sat up in his huge bed and reached for a glass of water positioned next to a photo. The photo was of himself and his friends during a better time. Now he was alone in this big house. Too much food for one man.

Dean left his bedroom and roamed the halls of his empty home. He had not used his wheelchair in many weeks. He had nobody to pretend for now. Without thinking he found his way into the living room. As he walked past the fireplace his fingertips dragged over its black brick surface. He longed for the heat that once slept here. He longed for any warmth at all.
The wind outside was strong. Window shutters in the distance slammed and banged and kept children awake. Dean was lured into the kitchen. The neon white light of the refrigerator slipped out and cascaded across the darkened room. He must have forgotten to close it.
Dean shut the door, but to no avail. It popped back open. He pushed again. Harder this time. It popped back open. Dean gave it one more shove, grunting as he did so. Yet again, it popped back open. Opening the fridge revealed more food than what Dean knew what to do with. Vegetables and fruits and meats and liquids. If he still had friends, one of them could make a meal out of all this stuff.

Food and drinks splayed over the kitchen floor as Dean dropped to his knees and frantically dug everything out of the fridge. He threw watermelon and lettuce and jugs of milk carelessly. By the time the fridge was empty, the kitchen was painted in food and drinks.
The white light vanished as the open fridge turned into a coffin of blackness. Dean peered into the blackness. He dare not reach into it. But he could feel a warmth from the darkness. A coziness not unlike his bed. Not unlike the people he loved.
The darkness offered him something. It told him he didn't need to be afraid. He could have everything he was forced to give up. All he had to do was pick up the phone

Nobody cared what his name was. He didn't care either. Not yet at least. No, one day they will. One day when his screenplays hit the big screen. Then they'll care who he is. All he was now was a man in a jail cell. He didn't want to be crazy. And, yeah, he didn't want to be in jail either, but at least here people would listen. They had no choice but to listen.
The Dog Guy told his cellmate all his movie ideas. And his cellmate would shoot down every one. The cellmate was in the middle of pointing out the similarities between Dog Guy's newest romantic comedy and the movie "Pretty Woman", when a guard pulled him out. For good.

The following days were grueling. Dog Guy's new roommate wouldn't listen. He would hit. He would scream. He would pick Dog Guy up and put Dog Guy down. He did everything but listen. And having no outlet for his stories made Dog Guy antsy. It put him on edge.

He cycled through every breakout movie he had ever devised. He could crawl out through the sewer. Or maybe he could sneak out with the laundry truck.

Dog Guy's escape was eventually brought on by his roommate beating him to a pulp. Dog Guy's story about pilgrims and aliens must have triggered something in the roommate. The guards had to bring Dog Guy to the infirmary. Dog Guy fought as they tried to sedate him, he begged them not to let him sleep. "Don't make me dream," he screamed, "I can't remember when I dream".

Darkness found him not at the end of a needle, but in the depths of his captor's eyes. When Dog Guy saw it, he made it his mission to have it. This beautiful darkness. Dog Guy scratched at the guard's eyes. He broke the other guard's head against a sink. He dug the accused needle into the doctor. Nobody would make him dream.

But this darkness in the eye of his tormentors. Perhaps it could help him imagine his next masterpiece. Perhaps it could make the fantasy real. All Dog Guy had to do was pickup the phone.

It took three months to clean up all of Howard's tape. And even then the job wasn't completely done. Tapetown's roads may have been cleaned but their buildings and street lamps were covered in the red sticky samples of Howard's body too. Patty was no longer the mayor. The town voted to kick her out of the role, but many still showed support in helping her clean up her long-lost husband.

Nobody really knew how Howard ended up like this. This man was well past the age to be transmogrified into an unholy abomination, and further to the point: the man was retired. Howard hadn't touched a tape-making machine in over twenty years. Then again, the tape giant had been a Tapetown attraction since the town's founding in the late 1910's.

Maybe there was a curse. Or maybe Patty's inability to let Howard relax for the rest of his days drove him into becoming one with their literal tourist traps. It didn't matter to her. She may not have been mayor and she may not have had the answers, but she had Howard. Over the trees and in the lake and under her shoe and in several hundred Home Depot buckets. She had him everywhere. She would tell her friends, "It's like he's home". Maybe because he was home. All over it.

Her only regret now, in this bypass of her life, was Patty's vendetta against the people who tried to set Howard loose. It was their fault he got out. Their fault Howard fell apart. And after all she did to accommodate them. Patty almost saw herself in that girl Vana. And a younger Howard in that Bale boy too. But to leave at Howard's time of need. Unforgivable.

The thought of those two out on the road drove Patty crazy. They were young and free and neither of them were made out of tape. If they stayed, maybe they could have helped her fix Howard. Maybe they could have helped her stay mayor.

Then the whole town wouldn't be slinging their pity on her. Helping her just to save face or avoid being guilty. But Bale and Vana got to avoid guilt. Avoid responsibility. And that did not sit well with Patty. She was not happy with how things ended with those two. Not until she picked up the phone.

Shadows ran like raindrops down a glass wall. Streams of colorless aura painted the streets of Lillipatton. This circuit board of emptiness acted as a map for the weary travelers brought here. A man with psychic powers. A criminal in a dog mask. And a woman covered in tape.
"I suspect neither of you brought me here?" Dean asked.
Patty put her hands on her hips, "Now, whatcha thinkin' there, bucko? Me and Dog Guy here couldn't organize a little get together?"
Dean shook his head, "Because a moment ago I was getting dressed. And now?"
"You're here," Dog Guy finished.

The lines of black united them, and they were pushed into the center of town. Absent was the sparkling water fountain of the past. Now lay a large lily pad over a swamp of sewer water. Against railings and scaplulting sat a beast of enormous size. Its black, leathery skin shone from the moonlight. Its deep and dark eyes could swallow your soul. As it breathed, you could hear the gurgling and digesting of food once eaten. If it were food to begin with.
"Perhaps it was this creature that brought us here," Dean pondered.
Patty tilted her head, "Looks like a big ol' pollywog to me".
"Like the giant ape in my jungle movie pitch," Dog Guy added to no interest.
The monster leaned forward and observed the trio. With a speculative glance, it then lifted one of its huge arms to reveal a broken street lamp. It lifted the lamp like a staff and illuminated the town square. What mattered wasn't what was lit by the light, but what shadows it created. Formed from the shapelessness surrounding the light, The Shadow Man appeared. Ringing phone in its hand. No voice to speak of. But its message was clear. Now was the time to seek revenge on Bale. Now, at his most vulnerable. And with these enemies of Bale it was more possible than ever. The psychic. The tape woman. The dog man. The frog. The boomerang. Yes, also in the town square was a man in black spandex suit with a boomerang emblem on his chest.

The job was understood. The accomplices were assembled. All they needed to do was find Bale. And The Shadow Man was part of Bale, he knew where he would be next. Easily enough, Bale was going to retrace his steps. Making it easier for his foes to find him. Easier for them to corner him. And when his allies had Bale where he wanted them, The Shadow Man would finally get what he wanted. Bale would have no choice. He would have to pick up the phone.

Chapter 25: Brother's Beach

A drive to the beach was supposed to be fun. Pop music and wind through the open windows. The sun beaming down on your bright little car. Speeding down the highway and looking for a good time. But without Vana, Bale could not relish in the sea salt air. His new rental car smelled too much like leather anyway.
If Vana was driving back home to the Boardwalk, the easiest route for her would be to go back through towns they'd already visited. Driving down that route took Bale back to Brother's Beach, which remained teeming with life and levity. Blue and Red had done a good job of keeping the beach clean of trash, and cleaner of bad people.
Friends and strangers alike were tossing beach balls and splashing water on one another. But the jazzy tunes of the beach goers meant nothing short of radio static for Bale. He was sweating in his car. Sweating on his old leather. His hair was straggly and combed over his forehead. His eyes hurt. It felt like he had been driving for days.

He needed to get Vana back. Even if it meant driving onto the beach because his vision got blurry. His tired eyes blinded him to the screaming masses dodging his car as it drove over bonfires and through volleyball nets. Bale's head fell onto the steering wheel as a cluster of stones grew closer and closer.
Bale woke to the sudden shock of his car hitting something. Not the rocks. His head shot up to see what he hit, who he hit. But it was Big Red, who's muscular red arms held the car as it continued to accelerate forward. Bale took his foot off the gas just as his door flew off. Big Blue ducked down to look inside the car. His expression of exhaustion turned into one of sadness, a familiar expression for Blue. He reached in and pulled Bale out. Bale's vision faded again and he fell asleep as Blue carried him across the beach.

In his dreams, Bale was under the ocean. The absence of sound occasionally broke with the motion of crustaceans scuttling past him. He reached out to the creatures and was surprised to see his hand was a claw. Was he like them? A lobster on the ocean floor? From this far down and with the light of the sun Bale could see the ocean floor for miles. Fluorescent pink coral, bright purple foliage, and schools of neon fish swimming through the sea.
Bale scuttled after his lobster brethren. He crawled under the swinging limb of a concealed octopus. Overhead were jellyfish which floated like balloons. Passing by a cliff, Bale could see a pair of stingrays chasing each other.
When he finally caught up to the lobsters, they were digging in the sand and plucking shiny objects out of the ground. Wedding rings and spoons and coins. Bale wanted to dig too. As he pierced his claw into the sand and scooped it out of his way, Bale's sight was set on black device in the dirt. He dug further and used his claw to grip and pull the device out. It was his cell phone.

Bale woke up to the sound of a phone ringing. He laid flat on his back atop a hard, wood surface. A gravelly voice asked him not to shake so much. When Bale looked over his chest he

noticed a glass of beer sitting on his stomach. The gravelly voice belonged to a diminutive man with a flush of red hair and teeth with gaps so long you could fit a football between his molars. Across the room Bale could see Big Blue answering a phone. Big Red was on the other side of Bale, across from the short guy. He told Bale what happened and how they brought him back to Doc's Bar after he passed out. The short guy-Doc-gave Bale a clean bill of health.
"Ye might be need'n more sleep, lad," he suggested.
"Could you take your drink off me?" Bale asked.
Doc chuckled and took his drink off Bale, "Next time," he said, "I'll use a coaster".

Bale apologized to Red about the driving incident, "You're sure you're okay?"
Red laughed, "Dude, this was not my first time getting hit by a car".
Blue finished his phone call and joined in, "And it probably won't be your last".
"What was that call about?" Red asked.
"Some crazy lady causing crazy problems across town," Blue looked at Bale, "Come along and fill us in".
"Come along?" Bale said, "I can't. I have somewhere I need to get".
"That's a no go on that, bro," Red announced, "Head injury + sleep deprivation + busted car in need of repair - our confidence in leaving you alone-".
"Equals," Blue added, "you're coming with us".

Inside their silver Jeep, Red and Blue let the fresh wind brush their faces happily. Seeing them together, it was easier to tell they were brothers. Even if one looked like an oversized smurf. Bale sat in the passenger seat while Red tanned in the back seat and Blue drove with one strong arm at the wheel, his bicep becoming a bridge from his sunglasses to his windshield.
Bale explained his story and Red chuckled in the back seat, "Caught between two loves, I know that feeling, bro".
Blue replied, "He means our older cousin or our aunt. Both of which he considered taking to our Middle School formal".
"Hey! Shut your mouth! Cousin Gretta was cool".
Blue side-eyed Bale, "Why didn't you tell Vana about Francine?"
"I did tell her".
"After she had already left with you?"
"Well, yeah".
"Do you think if she knew about Francine before you left the boardwalk she would still go with you?"
Bale didn't reply.
"Maybe," Blue said, "you didn't tell her because you were afraid she'd reject you".
"What does anything of this have to do with anything?" Bale asked.
"You went on this trip with Vana, right? What would have happened if she didn't want you? Would you have gone home?"
Bale didn't reply.

As the trio pulled up to the scene they were welcomed with a tornado of fabric whipping at everything in sight. Cars were dented, street lamps were wrapped up, and civilians clung to the ground, all by the wake of huge pieces of tape. Bale knew as soon as he got out of the jeep that Patty was in town. When the tornado settled she stood on the main street with a banner over her head reading "Patty is in town".

With a swing of her arm, tape erupted from Patty's tape-crafted trenchcoat and it spiraled into a drill. Blue and Red moved just in time as the drill pierced their jeep. Patty cackled, "Whatcha boys think about my new coat? Pretty swanky, huh". Blue and Bale found cover behind a tipped over hotdog cart while Red rushed from the right. With his enormous strength there was no doubt Red could overpower her, but the problem was reaching her. Red lept into her only to be stopped by a wall of tape which sprung from Patty's back. Red tried to rip out, but to no success. He became a cocoon of tape on the ground.

Bale shouted, "This isn't the kind of thing a Mayor is supposed to do, Patty".

"I'm not the mayor anymore, hun," she replied, "Thanks to you and your little gal pal, nobody in Tapetown pays me any mind". Patty held her arms in front of herself and small strips of tape crawled out of her sleeves. They twisted and grew and bent into horrible spiny fingers. "But after I'm through with you," long tape tentacles protruded from her back and carried her over the street, "I'll show those townies the same hospitality".

Patty cut the hotdog cart to pieces as Blue and Bale scuttled away. Patty fired her tape claws like porcupine spines, lodging them into the sides of buildings. Another spike flew through the air towards Bale, but he hit the ground painfully and avoided the shot. When Bale looked up, Blue was on top of him. The tape spike stuck out of his back.

As Blue collapsed, Bale grabbed him and dragged him into an alleyway. He pleaded to him, "Blue, come on. I can't stop her without you and Red".

"You can do anything Bale. You have the strength".

"No, Blue. I..I don't. I lost my strength".

Blue took Bale's hand. "Do you still have her name?"

Bale thought for a moment. He could feel the ink on his skin. He nodded.

"Then right now," Blue's eyes closed, "you have all the strength you need".

Bale fought back tears as the whipping and ripping sounds of tape grew closer.

"Oh, Bale dear. Why dontcha quit yapping with yer friend and ohow a former mayor some attention?"

Bale grit his teeth, "You want my attention, Patty". Bale's fists clenched, his tears stopped, and a fire in his heart ran through his body like a herd of buffalo, "You got it".

Bale ran through the flurry of tape tendrils which shot out of Patty's coat. He dodged, ducked, dived, dipped, and dodged every strip of sticky surface until he reached the source. He hadn't thought much as to what he would do once he reached Patty, but Bale understood her tape powers were coming from her coat. Once he was close enough, Bale gripped the coat and pulled as hard as he could, swinging Patty around and causing her to fall down on top of him. The tendrils of tape flailed widely. One strip flew across Bale's face and left a long cut. This happened again to Bale's neck. Then again to his stomach. Holding her wasn't helping anything.

Bale shoved Patty off and got a short distance away from her. As Patty lifted herself up with her tape arms she swore at Bale and then immediately apologized. "Now why do ya have to go and make this difficult, hun?" she asked, "Dontcha know how hard this is already?"
Bale shook his head, "What is your problem? You got your husband back, didn't you?"
"In ribbons! I got him back in ribbons," she raised herself up high, "And you got him tangled, ya know that? You couldn't leave well enough alone".
Bale was taken aback. The way she was speaking sounded like…Bale called back to her, "You knew he was in there? Didn't you?"
Patty bit her lip. She looked down for a moment, "I didn't know what to do. When he got…when he got like that. Covered head to toe. I thought, I don't know, I thought he'd want to be memorialized. He was finally the King of Tape".
As Patty began to sob, her coat tightened on her. At first she was comforted. She rubbed the coat and whispered her husband's name. But the security soon turned into a constraint. Her arms crossed and folded. Tape slung from out of her collar and zoomed across her body until it was wrapped in a straight jacket of tape. One last ribbon of tape went across her mouth as she collapsed.
Bale approached Patty, now that she was down. On the back of Patty's coat a face formed, with eyebrows and lips made from-you guessed it-tape. Bale stared at it, and the face stared back. Bale bent down to speak to the face, "I'm sorry about what happened to you".
"Not…your…fault".
"I'm…I'm sorry we left you. We should have helped you".
"Not…your….problem".
"I just…what are you going to do now? You're stuck".
"Not…stuck….I cling".
Patty was lifted from the ground by the tendrils of the jacket. The jacket extended into a human shape, a giant adorned with all colors and textures. In the center of its body was Patty, snug tightly against the heart of the man she loved.
As the giant began his pilgrimage, he stopped to look over Big Blue. From the giant's hand came strings as thin as eyelashes. They burrowed into the wound on Blue's back. Whatever was happening, it ended with Blue's open wound being sealed with tape. The giant nodded to Red as he began to stand up, and then it stomped away. Wherever it would end up would be better than where it started.

Chapter 26: Lillipatton

The sound of rain soothed the frogs of Lillipatton. It broke up the usual days of gray skies and hot nights. The pitter patter of raindrops hitting the stone streets and alleyways. It was a reminder of a time before. Before the bog washed over the town and drove the humans away. The tree logs clogged once busy streets, and fauna cascaded from rooftops, the only safe place for those free from the bog. There weren't many of them left, these special frogs. Their powers were drained by the miasma they breathed. Their growth and reproduction was stunted by the presence of the bog's manipulator. One of their very own kind.

The glistening rooftops became stained by the pelting of gooey limbs as the Bog Monster tried yet again to climb the buildings. And yet again it was met with opposition, for what it sought was a colony of frogs. What it got was an army of Frogfolk.
Spears made from sharpened wood stung into the hand of the monster. It shrieked, but continued its climb. It stunk of sewer juices and humidity. A voice croaked "Again," as another volley of spears hit the same hand. The Bog Monster slammed another hand onto the roof, hoisting itself up with its incredible strength.
"Hold," the voice called out. The Frogfolk did as they were told. Some did not like this command, while others had no courage to disobey it. From beneath the cover of the bell tower lept a frog the size of a human child. In her arms she held a wooden staff with small poisonous needles protruding from the end of it. Her skin was smooth and blood red. Her eyes were as dark as the abyss. A black T-shirt with "Aerosmith" written on the front decorated the champion of Lillipatton. The comeback kid. Their last hope. Her name was Plum.

"The monster got closer tonight than it ever has in the past," Coatox claimed. His flat fingers spread across the map of Lillipatton. He, Plum, and the other sixty Frogfolk were stuffed into the belltower. In the center room, on the center floor is where a small cadre of Frogfolk talked strategy. In other parts of the belltower Frogfolk repositioned traps to keep the bog out. Their strongest tool was the bell itself. If the bog monster ever got too close to the tower, all the frogs could croak at once to trigger the bell and ward the beast off with a magnitude of vibrations.
"So what do you suggest we do now, Coatox," another Frogfolk named Mebrama asked.
Coatox replied, "The bog monster only grows stronger. We must take action and cease this cowardice".
"This so-called cowardice has kept us alive," said Quaxo, she leaned forward over the map, "Or did you forget what happened to our last leader? The one who so boldly took on the bog monster head on".
"I did not-".
"We lost nearly fifty of our kind in that battle! We lost so many younglings".
"I did not forget, Quaxo! I did not forget".
The room fell quiet. Plum continued to roll her nametag between her fingers. Coatox went on, "It does not please me to suggest such a direct tactic. But we all know the bell is our salvation. And if tonight is any indication, the bell might not be enough. Nor will any newcomers," he shot a look at Plum. Plum paid him no mind.

Quaxo calmed herself and asked, "Your plan then, Coatox? The same as before?"
"The same as before".
Plum spoke from her corner, "I know nothing of this plan".
"Of course not," Coatox rolled his eyes, "You're too new to have been here for its conception".
"Do not let his animosity cloud your curiosity, child," Mebrama said, "This plan was devised shortly after we discovered the bell could hurt the beast".
"If you wish, I can recollect-" Quaxo added.
Plum cut her off, "With all due respect, ma'am. I'd like to hear Coatox tell it". Quaxo seemed disappointed. Coatox cracked a small grin.
"Very well," Coatox replied.

The bell created vibrations from the sounds of all the Frogfolk croaking at once. Even as far back as when they were all normal frogs, the song of their people meant salvation. It was one of the only things they kept when the humans monopolized their swamp and turned it into a tourist trap. Some say the ancient properties of that swamp remained after the humans desecrated their land. And those ancient properties unlocked the hidden abilities of the frogs.
Even down to their voices, which evolved just as their bodies did. The Frogfolk had the tools, they had the skill, now all they needed was the timing. In the dead of night is when the bog monster was its most furious, but during the day it was far more passive. No lone frog, no army of frogs, could kill the monster during either time of the day. But if the bell could be triggered close enough to the weakened beast, there was a chance at killing it.
It would be too slow to run. Too weak to fight back. And too stupid to stop what was happening to it. Plum listened as Coatox laid this plan out and quickly saw the flaw. The bell was very, very heavy. It would take at least thirty of them to lift it off the tower, maybe another ten to move it to where the bog monster rested. And after losing so many of their members, the Frogfolk could not risk endangering their ranks again.

"Which is why this plan will not work," Mebrama interjected, "We cannot lose more of our kind".
"There is no other way," Coatox insisted, "If we must die to free ourselves-".
"What use is freedom if we have to die for it?" Quaxo asked.
"You forget, Quaxo. That the fundamental belief of freedom was something our predecessors died for".
"And you forget, Coatox, that the frogs did not die for freedom. The humans did. And their sacrifice may have benefited them, but they used that freedom to enslave us. To weaponize us. For you to use those ape people as examples-".
"Quaxo," Mebrama stopped her. He looked over at Plum, as did Quaxo.
"No, it is fine," Plum said, arms folded and eyes shut, "Please, regale us with your criticism of humans and how none are good".
"Now, Plum. That's not what I meant".
"Why be coy about this, Quaxo? Plum was raised by a human," Coatox shrugged, "And we all know it. It is simply another reason not to stake our hopes in her".
"You will need to stake all your hope in me, Coatox," Plum walked up to the table. She laid a hand on the map and leaned forward, "Because I am the only way your plan will work".
Coatox laughed, "Oh, really? How do you intend to do that? By carrying the bell?"

Plum shook her head, "I'm going to do what I have been doing here. I'm going to buy you time".

Sunrise. Warm waves of amber light rolled into Lillipatton. The illumination was limited. The warmth was drained from the sunlight by the mass of black slime which sat in town square. The bog monster kept a heavy breath. Inhaling by splitting dioxide from the air, exhaling a stench so foul it could burn eyebrows off. It leaned its back against a tall bank and its bottom legs spread out far enough to enclose the square. The water fountain which sat in the middle of the square was gone and replaced with the stony remains of what once was.
Plum spent hours creating sacks of poisonous needles. She tied the bags to her waist and fashioned a blow gun from an old toilet paper roll, a rubber band, and a crushed soda can. She loaded the roll with needles, pulled back the soda can, and finally released the soda can and allowed the rubber band to sling the flurry of needles at the side of the bog monster's head. It turned very slowly. Once its huge red eyes locked on Plum, the monster swung a heavy arm towards her. She was quick enough to avoid it and the bog monster simply tore down an old apartment building. The monster shifted its weight and stomped after Plum as she ran along the buildings. Another shot of needles did little to stun her foe, so Plum had to think quickly on her feet as the monster crushed a rooftop flat with a downward swing of its hand.
Brick and roof tile slid down and so did Plum as she became overtaken by the bog monster's black liquid. It began to swallow her. She became slower as she struggled. With her wooden staff, Plum used its hooked bottom to link herself to a metal railing. It took all her strength to pull herself out of the bog.
As she gained back her footing she could feel the monster gaining on her. Getting closer. Bits and pieces of slime drizzled down on her from above. Plum croaked loudly. Croaks from the belltower echoed back. Plum became emptied when the bog monster tackled forward like a train. It pinned Plum against a brick wall and the waves of black evil washed over her again.

Through the blackness around her, Plum could see it. The shiny, golden trophy the Frogfolk relied on. The gold bell became larger and larger until the blackness blinded Plum. The sounds of slothing and heavy breathing was briefly split by the sound of metal hitting pavement.
She could not feel much. But Plum could feel the bell. And so she croaked. She croaked harder than she ever had before. Even when the sewage filled her lungs she cried out-not in fear-but with ancestral pride. In hope, that her kind would not be subjected again. She had lived for too long. She had been given too many chances. If Vana dropped her off here to help only for her to die now, then her freedom was not worth it. Not if it meant the job wasn't done.
The croaking became clearer. It became louder. And the slimy substances around her inflated and thinned. The darkness was no longer thick. And the music to Plum's non-visible ears was one ceremonially sung by the rest of her Frogfolk. The bell shook in a tantrum and the croaks fueled the engine of the bog monster's demise. With a "pop", the bog monster would not cover the town of Lillipatton again. Not alive, this time.

"I could hear the bell from the intersection outside of town," Bale explained, "I guess whatever you did, it worked".

"Yes. And thankfully at the cost of no Frogfolk," Plum replied from her miniature wheelchair. In the time that had passed, Bale had entered Lillipatton. His welcoming was not friendly, but his connection to Plum-the hero of the Frogfolk-was enough of a recommendation for Coatox to give him no more than a distant glare. Bale and Plum stood in the town square, where other Frogfolk cleaned up the remains of the bog monster.

"Did you know the whole time? About Globulous?" Bale asked.

"Yes. But I did not want to tell the Frogfolk," Plum said, "The last thing any of them needed to know was the origin of the monster".

"Is it my fault this happened, Plum? Should I have tried harder to raise Globulous? I mean, Vana was great to you and now you're a hero".

"Do not blame yourself, Bale. The frogs of Lillipatton were never meant to fight the way some of the humans made them. And, to your credit and my mother's, you did not want us to fight in the first place. Globulous simply lost his way".

"Still. With what happened with Vana, it doesn't make me feel good to know my frog and her frog fought each other".

"I don't like it either. But I choose to recognize this tragedy as an opportunity. The bog monster scared off the humans, the Frogfolk destroyed the bog monster, now our home belongs to us. I owe a great deal to you and Vana, I stayed because of what I learned from you two".

"What did you learn?"

"To help people when people need help".

Bale smiled. As Plum followed Bale back to his rental car she filled him in on everything she knew about Vana's drive home. Plum revealed how sad Vana sounded. She shed no tears, but whatever light existed in her voice was gone. Vana did not want this ending, but Plum didn't know how to help her. Plum missed Bale just as Vana did. But this problem was not one she could solve. That part was up to Bale.

Before getting into his car and bidding Lillipatton goodbye, Bale said to Plum, "Earlier, you called Vana your mother".

"Yes. I suppose I did".

"Plum, what does that make me to you?"

Plum smiled. "You are my poppa, Bale".

Chapter 27: Longhill

"Direct your attention to the tall drink of water over yonder. The man so casually leaning against the railing that which overlooks the crystal lake. That man is named Gunner McGavin, and once upon a time he was a national treasure. A legend in the National Football League. One of them Wheaties box athletes. Truly, he could not have fallen harder. When his obsession with that glorified piece of jewelry destroyed his marriage and his career, all for nothing as his team didn't even make it to the Superbowl, he scraped every piece of notoriety off his back by trying to coast off the success of players more popular than himself. His neglect of the people around him-outside of what they could offer-left him in the hands of dangerous people, individuals who'd sooner squash their problems themselves rather than make a publicity stunt out of it. Gunner was beaten by six men in a garage after he tried blackmailing a coach into trading him onto a more successful team. The man would need a cane for the rest of his days".
"And what about now? How is he now?"
"Gunner runs a card shop next to Mrs. Tula's diner. He hardly brings in the proverbial bacon like he used to, but the man would seem to be at peace. No jewelry, no loved ones, but as you see him now he finds the pleasantries in simply gawking at a body of water".

"I see. I've met Tula. What is her story?"
"Ah, Mrs. Tula. If God could pick an angel for which every other angel aspires to be, Tula would be that angel. Before Longhill, Tula was a nurse a few cities over. What you have to consider though is the date at which she held this occupation. Spry as a newborn buck she may seem, Tula is an aged delicacy. Back in her days of medical profession, women were not paid as much as men like you or I. Nor did she ever receive the respect in this workplace which she so desperately deserved. Tula sought to it that every patient imprisoned in the American hospital standard was treated with dignity. No patient would be made an example of worse things to come to other patients with better health conditions. No doctor would so flamboyantly flaunt their vernacular understanding of modern medicine to a patient without a more mundane explanation being provided. Tula cared about the people more than she cared about herself".
"So what happened?"
"She cared too much. A patient was under and a surgeon got cocky, thinking they could make their mark in the medical profession by fixin' somebody better than what was agreed upon. The patient had a very detailed description of what would happen to them, an agreement which he expected the surgeon to honor".
"And he didn't".
"Correct, sir. Tula, as she worded it; busted into that room like a bull on ketamine. When her opinion fell on deaf ears, she took her quarrels to the Chief. The surgery was postponed, the surgeon was put under investigation, and Tula was fired for interrupting a careful procedure".
"And the patient?"
Sheriff West shook his head, "Didn't make it. Tula could never bring herself to put the blame on anyone else".

"You seem to know a lot about the people in this town, Sheriff," Dean asked, "But what do they know about you?"

West closed his eyes and bowed his head, "Less than I'd like, stranger. See, I married my highschool sweetheart back in my hometown. Thought I was in love. Shortly after my twentieth birthday she and I had my firstborn-Riker. A month later, we were wed in front of the whole town. Including my new father-in-law who swore he'd kill me one day. Then Iraq happened and he came around to the idea of me livin' with his daughter. Mainly because I wouldn't be livin' with his daughter. That time of my life, well, to say it was wasted would be upfront to my country. But I did not enjoy it. I did not enjoy killing people I did not know. Being away from the people I loved. I was afraid I could not function in their world any longer. My fears were mute, for I was not welcomed back into their world. The father-in-law I had once won over had made acquaintances with a new young man who found his place next to my wife. Just as bad, the new recruit became a father to my boy and my unborn child. I believe they named her Yasmin".
"And you ran here? To escape?"
"Escape would imply I was being held there. Not the case. No, that town had no place for a guy like me. Bitter at his family. Bitter at his country. What purpose could I serve to my community so strung up like that? No, I'd be no better than the soulless patriots who put me out to the pasture to hunt for oil, or whatever that spat was about. Longhill was my chance to start over. Met myself an older gent much like me. A soldier. A family man. He was on his way out, so he let me in," West looked at the badge on his shirt, "he showed me there was something more to authority than fear or possession. He taught me how to be a symbol. The kind of man I needed when I was unsure in my life. Do not misconstrue my words, Mr. Dean. If given another chance, I would not change a thing about the path that led me here today. If not for the shotgun wedding, the babies, the war, the rejection, I would not have Longhill. I would not have my wife Pam. My friends and neighbors. Hard as times were, I wouldn't give them up for anything".
"That's very beautiful, Sheriff. Thank you".
"What's that?"
"I said thank you," Dean repeated, "for sharing your story. As well as the story of every person in Longhill".
"If you do not mind my unraveling of this here pow-wow," West said, "What would procure your curiosity?"
"It's simple really," Dean crossed his legs, "I plan on killing someone. And I'm going to use your town to do that".

Drake was one of Longhill's youngest civilians. He moved out of his parents house four months after his twenty-first birthday and made a new home for himself above his parent's garage. His parents held out that space for his grandparents whenever they decided to visit, but those occasions became further and farther between.
Drake began paying his father two-hundred dollars a month to rent the space above the garage. He would pay for his own food, pay for his own phone, and pay for his own insurance. The space wasn't big, but he didn't need it to be. Drake was a busy body, he could never stay in one place for long. When he was a kid, doctors diagnosed him with ADHD. If you asked him now, he'd say they were exaggerating. But if you saw his prescription list, he's got it bad.

Between working and playing basketball with his friends, Drake came to Mrs. Tula's diner almost every day. Tula would give him free drinks as long as he helped wash dishes on the weekday nights. Things had changed recently though. Now anytime he came by he'd need to be really quiet and hide under the tables like everyone else.

Today was like that too. But today a man walked into the restaurant that Drake hadn't seen since Sheriff West took all those men to go hunt the monster. West and his posse came back with their tails between their legs, but this new guy didn't come back. Until now. Guess that meant Drake owed his buddy ten bucks. They bet on whether or not the monster ate all of the Sheriff's new recruits.

Drake watched as the new guy ducked behind the counter to talk to Tula. The new guy wasn't looking so hot. His hair was greasy and long and stringy. He had on these church pants and a white button up drenched in sweat. The last days of summer were often the hottest in Longhill. Drake couldn't hear what was being said, but he only had a passing interest.

Something possessed him to be more interested. Drake couldn't understand why, but he needed to get closer. With a slow crawl on all fours he made his way up to the counter and sat on the other end of it, out of sight from Tula or her friend.

"...here yesterday…" Tula mumbled, "took her pumpkin pie…."

"Did she say anything about…"

"...and that you were….said you would be happier…"

"And what did you say when…"

"...crazy to think….meant for….don't just happen…."

They were talking about a woman. Vana. Wait. How did Drake know who Vana was? Why did he even crawl over here? He came to get lunch before work. "Oh, crap," Drake said aloud. He sprung up and before the other customers could shush him he frantically put a twenty on the counter, said "see ya" to Tula, and ran out to start painting Mr. Brand's fence like he promised. Part of him wanted to go back and listen to Bale more-even if he had no idea who Bale was or why he knew his name-but Mr. Brand promised to give Drake his old beat-up Pontiac if he painted that fence.

Carmine came to America with her family when she was a teenager. A small town in the middle of nowhere was a step down from Venice, in her opinion. She always told her parents she'd go back to Italy one day. After high school. And then after college. Then after the wedding. And then after Fanti was born. Now she was in her early thirties, working from home, and cooking for her husband and son. The closest she felt to her home country was microwaving Chef Boyardee.

Today she was driving Fanti to his soccer game. Soccer was one of the few interests she kept between countries, and she was happy enough to pass it along to her son. Fanti just loved to kick things. As she was driving she drowned out Fanti's loud spaceship phone game by running through the newest catalog of blouses coming to her store. The streets were packed with cars, so that kept her mind busy too.

In front of her was a dark blue car older than she was. Driving it was Bale. Has she met him before? She had to find out where he was going. She veered off her original course and followed Bale towards the woods. Fanti tried to tell her she was going the wrong way, but Carmine snapped back at him with words that didn't belong to her.
Fanti's crying and screaming in retaliation only made Carmine angier. She couldn't follow Bale and find out what he was doing with all this noise. She could drop the kid off in the woods somewhere. Or better yet, stop Bale from driving.
Carmine accelerated and rammed her car into the back of Bale's car. Bale yanked his wheel in one direction, then the other, then the one before that one, and then he tumbled. Bale's car was upside down in a ditch on the side of the road.
"All I have to do is hit him now," Carmine said to herself. She had her car sideways on the empty road, pointing right into the ditch. Her foot slammed on the gas, but she made no forward movement. She cursed under her breath and looked down. Her other foot was on the break. Another bad word. Another scream from Fanti. He was so scared. What was she doing? Carmine took her foot off the gas and snapped her head back at Fanti. "I'm sorry baby," she said, "are you okay? I'm sorry". Fanti sniveled and whimpered and held his soccer ball in his arms. Instead of being black and white, his ball had the colors of the Italian flag on it. Fanti got it from his grandfather for his last birthday. It came with a note saying "a little bit of home".

There was something about nature that put Arnold at peace. He had spent most of his life bent out of shape over a debt he had to pay or a check he had to chase. Out here though, none of that mattered. No, out here all that mattered was in front of him. The trees and the creeks and the birds and the sunlight. That's all that mattered.
No. Nothing mattered but revenge. Arnold drifted his binoculars across the forest until he saw Bale limping down a dirt path. In his condition Bale couldn't run. Perfect. From his duffel bag, Arnold pulled out a pistol. He had always hoped he'd never have to use it, after all he only ever came out here for the quiet. And there's not much louder than a gun.

He wondered how it might feel to be shot. Arnold never knew the sensation. Neither did Dean. There was one time, Queen got shot by a robot because Dean's connection to Lucien had "hiccuped". After she was all patched up she described to her teammates that the stinging feeling in her hip was constant. "It's like someone left the light on all day," she told them, "and it still burns when you flip the switch off".
Stalking Bale through the shrubbery, Arnold tried to call out for help, but his mouth would not move. Someone else had him strung up like a puppet. The only way out was to end Bale's life. But was taking the life of a stranger something Arnold could live with? He had no time to ponder this as his hand lifted the pistol.
He grit his teeth. Arnold used his other hand to push down on the hand with the gun. Wincing and straining to overcome his own strength. His finger on the trigger recoiled sharply and suddenly as the trajectory changed. The bullet didn't hit Bale's back. It hit him in the ass. Arnold let his jaw unclench. He let his arms fall low. And he just watched as Bale threw himself onto the ground and cried out in pain. Through swearing and screaming, Bale dragged out a

name as he shouted it. Arnold remained still, but his legs burned. He wanted so desperately to run over and get Bale to a hospital. Luckily, someone else would enter in his place.
That someone appeared to be a giant bear monster who, upon the mere sight of, scared Arnold back further into the forest. He didn't know a lot about the monster, always passing up the chance to join Sheriff West and his crew to go hunt it. "What if it's not a monster, Sheriff?" he would ask, "Then we'd just be hunting an innocent animal". His pacifism didn't win him points in the community, but Arnold didn't believe in murder. Losing your mother to gun violence will have that effect on you. The thought of which could not exit Arnold's traumatized head as the entire jog out of the woods he thought less about the monster and more about that poor man he shot.

It was sunset and Dean had all the cards in his corner. Using his mind control powers, he forced every citizen of Longhill to stand outside on the main road and wait. In their hands were firearms, hatchets, baseball bats, and two or three of them had honest to God pitchforks. Longhill didn't even have a barn or anything, it was weird. Beyond the stern faces of Sheriff West, Tula, Drake, and the other civilians, there was Dean. Standing behind all of them. Children in the front, adults in the middle, Dean in the back curling his non-existent mustache. He knew what was to come. He didn't need clairvoyance to know. He didn't need to peek inside Bale's mind either. Because he already had all the information he needed from the town.
"...so myself and my posse procured Bale and escorted him up to yonder cave where he made acquaintance with Supay-" Sheriff West had said.
"Supay? Is that a friend of yours?" Dean asked.
"Correct, Supay is my trusted friend and confidant, as well as an ally to the gentlemen in this here town".
"If he's such a good friend why does he live all the way in the woods? In a cave?"
"Well, see, Supay happens to be the Incan God of Death and by classification is sworn to inherit the underworld and all assembly of demonic individuals".
Dean had to process that bit.
West added, "He's, uh, he's going to be a massage therapist".
Dean did not need to process that bit.

Dean knew about Supay. And he knew Bale would go to him and ask for help. And, as he predicted, Bale and Supay arrived on the main road, walking towards his Longhill army. Bale walked unevenly and winced with every step. On account of the bullet in his ass. Supay was tall and proud. His horns shimmered in the sunlight. As did his ferocious claws.
Upon seeing the mass of people, Bale called Dean out, "I don't know who you are, but nobody here has to get hurt".
Dean shook his head, "Of course, I almost forgot myself". With nary a strain Dean unlocked all the memories of Eastchester in Bale's mind. Like running a stick through a metal fence the bits and pieces rang loudly in Bale's head. He stumbled, but stood his ground. Bale put a hand on Supay to help keep himself up.
He turned to Supay, "He can get in your head," he told him, "he can make you think or forget anything he wants".

"On the contrary," Dean called out, "other than that memory block, there is not much I can do in your beehive of a mind. And as for you, monster," he pointed at Supay, "I'd be stupid to try and fester in the mind of a God". Supay nodded and kept himself silent. Dean went on, "That's why I'm not going to kill you with my mind. I'm going to use this town to tear you both limb from limb".

With a wave of his palm the masses ran towards Bale and Supay. Before Bale could form a thought, Supay ran into battle with no hesitation. There was also no sight of remorse. A lumberjack named Hugh was impaled by Supay's long claws. Bale gasped in disbelief, but could not find the power to run or stop Supay from his rampage. A neck was torn to shreds, a spine was plucked from someone's back, Supay breathed lava so hot Bale's neck hairs burned a little bit as this lava barf found its way over the faces of three barbershop employees. Supay went to the extreme of melting every firearm the crowd had with his volcanic gust breath.

When the bloodshed was over, only Dean remained. He was stunned. When West told him about Supay, he expected Bale to recruit the monster, but believed making Supay's nearby neighbors human shields was the only way to stop him. Now though, Sheriff West's legs were hanging over a railing and his top half was on top of a parked car.

Dean shook his head. "N-n-no, n-not again," he mumbled, "you can't do this again".

Bale walked closer, but kept his distance from Supay.

Dean went on, "Everytime I think I have you, something gets in my way. First the shadow man, now this thing".

Bale could press about the shadow man, but words could not leave his lips. Not while the blood and vile of the innocent sat around him. Bale wanted to rake Supay over the coals for what he did to the people of Longhill. People Supay had come to love. Bale had to stifle those feelings. Dean was here, and if the run-in with Patty was any indication, Dean was probably sent after him too.

"Why?" Bale asked. He asked again, louder this time. His voice cracked under the pressure of the situation. He believed at any moment Dean could snap his psyche like a carrot. But just as likely Supay could separate Dean's head from his neck.

"Because the day I met you was the day my life fell apart," Dean replied, "for the second time".

"You were brainwashing an entire town into loving you. You brainwashed your own friends," Bale shouted. Supay was already in a lunging stance, but Bale could see his back legs tighten.

"Eastchester was safe under my guidance, Bale. Nobody had to pay for anything. Nobody ever got into arguments. Everybody got along and anyone who didn't was simply asleep until I needed an audience for my Foremen". Dean opened his arms and gestured to the street of corpses. "You may think what I did was wrong, but the people of Eastchester never had to die for serving me. Not like these poor men and women".

Supay's claws dug into the street like the ground was made of foam. Supay's big, crazy eyes never moved from where Dean stood.

Dean did not move. He was positive the work was done. He had no hostages left to throw, he had no sure way of manipulating his enemy's minds, effectively he was going to die for a shadow man that nearly killed him already. "But it will be worth it," he thought, "Bale's hope in the kindness of others will be destroyed by Supay's actions. The monster might just kill Bale and keep the whole town under wraps". Dean had nothing else to live for. This fight was the last real

effect he could have on the world. And even if he couldn't kill Bale, body or mind, Bale's soul could never recover.
Maybe Supay could read minds like Dean could. Or maybe he could just read a man's body. He was a massage therapist, after all. Or perhaps the end didn't mean anything. This man in expensive clothing came to this small town with the intention of using innocent men and women as his ammunition. All to kill Bale. Too many people died because Supay couldn't stop Dean sooner. Because despite wherever you come from, or wherever you go, the devil will follow you. In one way or another.

Dean died moments before the sections of his body could fall apart. Supay did to him what a dicer does to veggies. In all his travels Bale had seen some weird stuff, but this wasn't weird or fun or goofy. This was horror. This was the cherry on top to an already bloody evening. The sun hadn't even dropped past the horizon and the main street of Longhill was already drenched in blood. Bodies piled over one another like dirty laundry.
Supay stood over Dean for a few minutes. Supay didn't need to breathe, but he could. And he did profusely. Demon or God or whatever he wasn, he wasn't a killer. At least, he never believed himself to be one. To be capable of all this. Worst he ever did was eat someone who was already dead. Someone nobody would miss. And who would miss the people of Longhill if everyone in Longhill were dead? Supay couldn't turn back to face Bale. Because then he'd have his answer. And nobody else had to die today. Not by Dean. No by the claws of a God. A God of Death, to be clear.

As the God of Death, Supay could use his powers to revive everyone in Longhill. The people of Longhill woke up the next morning confused and misplaced, none of them had any memory of anything after Dean came to town. Bale was too traumatized to say his goodbyes. He was too horrified to confront Supay. He could not see Longhill the same way. He never got any answers as to why Dean came here for him, or how he knew about the town. Bale didn't even know where Dean's body ended up. He would try to move on. To forget about the whole town because of the memory attached to it. But he could not forget the fear of it all. The fear that locked his doors.
As for Supay, he never left his cave after what happened. In fact, he caved the whole thing in. Sheriff West and his buddies couldn't visit Supay anymore now. And with no explanation, some of them believed Supay went back to wherever he came from. They were wrong. Supay was still in that cave. And so was Dean.

Chapter 28: Scene

1. EXT. VIETNAM. MORNING.

Open on the face of a man as he looks straight forward. The man is lightly sweating and as the camera pulls out we see he is dressed in an army uniform. He is breathing steadily.

Pull back further to reveal the jungle around him.

Cut to an angle looking up at the man from the ground. Cut again to an angle looking down from over his shoulder. Reveal the man is standing on a landmine.

Cut back to the man's face. He looks up and stares straight ahead.

THOMAS OLIVER. 24, a dark-haired white man with Native American roots. He has a past of juvenile delinquency, but a heart of gold. He desperately wants to get back to Brooklyn and back to his wife Katherine and his son James. Gun in hand, motionless, he stands atop certain death.

2. EXT. VIETNAM. AROUND NOON.

Tracking shot. Follow three soldiers as they crouch and walk through the jungle. The ending of the shot groups the three behind some boulders.

Behind the shoulder shot setting the middle soldier in the foreground and the lone soldier atop the landmine in the background. Camera shifts focus from the hidden soldier to the standing soldier.

JASON SCOTT. 30, he is an athletic white man with a five o' clock shadow. He follows orders to a fault. Isn't afraid to speak his mind even when it's out of line. Commanding Officer, he treats his men like brothers. Better than he treats his own kin back home in Iowa.

WILLIAM CRANSTON. 28, William wears thick glasses. He just barely passed the entry bar into the army and he only joined because his friends Paul and Jay. Paul and Jay died on a beach when they were shot by enemy soldiers. William is skinny and tall and quiet. Some folk think he's wrong in the head. Nobody ever asked him about his family.

ZACKARY TAYLOR. 22, Zack is the kid brother of the group. He is a thin black man, his hair is short and curly. Zack spits through the gap in his front teeth. If it weren't for his big mouth, Zack wouldn't have caught so many beatings back home. He joined the army not only to escape the racial prosecution he faced in Montana, but also to escape his drunk father.

Jason, Zackary, and William peek over the boulders. We switch between a shot looking at them head-on, and a shot looking at Thomas straight-on, with the three men in the background.

>   JASON
>   Private Oliver, you're out in the open. Fall back, now.
>
>   THOMAS
>   Can't do that, Lieutenant. I'm standing on an active landmine.
>
>   ZACK
>   Jesus Christ.
>
>   WILLIAM
>   It could be in an inactive state.
>
>   JASON
>   Say again in our language, man.
>
>   ZACK
>   Sir, I think he means it's a dud.
>
>   THOMAS
>   Sure don't feel like a dud.
>
>   JASON
>   Private Cranston, take a look.

3. EXT. VIETNAM. AFTERNOON.

Headshot of Thomas. Sweat becomes more frequent. Breathing becomes heavier.

Shot changes quickly over and over to show the locations of the other soldiers. First of these shots is above William's shoulder as he identifies the writing on the landmine. Next shot follows William as he leans up and onto his knees. He pulls out a notebook and flips through it, getting the dirt on his hands on every page. This bothers him.
Next shot is over a boulder wall. Jason's head pokes up from the rock wall. Now he is on the opposite side so his back is to Thomas. Next shot is wide, showing Thomas' whole body facing forward, William reading while on his knees beside Thomas, and Jason with his back to the camera and his chest on the wall. In his arms is a rifle.

>   JASON
>   Whadda' got, Cranston?
>
>   WILLIAM
>   …Appears to be some sort of recent model…
>
>   JASON

>   Damn it, Billy. Speak up. A man's life is at stake.

>   WILLIAM
>   Yes, sir. Sorry, sir. The mine is newer than the ones we've encountered already.

>   THOMAS
>   That make much of a difference?

>   WILLIAM
>   Incredibly. The shrapnel range is four times as far, the sonic impact of the explosion has a
>   further radius too.

>   JASON
>   The mechanics, Cranston. How do we undo the mechanics?

>   WILLIAM
>   Ah, yes, sir. Well, as long as the panel is pressed down the interior won't explode-

>   JASON
>   I know how a damn mine works, Cranston-

>   THOMAS
>   Let the son of a bitch get to it!

>   JASON
>   Don't you move, private! You move and you'll die and take us with ya! Private Taylor will come
>   back to rescue nobody. If he comes back at all.

4. EXT. VIETNAM. SUNSET.

Shot of the muddy ground. Water hits the ground creating a little more mud. We lift the camera up to focus on a rag being soaked and twisted by Jason. His body language has gone from "on guard" to "standby".

Next shot shows the above chest of Thomas and Jason. Thomas isn't wearing his helmet anymore, revealing dark hair matted to his head. The sweat has made his skin shiny, the sun has burnt him into a pink color. Jason takes the wet rag and wipes Thomas's face down. Mosquitos the size of ball bearings buzz around both men's faces.

Shaky camera now. Camera faces William as he grabs rocks off the ground and puts them in a small bag. The camera changes shots to focus on his dirty hands, shaking and struggling to grip the stones and lift them. Next shot shows him tossing the bag in his hands. Testing the weight.

Shot changes to a back and forth between Jason and Thomas.

                             THOMAS
                Lieutenant. Has Private Taylor come back yet?

                              JASON
                       No word on Taylor, Private.

                             THOMAS
                         You think he's dead?

                              JASON
        Hard to say. The enemy hasn't found us yet. Maybe they haven't found him.

                             THOMAS
          With all due respect, sir? Nothin' saying they haven't found us out here.

                              JASON
                        Think so? How you figure?

                             THOMAS
 Back home, me and the boys-when we were kids, ya know-we'd pick fights all the time. Most
days we'd kick ass. Other days we'd lose. We didn't like losing. Our biggest kid though, he came
up with a plan. A way to make those other kids easier to beat. A way to make them lose sight of
                              what was coming.

Gun shot. William falls to the ground. His bag of rocks flies out of his hands and scatters across
the grass. Jason dives down and huddles behind some bushes. This is all shown in very quick
camera cuts.
Thomas begins shaking. We follow his glance down to the bag of stones on the grass.

   5. EXT. VIETNAM. EARLY NIGHT

Full body shot of Thomas. He is shaking throughout his body. His jacket is unbuttoned. His
golden cross necklace is clearly visible. Sweat glistens on his face, neck and chest. His eyes
are closed as he tilts his head upward and mouths prayers to God.

Next shot shows Jason, sitting against his rock barrier. His jacket is open too. With his helmet
off, he loads rocks into it one by one, each plucking of a stone is shown via a shaky camera.

Shots jump between the two men's faces as they talk.

                              JASON
   Private Oliver. I think my helmet might be heavy enough now. We can…we can use it to…what
                         the hell did Cranston say…?

THOMAS
Trick the mechanism, sir.

JASON
Right, right. Man, I should have listened to that guy more often. Can't apologize to a corpse, can I?

THOMAS
Doesn't matter, sir. If he's alive or dead. We're all going to die here.

JASON
Not yet. Ya hear me, private? Not yet we're dying. Just gotta use…use my helmet…and get you out…

THOMAS
Then we'll get shot.

JASON
You don't know that.

THOMAS
Or we'll get ambushed. Or they'll tie us up and drag us out and slit our throats in front of the whole damn village-

JASON
You don't know that! You don't, private.

THOMAS
They got him, sir. They got them both. Cranston. Taylor. Now you and me.

JASON
We…we were supposed to win this war, Oliver.

THOMAS
Maybe we will. You and me though? No. No, we're done here.

JASON
You don't…you don't know what you're talking about, kid…neither do I. I just need to rest. I just need to rest, that's all. Private, finish your story. What you were telling me earlier.

THOMAS
Right, yeah. My pals and I, we didn't like losing fights. So one day…one day one of us comes up with an idea. We, uh, we spread this rumor about one of the rival gangs. We say to people,

we say "Don't trust that Robbie Santo kid. He's been messin' around with Adam Park's girlfriend for months".

(Laughs)

Yeah, he, uh, he didn't bounce back from that. People kept on saying stuff like that. People outside the gangs. Robbie and Adam, they went at it hard. Both of em' took their shit and walked off. Their gang had less muscle, or we'd end up with two weaker gangs. Point was, we never had to lay a finger on nobody until it was all said and done.

JASON
So you set up a bomb.

THOMAS
And we just waited until it went off.

JASON
Wow. Kid like you, Oliver. How'd you end up here?

THOMAS
Never was proud of where I came from. Figure'd this'd be a way to get out of it.

Jason doesn't respond. His eyelids are heavy. Use black bars over the camera facing Thomas to illustrate Jason's struggle to stay awake. Cut to a side profile of Thomas's mouth. Cue tears running down his sweat covered cheek.

THOMAS
You should rest, Lieutenant. You've been awake for a while.

JASON
Can't...gotta watch you...

THOMAS
Well, I'll watch you, sir. And I'll wake you up and we can take turns. We can take turns, alright?

JASON
No...I...I just need to...rest my eyes for a bit. We'll, uh, we can figure this out in the morning. Just need....to rest my...

THOMAS
(Sniffle) Sir, yes, sir.

Camera focuses on Thomas's face. Tearful, he keeps his eyes closed. Camera pans down his body, past his cross necklace, acoss an arm held down in front of him containing a pink letter sent to him by his girl back home. The camera stops and frames the shot between his knee and the grass under the landmine. Thomas slips his leg out and falls onto the mine just as it explodes.

We cut to black.

Dog Guy lowered the screenplay from his face and held it beside him. Through his face mask he looked at Bale, tied to a chair and bruised from the lashings of Dog Guy's pistol. He still had the receipt from Walmart. Dog Guy let the story sit for a moment, but then asked, "What do you think?"
Bale, black and blue, nodded a few times, "That's pretty good".
"You think so? For real?"
"No, yeah, that had me going. Like, as soon as the Cranston guy was on the ground looking at the landmine".
"Right, right, okay. So, you liked it?"
"Yeah, dude".
"You're not just saying that so I don't kill you?"
"Legit, man. I think you got something there".
"Oh my God, that's so good to hear. Thank you, man. Seriously".
"Where did you…where did you even come up with that".
"I heard a lot of war stories in prison".
"Did this, like, really happen?"
"No, I made it up. The characters are made up too, I'll probably change their names".
"What? To like real people?"
"No, it's just, like, they're placeholders. They're named after Power Rangers".
"So, you watched Power Rangers, but, like, no movies growing up?"
"Bud, I'm wearing a dog mask and holding you hostage with a gun I bought in a Twelve Items or Less line, I didn't have a consistent childhood".
"Okay, fair," Bale nodded again, "So, what now?"
"Well, I know an inmate who was jailed for tax stuff so he said he can get me in contact with a guy from Netflix-"
"Oh, no, sorry. I mean what's next for me?"
"Oh, well, I gotta kill you".
"Oh, really?"
"Yeah, sorry. I'm glad you liked my movie pitch though. I was planning on sort of skinning your face off and wearing it as a new mask, but now I feel kind of bad so maybe I'll just make the death thing quick, ya know?"
"You could not," Bale said quickly.
"What?" Dog Guy asked.
"I said you could not. You could just take your script to somebody and make a movie and forget all this?"
"You really think this is that good? That I could just walk away from this?"
"It's good, man. It's really good. You need to get that made".
"Give me a criticism".

"What?"

"Give me a criticism of my movie. I ask people all the time for stuff like that. Tell me something you didn't like about it".

"Well, obviously you'll flesh out the four guys more, right?"

"Yeah, of course".

"Okay, well, maybe when Thomas tells a story about his past, you could do a flashback sort of thing? So that the setting and events aren't just in the jungle".

"Okay, that's a good idea. What else?" Dog Guy leaned over his desk and wrote notes on the bottom of his screenplay.

"Well, I know the movie about Thomas, but I kind of want to see the other characters do stuff too. Like, it's suspenseful that Zack doesn't come back, but maybe we can see what happened to him?"

"Yeah, but leaving it up to the viewer's imagination makes it scarier".

"I guess, but you're not making a horror movie, are you? It's a suspense story".

"I don't know".

"You can still kill him off, but it might hit the audience harder if you show how he dies. Or, maybe he doesn't die. Like, they think he tied, but he just got slowed down and Zack is the one who finds the guys after Thomas sets off the bomb".

Dog Guy looked up from his paper, "I like that. That's actually kind of good. Like, he's the one who was there to remember these events".

"You could even switch the narration to him. Or, if there is a narration, we think it's Thomas the whole time, but it's really Zack".

"Yes, dude. Yes," Dog Guy went back to writing notes.

"I think that would be dope. And it's gotta be him, ya know".

"Cuz he's the kid, right? He's the youngest guy on the team".

"Yeah, but like, you gotta remember you're writing a movie. You're writing a movie, like, right now. This decade. And it would be kind of messed up if you killed the only black guy in the movie off screen".

"Oh, God, I didn't even think of that. Good catch, man. Good catch".

Dog Guy stood up straight and listed off some notes he made. He tossed some other ideas out there and Bale went back to nodding. "This is great. This is really good," Dog Guy said as he looked at his masterpiece, "Thank you, Bale. Really, you've been a big help. Maybe   maybe you were right before. Maybe I can walk away before this-".

Just then the boarded up door to the abandoned apartment flew open. Sunglasses marched in, covered in cuts, bruises, and running blood. He toted a sawed-off shotgun and grit teeth as in one motion he blasted a hole through Dog Guy's upper torso. The maniac fell to the ground and painted the adjacent wall with his blood. After the booming sound of the gun, the only sounds in the room was the heavy breathing of Bale's savior and the streaming blood of Bale's foe-turned-friend.

Sunglasses untied the trembling Bale from his bindings and helped him to his feet. Bale couldn't take his eyes off of Dog Guy's corpse. His screenplay soaked it's author's blood. Bale shook his

head. Slowly at first. Then he shrieked and shoved Sunglasses. But the man would not budge. Not for Bale at the Sendoffs club, not for Bale now.
Bale pushed again with similar impact. He swore and he yelled and threw up a little. First on Sunglasses' Nikes, and then again in the corner of the room. Bale figured if he splashed Sunglasses' shoes again he'd be the next person sprayed across the wall.
"Alright," Sunglasses said, "Let's go".
"You killed him," Bale shouted, "You just freaking killed him. Blew his brains out".
"Technically, I blew his chest out. Besides, he was gonna kill you".
"No! No he wasn't. I talked him down. He was gonna just walk away".
"Come on. Walk away? After what he did to you? After all those people he killed to get here?"
"You don't get it, man. He wrote a screenplay".
Sunglasses lowered his shotgun and looked down at Dog Guy. He shook his head. He used his open hand to rub his eyes under his sunglasses. Then he used that open hand to slap Bale across the face. Bale fell onto the floor like a mic stand. Sunglasses looked down at him now, "Get yourself together and quit talking crazy. We need to go. Lord knows who else you managed to piss off".

As they walked out into the hallway of the old building, Bale followed behind Sunglasses and noticed all his battle damage.
"What happened to you?" He asked.
"Same thing that happened to you, except I'm tougher than you".
"But, who did this to you?"
"The Black Boomerang. Dude, was annoying as hell".
"The Black Boomerang?" Bale stopped and they looked at each other.
"Yeah. Black Boomerang. You know".
Bale shook his head.
"Come on. Dude wore a black spandex piece? With shapes all over it? The visor on his helmet was a big white boomerang, man".
"I have no idea who you're talking about".
"Dude said he knew you".
Bale shook his head.
"Said he was part of it. Part of all this".
Bale stared blankly.
"What the Hell. For real? This man nearly did me in and you never met him?"
"I never met him".
Sunglasses shook his head. Roles reversed. He looked down the hallway and made a disapproving noise.
Bale asked after a while, "So, what? Did he like, throw boomerangs at you or something?"
"No, no he did not throw boomerangs".
"So what did he do?"
"He could-goddamn it, this is stupid-he could launch himself really far".
"Okay".
"And then, like twenty feet from where he jumped from, he could just hop back".
"He could throw himself?"

"Yes".
"And then come back to where-"
"Where he threw himself from, yes".
"Like a boomerang-"
"Like a boomerang".
Bale and Sunglasses stood in that hallway for about a minute and a half. Looking at each other. Looking away from each other. Handling the gravity of what had happened to them today.
Finally, Bale spoke, "This, uh, this chapter really should have been about you".

Chapter 29: The Boardwalk

It had been a long drive to the Boardwalk. Bale spent most hours awake and on the move. Only stopping on the side of the road for short half hour periods to regain his strength. Along the way he listened to motivational tapes Big Blue gave him. Most of them were in French, so he listened to the British ones on repeat. In the passenger seat of his car was a box full of finger sandwiches Tula prepared him. They were assorted and Bale didn't like tuna. He would have told Tula, but he was still traumatized from seeing her head get chopped off.
Bale wasn't big on energy drinks, he preferred coffee. But after Lillipatton became overrun with Frogkin, Plum gave Bale the local grocery store's supply of energy drinks. "Not like we have a need for them," she told him, "I'm half sure drinking one would kill me". So with caffeine, protein, and the soothing encouragement of Michael Caine, Bale reached his destination without the hammocks under his eyes.

Time had changed The Boardwalk. As did the season. Bale first came here in the Summer, when everyone was on school break and when various MTV reality shows were filming on location. Autumn graced the Boardwalk with nothing more than cold breezes. The beach crowd remained, albeit quieter. They bundled up in their coats and boots and drank their hot mocha lattes. They came not for the sweaty, sticky, sun-kissed bikini models. No, instead they came for dramatic photos by the ocean. The local history of lighthouses and boats and big rocks Pilgrims used as compasses or something.

The history of The Boardwalk was not something Bale had any interest in. The closest he came to learning anything was being stuck behind one of those tour buses where the tour guide is either quiet as a churchmouse, or as loud as the announcer in a boxing match. When traffic cleared and Bale found a parking space he practically flew out of his rental car.
He could feel the cold air cling to his face as he huffed it down to the wooden walk of entertainment. Most of the shops were either closed or selling something else. The bar Bale had been trampled out of was now a little bistro playing jazz music out of a bluetooth speaker.
"Excuse me," Bale asked the barista, "I was here a few months ago and there was a bar here".
"Vivid memory, brosef," said the barista, his wild and curly hair covering his eyes, "but as the present would inform you, this particular location is rented by yours truly".
"Does this happen a lot? Businesses being replaced?"
"As common as the high tide, brotato. Time changes the atmosphere, ya know? This time of the year folks want to wind down, sit a spell, and reflect on their life".
"Yeah, well, I gotta be somewhere so thank you-" Bale turned before finishing his sentence. The curly haired man appeared behind Bale just as he turned.
"If I could offer a totally free piece of advice, brobocop? Nobody, ever, like, in the world, ever regretted having time to think".
Bale thought, as he was instructed, and gave the moment a chance. He asked for a large coffee.
"The advice is free, bromancing the stone," the curly man smiled, "but a large is called a Grande and it's eight bucks".

Bale sat at the edge of the docks. On a bench that wasn't there when he first came down here to toss his phone in the ocean. The bench had that "new seat" smell. Sitting there was not comfortable, and the coffee was too bitter for Bale's liking. Maybe he grew attached to the gas flued taste of "Riptide" or "Sharkpunch" or whatever those energy drinks were called.
Even after all this time, with everything he had gone through, Bale didn't feel happy. Not as happy as he was with Vana. Then he thought a lot about Vana. And how she was here. Or maybe she wasn't. Either way he was wasting time just sitting here and thinking about stuff. Bale got up and ran, leaving his coffee on the bench. Probably smarter than throwing it into the ocean or something stupid like that. "Thinking is stupid," he shouted as he ran by the barista.

The tattoo shop stood where it once was. The lights were out, a "closed" sign decorated the front door, but it was here. Bale put his hand on the door and pushed. He kept pushing and nothing happened. Was his confident strength gone? Or was this door secretly Sunglasses in disguise? Bale sank to his knees. The shadow underneath him felt cold, but firm. Like he could sink into it at any moment. Bale's hands fell off the door and to his side. They grazed the wooden floor.
Did she really leave? Did she even come back here? Maybe she met someone else. Someone who could make her happy in a way Bale couldn't. Some perfect angel-man with no baggage, no gripes. Just a clean slate and a blank schedule. Or maybe she met someone with a plan. Someone with a 401K and enough vacation time to film a Christopher Nolan movie. Vana would appreciate that joke. Maybe she met a comedian who could make her laugh a soliloquy and smile a horizon. Someone better.
Bale just sat there listening. Listening for any sound that wasn't coming from his voice. But he didn't hear Vana. He didn't hear her words of affirmation. He didn't hear his father's forgiveness or Fran's admittance of guilt or his mother's shame of controlling him. Nobody said "sorry" and nobody told him he was enough. The only thing Bale could hear was a slow, growing ringing sound.

The door opened slightly. Bale looked up to see Vana's face in the open door. She looked down on him expressionless. Bale spoke her name, "Vana".
"Hello, Bale," Vana replied, monotone as her expression.
"The door…it wouldn't open. I kept pushing and I just…I couldn't-".
"You were supposed to pull".
Bale's eyes darted to the front of the door. At the very top in tiny, red letters was a message that said "Please Push. Or don't, I'm not your mother".

Bale followed Vana inside. The tattoo parlor was cold and quiet. The black-tinted windows kept the place cool and dark, and the only scent in the air was the smell of chemicals in the corners of the shop. Vana walked in automatically. No sway or switch up. Her movements were set in stone. She stood in front of her station and motioned Bale to sit down in the chair. Bale did so.

Sitting there, Bale tried to explain himself, "Vana, I'm sorry about the whole thing with Fran," he said, "I was going to see her to tell her I wasn't interested. I told her I wanted to be with you, Vana".

Vana did not reply. As Bale talked, she pushed the chair in a reclining fashion and rolled over her set of tattoo equipment. Bale continued, "I don't blame you for leaving. I know it was a lot. And I know I should have told you I was leaving. I just didn't want to stress you out".

Vana readied her ink and pulled up Bale's shirt. She looked at the tattoo of her name on his side. Bale tried to keep talking, but he could feel the needle hit his skin. He asked what she was doing, but Vana did not answer. She began dragging the needle across Bale's tattoo. Despite his pleads for her to stop, Vana successfully drew a line through his tattoo. Bale had tried to lean up, but Vana had her palm on his chest. Bale could not understand how Vana could keep him down with only one hand. It felt like an engine block was crushing down on top of him. "Vana," Bale grunted, "Why?"

"Because, Bale," Vana looked up to make eye contact, "You never called us back".

With her free hand, Vana slammed her tattoo needle into Bale's chest. Hot ink splattered out of the needle and covered the room. The hot, liquid intensity shot pain through his body. His screams painted the room. The ink painted the room. Literally, this time. The shop interior became completely black. But Bale could still see Vana, who's skin began glowing brighter and brighter. Vana's jaw unhinged and fell slowly. Her eyes rolled back into white globes. As the whiteness of her flesh began deteriorating, the black mass behind her became present. The complexion of a starry night sky. Piercing white eyes. One fist, a block. The other, a beacon containing a glowing square and a ringing that would not cease.

The Shadow Man leaned into the needle and pinned Bale down as the man kicked and shook. Bale screamed out louder, only for his lungs to become filled with shadow. The monster demanded Bale call him back. Over and over. Instinctively, Bale reached into his pocket and grasped the kaleidoscope. A chromatic tsunami bursted out from Bale's hand, swallowing the shop in a battle of light and darkness.

Freed from The Shadow Man's grasp, Bale lunged onto the monster. He gripped it with the force of the man who could lift the ocean. Bale screamed again, this time in rebellion, he asked where Vana was. What did The Shadow Man do with her? But the monster simply replied, "Call. Me. Back". With a grunt of aggravation, Bale put a foot on the monster's chest and his hands over its shoulders. "Tell me where she is," he told the creature, "Or I will rip your arms off". The Shadow Man repeated himself.

Bale pulled its arms off and threw them aside. The ringing stopped only briefly, as new arms grew to replace the old ones. In fact, arms kept growing. They kept growing until the Shadow Man was a ball of writhing arms all swinging their wide blocks. Bale became pelted by the arms, he walked back further and further. As his strength vanished and his body neared the front door, Bale could hear a sound behind the ringing he hadn't noticed before. He could hear Vana. And he could not leave her behind.

Bale fished the kaleidoscope out of his pocket again. The toy wasn't in the same shape it used to be. Some of the glass was broken. Some of the plastic was bent. But its condition wasn't why he kept it. This toy represented a freedom Bale never knew. And The Shadow Man represented a past Bale chose to leave behind. The ringing and the crying of his loved one became interchangeable. And just like sound, colors became one and before Bale was a tunnel of darkness. One direction. One path. In a quest to find what he wanted, Bale's destiny finally became clear. If nothing else, Bale had to destroy his past in order to decide his future. Dashing down the tunnel like a marathon runner, Bale came out the other end into a place he had only briefly visited: The Rescape. He and The Shadow Man stood atop monoliths of unidentifiable people. The representational bodies of these people twisted and held one another to form these huge pillars. The sepia sky was lined with dark brown dots and thin crinkling lines. In the Rescape, The Shadow Man became much more detailed. Too detailed for Bale's liking. For standing across from him was no simple shadow, but a man. A man with long, straggly hair, a suit too big for him, and the eyes of an insomniac.

The mirror image of Bale struck a chill down his spine. The Shadow Man had his face. His briefcase. His cellphone. Wet from the ocean, plagued by rejection, The Shadow Man would make his last stand here and now. "Call. Me. Back".

Chapter 30: The Rescape

Here, memories were power. And if this fight were a card game, let's just say Shadow Man and Bale were playing with the same deck. The Shadow Man's briefcase swung open, unleashing the ghostly spirits of Bale's family. His father appeared as a minotaur-like phantom. He charged at Bale. In the past Bale would have run away, but with something to fight for, Bale found himself fearless in the eyes of his predecessor. He grabbed the ghost by its horns and dragged it to the ground. It bucked and kicked and changed shape as it evaporated in one second, and appeared behind Bale the next.
The ghost of Bale's mother appeared as a large spider. It crawled around the pillar and snuck up behind Bale. With a lunge, the mother spider was caught by Bale's legs as he fell on his back. The spider's sharp legs brushed against Bale's face, scrapping him like rusted metal barbs. The pain was ample. Bale pushed the spider over the edge only to watch it become a cloud and find its way back to the side of the pillar.
The father ghost returned and grabbed Bale from behind. Always over his shoulder, these facsimiles of his kin. The ghost father slammed Bale over his huge knee. The phantom then threw Bale off the tower. The neverending fall was prevented by the web noose his spider mother slang around Bale's neck. This kept him from falling, but it began to choke him as he helplessly hung from the tower.

Bale grabbed the web rope and lifted himself just enough to breathe. Just enough to spot the spider crawling down the web line. Beyond her, the bull father ghost loomed over the edge of the tower. Bale stupidly looked down. Indiscriminate pipes of human memories lay beneath him. It was certain death if he fell. Although, it was less certain than if the spider reached him.
Bale got himself loose and dropped. As he fell, Bale grabbed the side of the pillar. His hands dug into the mannequins like he was digging in soil. At first this was comforting, it meant Bale could just climb back up. But the longer he kept his hands buried the more memories invaded his mind.
As he grit his teeth Bale remembered to hand Danice those transcripts before he left the office. He questioned if he'd be able to make it to dance practice, or if he wouldn't have time since he had to wrap all of Timmy's gifts. He searched for stability in the memory of his trip to Cuba with Miguel and how wonderful that getaway was. But now he had his sister's bachelorette party to worry about. What if Linda showed up? Would she freak out after what happened between her and Carol?
Bale couldn't think straight. Too many memories clogged his mind. The suffering ended when his spider mom finally fell atop him, sending the two of them plummeting into the beige nothingness. Face-to-face with this imitation of his mother, Bale reached back into his mind and tried to find some memory of value. Something that could save him.

Bale and the spider broke through a roof and into the living room of his parent's house. Pieces of roof littered the otherwise cozy atmosphere, and the spider mother broke mom's coffee table. She always hated that coffee table anyway. The spider lunged at him and pinned him against the wall. It shrieked in amusement. How could Bale fight this thing? How could he hurt his own mother?

Bale turned away and spotted a family photo on the wall. Maybe he couldn't bring himself to fight his mother, but he knew someone who could. Suddenly, the doorbell rang. The spider mother dropped Bale to the floor and then crawled over to the front door. The door flung open and a huge bird stomped in. It buffed its chest and radiated bravado. Its astute eyes targeted the spider. And with a quick snap, the bird locked its beak atop the spider and lept back out into the sepia endlessness. Bale stood in the door frame and waved to the bird, "Thanks, Grandma".

Bale crawled his way up the metaphysical pillar and encountered his doppleganger once again. This time though, his minotaur father did not blindside him. He simply stood behind the Shadow Man with his arms crossed. Bale knew how to deal with these parental demons now, but he also knew his father had little regard for anyone in their family. With one exception.
Bale thought hard and envisioned his brother. He tried to remember the last time he had seen him. He remembered the dark blue uniform. He remembered the white cap. Bale could only ever recount his brother as a soldier going off to war. So that's what he got. A soldier in a war. Bale's brother appeared from the Rescape as young as the day he left. He didn't speak, but the glance between Bale and this figment of his brother spoke volumes in his heart. His brother smiled. The Shadow Man screeched. Fed up with Bale's resistance. The monster threw his minion at the brothers. Though weary of his master, the father minotaur ran head-on into the boys. Bale took his brother's hand. The two shared a knowing nod, and together they used their connected arms to trip the bull and send him flying off the tower.
With no trauma left in the tank, The Shadow Man resorted to old tactics. The creature melted into the floor and spread itself out, littering darkness around the Rescape. Bale gasped, "He's trying to bring us to his world". Bale looked to his brother, who began to fade away. "What...what am I supposed to do," Bale asked. Bale knelt to the ground and felt the remaining texture of the memory pillar. This time he was not clouded by the memories of others, but reminded of a time he shared with Vana. "Let me show you my world," she said, "Before we go back".

The darkness rolled out like spilled ink around the corners of this realm. The Shadow Man was becoming bigger. Omnipresent. The transition into the Unscape was approaching, and there, Bale would be a flea before a God. The Shadow Man became aware of a noise in the quiet, a ripping sound. It lifted its head. Vana was in the darkness, pulling and tearing pieces of black off the walls. Another rip. Across from her were Bale's parents tearing pieces of the ground up. Bale's brother returned and hastily pulled piece after piece of black off the walls to reveal the Rescape beyond the cover.
As pieces of blackness were pulled, more people came through from the Rescape. Big Red and Big Blue, Supay and Tula and Sheriff West. Sunglasses kicked a hole through the darkness and Plum cut through it with a swing of her spear. Bale's parents reached into the empty darkness and took hold of something. Someone. They pulled hard and yanked Bale through the barrier. Another screech from the Shadow Man was cut short when the intruders began to bombard him. Francine stomped the back of the monster's head. Hank appeared to elbow drop the monster, and Roma Phenomenon crawled up from the darkness to hold the monster down. As the Shadow Man tried to stretch and expand, Bale's memories sped to catch the monster

around every turn. His college roommate Dole appeared, his childhood friends Seymour, Rosie, and Carly lept in too. Frank The Dog bit the Shadow Man's ankle while perfectly balancing a cigarette in his mouth.

Bale was helped past the writhing tendrils of the beast by the memory of his parents. His father pushed him along as he did when he taught Bale had to ride a bike when he was six. His mother swatted the lashings away as she did with the rose bush Bale got stuck in when he was four. Bale's brother ran in front of him and showed Bale how to avoid the Shadow Man's attacks, just as he showed him how to avoid the ghosts in Pac-Man. They helped him every step of the way until he got to The Shadow Man.

Pushing all its attackers away, The Shadow Man grew as tall as a tower. It became a long spike with tendrils coming out everywhere. Each arm of the monster incapacitating one of Bale's allies. The Shadow Man hung it's head over Bale now, with the cell phone screen becoming a movie screen across the Shadow Man's face. A blinding neon light shone down on Bale, forcing him to cower and hide as his vision was stripped.

"YOU SHOULD HAVE CALLED US BACK," the Shadow Man said in a booming, computerized voice. "YOU SHOULD HAVE. YOU SHOULD HAVE. YOU SHOULD HAVE".

It repeated over and over, each time the wave of light atop Bale became heavier and heavier, knocking him to the ground. The screams of his allies were overshadowed by the Shadow Man's tauntings. Bale could not even look upon his memories. There was only noise and blinding light. Bale reached into his pocket. He felt the kaleidoscope. He felt it melt into hot plastic slime as the light above him set his clothes on fire.

"THE TOY CANNOT SAVE YOU," the Shadow Man said, "YOUR PAST CANNOT SAVE YOU. NOTHING CAN SAVE YOU".

Bale shook his head. He swore out the Shadow Man. He rejected its will and reached deeper than he ever had before. No muscles. No family. No toys. But maybe he didn't need any of those things to conquer whatever this was. Maybe the power he carried this time wasn't in his pocket. Maybe it was on his skin.

The Shadow Man's light began to run over some force field like water over a dome. The barrier was an array of mystifying colors all blending together. Within the bubble, Bale looked up and saw her. The woman he loved. Vana looked a bit different inside the kaleidoscope dome, it appeared there were multiple versions of her all standing in the same place. This could have been a compilation of Bale's memories, or it could be that there were parts to Vana he just never knew about.

Regardless, his love had one hand stretched up to create the force field, and another reaching towards him. Vana lifted Bale up and their eyes met. Time stopped. Colors muted. There was nothing. There wasn't even a visual representation of nothing. There was just her and her breath and her smell and the little curl under her eyes when she smiled. There was the car radio they jammed out to. There was the sleepless nights they would just stay up and talk. The nights they couldn't keep their hands off each other. There was the things neither ever said, that neither had to hear. There was only them. Bale and Vana.

"I see what you mean," Vana said. She looked up and around the bubbles, "These really are pretty colors."

A beam of multicolored vividity blasted out of the dome and through the monitor head of the Shadow Man. Vana and Bale held hands as they walked along the Shadow Man's body, which began to sink like a balloon with no air. Around them, their allies regained control and began tearing pieces of the Shadow Man off. By the time the two reached the Shadow Man's head, all that remained was the humanoid shape they had come to recognize.

"You…didn't call us back," the Shadow Man pathetically whimpered. It was on its hands and knees.

"How do you want to do this," Vana asked, "We could probably do another rainbow beam thingy if we tried".

"No, I don't want to hurt it anymore," Bale replied.

"What? Bale that thing has been trying to kill us the whole time,".

"And it could have, Vana. It could have killed you when it caught you".

"But it didn't".

"Right. I don't think it wants to kill us".

"So," Vana turned to look at The Shadow Man, "What do you want?"

Bale knelt down in front of the Shadow Man. The Shadow Man lifted its hand, revealing its cracked cell phone screen. Bale took its hand and brought the phone to his ear.

"I…want to play games. I want to look around. Watch people. Laugh. Drink. Walk. I want to throw myself into the world…a hundred more times".

"Bale," Vana asked, "What did it say?"

Bale nodded to the Shadow Man, "I know what it wants now".

How he did it didn't matter. What it meant mattered more. Escaping the Rescape. Bidding adieu to these figments of his past. Freeing his woman from the clutches of the Unscape. All while allowing The Shadow Man to enter his body through every opening, but mostly his ears. Vana questioned if what he was doing was smart. If it might end up hurting him. But Bale knew now what he didn't before. Throwing his life into the ocean didn't end it. That simply separates it from everything new he would experience. The Shadow Man was not angry for the sake of anger. It was alone. And scared. It didn't want to be left behind.

Bale could not have this much fun or excitement if the life he lived before didn't exhaust him. He would not have loved Vana if he didn't love Fran first. He would not be eager to travel if he hadn't been stuck in one place for so long. He would not value his freedom if he never felt like he had none. You can't throw your past away and start a new life. The past is part of that future.

Chapter 31: A Good Place

"So, what exactly happened there," Vana asked. She and Bale were sitting at a table outfront of the coffee shack from earlier. The sun was still setting, but the barista lit some tiki torches to "get things in the mood, brobama".
Bale had a fruity smoothie drink, Vana drank a tall iced coffee. Bale replied, "I absorbed the Shadow Man. I think".
"Okay, but what does that mean?"
Bale looked at the ground. Vana looked too. Their shadows were cast onto the boardwalk. Bale's shadow moved without Bale moving. It waved at them.
"That's going to take some getting used to," Vana said, "So you think it-I guess "he"-is going to be okay?"
"Well, I know one thing," Bale watched as The Shadow Man's hand fell onto the hand of Vana's shadow, "He won't be lonely".

Vana packed her tattoo equipment into a briefcase. Bale used an empty box to gather up any leftover cleaning stuff or forgotten items. Vana's tattoo parlor was done for the rest of the year. She had already agreed to let a local artist construct the parlor into a greenhouse. After one of her employee's lets their boyfriend use it to shoot a music video.
"Remember when shooting music videos was cool," Vana asked.
"I never did that," Bale replied.
"Never? Not even a talent show?"
"What would I do in a talent show, Vana?"
"I dunno, Bale. Maybe lift the ocean or punch a Sedan in half?"
She laughed. He laughed. They smiled.
"Aren't you going to miss this place," Bale asked her as she locked the front door.
"Not really. It's always right here".
"Well, what if it's not here?"
"Then I got my tattoo stuff".
"And what if you didn't have that?"
Vana smiled, "Then I guess I would only have the memory".
"Maybe that's enough," Bale shrugged.
"Maybe," Vana wrapped her arms around Bale's shoulders, "But I still think you should call your parents".
"Yeah, I know".
"And you should call Hank".
"No, I'm not calling him".
"Why? You don't have his number?"
"I have his number. He gave his number to everyone".
"Well, he did help you fight The Shadow Man".
"Like I said, he wasn't really there. He and everyone else were just illusions".
"Except for me?"
"Except for you".

"I'll never understand this crap".

Bale loaded the last bag into the trunk of the rental car. He looked over at Vana. The sun had finally set, and from the angle they were at you could see the whole boardwalk. You could see the city lights and the vast ocean, everything blended together. Like it belonged that way. Like it was supposed to be this way. The night was split by the lights of a hundred lives and a million stories.
Bale walked up next to Vana and held her hand. They looked out into the ocean together.
"Nights like these," Vana said, "Really make you want to throw your phone into the ocean".
"Har har," Bale mocked. He looked at her while she stared away. Her hair was different. She had some burns. She wore glasses now, probably for fashion. There was something new about her, all over again.
"You look different," Bale told her.
"Yeah, I, uh, I had an arc," she replied.
Bale nodded, "You'll have to tell me about it".
"I will," she tightened her grip on his hand.

Vana's apartment was cold and quiet and dark. But none of that bothered Bale anymore. Even if he couldn't see it, he knew his shadow was there. And so was she. Dressed in something comfy to sleep in, but too sexy to sleep in. And here he was. Finally shaven. Finally short-haired. Bale told Vana if the tattoo business didn't pan out she could be a hairdresser. Vana laughed, "I've met hairdressers. Those girls are way too stressed out".

They laid in her bed watching the ceiling fan spin. The window was open, letting the cool autumn air circulate. You could smell the sea salt even indoors. How anyone could leave this town was a mystery to Bale, but that's how he would sum up Vana too. She was mysterious, but you could hardly ever walk away from her. If you did, you would miss out on whatever she'd say next. And when it wasn't funny, it was genuine.

Vana got to see that in Bale too. He was a sad sack of a guy. But for little reason. It's like he had everything he needed, everything that should have happened to him. But he was incomplete, and that sentiment was clear. Vana was enriched that she got to be that missing piece. Bale fulfilled something she never knew she wanted either. Perhaps needing each other wasn't the way they'd describe each other, but the knowledge of being wanted made a difference. The knowledge of being anything less than your whole self without the other. Was that "need"? Was that a bonus? Was love really as complicated as everyone says it is?
Or was it this? Simple. Loose. One night under a fan, the next day under the sky. Bale and Vana were going to leave again. They were going to travel again. Across the country, across the world, maybe even across the galaxy. Another thirty chapters of experiences that could change them. Or of experiences that could fall on them. Reactionary approaches to challenges they would have never imagined.

But what kept them stable was one another, and the knowledge that the unknown is scary even when you're not alone, but when you're not alone it may not feel like a challenge. It may feel like another part of the journey. Somewhere along the way, Bale thought, it really became about that. The journey.

The End

Epilogue

"Aw, brodin of Asgard," the barista said to himself, "someone totally spaced". His attention was locked on a cup of coffee on a bench facing the ocean. He could tell in an instant it was a coffee he served. The aroma, the dark consistency, the company logo on the side of the cup. Satisfied with his deduction, he sat beside the cup.
"You know, little coffee cup, you and I are much alike. Like you, I was left behind in a scenic venue. It was a Denny's, but still," the barista looked off into the dark ocean. "Yeah, I bet whoever was drinking you probably didn't appreciate your taste. I've been there too. It was more of an artistic taste, but still". He gripped his fists, "but maybe, you and me, we can still prove our worth, you know? Prove we still have some value in this spinning mudball we call a planet. Whadda say, broprah Winfrey?"

Just then a seagull swooped down and attempted to pick up the cup with its mighty beak. However, this avian assailant lacked the strength, speed, or coordination necessary to perform such a daring act of competency. The cup simply fell off the bench as the dastardly sky rat vanished into the night sky. The cup rolled along the boardwalk, spilling its remains through the gaps.
"Little Coffee Cup," the barista shouted. He got on his knees, lifted the cup up, and pouted at the sight of its emptiness. He stood up and lamented, "Maybe now we're more alike than before, broliver and company," he held the cup in both hands, "We're both empty. Lacking the warm, liquid, sugar-free potential we once held. Except for me it's more metaphorical. But still".

The barista crushed the cup in his hands, "Curse you, Little Coffee Cup! Your existence has only reminded me how empty my life is! How I wasted it on hot bean beverages, when I could have been a musician like I always wanted". The barista's eyes welled with tears as he looked off into the ocean. "Damn you," he whispered. "Damn you, Little Coffee Cup," he screamed as he threw the crushed paper cup into the ocean.
It could not be seen in the dark waters. Or through the barista's tears. He stood and panted for a brief moment. Then he wiped away his tears, sucked up his snot, and stood firmly. If this experience had taught him anything, it's that he was wasting his life away doing something nobody appreciated. Something that prevented him from following his dream. Well, that coffee cup would be the last one he'd ever hold. Unless he was thirsty, but still. The barista turned and walked away from the dock and towards the rest of his life.

Subtle bubbles grew from the surface of the ocean. As the cold autumn night carried on, and the winds carried leaves of many colors, not even the loneliest of melancholy men, women, or children walked the cold, coarse beach. With a steady pace, it walked up from the ocean and stepped through the waves and the sane. It fell to its hands and knees and as the water left it on land. It looked up to the airborne leaves and made eyes out of their patterns. Its skin was as ever shifting as the ocean. Its arms and legs were thin and dark. Big white gloves, big black shoes. Something appeared sewn into its right hand. Something empty. Something crushed. Something tall in shape. Grande, you might call it.

Epilogue 2

"That was all really hard".
"I know it was. I made it that way".
"Why? Why couldn't you have, I don't know, just make it funny?"
"I tried to make it funny too. But it couldn't just make it one thing".
"But it was hard. Really hard. I almost lost. I almost lost everything".
"That's not true. You had nothing to lose".
"What do you mean?"
"I mean everything you have, I gave you. And what I gave you was made up. You had nothing because you are nothing".
"I don't believe that. You wouldn't have made me if I were nothing. If all of this was nothing. What about Vana? Or all the towns? Was all that nothing".
"I guess it might have been. Vana was based on someone. The towns were just ideas".
"What about me?"
"Well, I guess you are a part of me. A part of me that wanted to escape".
"Escape what?"
"Escape everything. Work. My home. My family".
"That's how you feel?"
"Not all the time. Not even most of the time. I don't know. Starting over somewhere. Being someone else. It all sounds romantic".
"But you have so much to lose. So much I thought I had. Why would you want to throw away what makes you real?"
"Why should my being real be dependent on what I have?"
"Is this what you want? To throw your life into the ocean and be chased by your shadow?"
"First of all: that's all just an obvious metaphor. And second: no, that's not what I want".
"But it was on your mind".
"Yeah, dude, I think about Pokemon all the time. That doesn't mean I want my dog to breathe fire".
"So, what am I supposed to think? I'm just a fantasy you'll never act on".
"That's not the point of you. Everyone can see you as a fantasy. You are an outlet".
"Well, where does that leave me? If I can't be a person, if I have to be an outlet, how am I supposed to live?"
"That's not up to you. That's up to me".
"And that's supposed to make me feel better? Would you feel better if someone was controlling your life? Like it was a story?"
"I don't know. Maybe I should find out".

Made in United States
Orlando, FL
30 August 2022